Edited by:

Staccato Publishing

Zimmerman, MN

First US Edition: October 2011

Second US Edition: March 2016

ISBN: 978-0-9972125-2-5

Printed in the USA

The Five Santas

A Dan Landis Mystery

A novel by Jay Mims

5 | The Five Santas

This Book is dedicated to Mrs. Rita Sanders who in elementary school made me promise I would dedicate my first book to her. Thank you Mrs. Rita.

For Mama and Daddy

Chapter 1

Red sky at night sailor's delight, red sky in the morning sailors take warning.

The morning sky blazed blood red as Dan Landis lay on his back, staring upwards. One foot was still aloft, and he took a moment to admire his Day-Glo socks. It was important for socks to have personality. The cold of the cement made his body ache from where it touched his skin.

Pulling his legs toward his chest, he rocked back and thrust his legs forward. Momentum pulled him to his feet. Mama Landis' favorite son couldn't do a lot of things right, but a textbook kip-up was one.

Maggie, his old partner, could always tell a bad day just by how the morning smelled. Currently, all he could smell was the bad muffler of the car that had nearly run him over.

"Merry Christmas to you too." Dan shouted at the car, shaking his fist for emphasis. The jack wagon hadn't even slowed down. In fact, he could have sworn the car had sped up. Brake lights flared at the corner and he ran for it. The guy probably had a gun.

No respect for pedestrians in this town, he thought while bolting around the corner. Or, he added darkly, us jaywalkers. It was the most wonderful time of the year.

As Dan stormed down the water stained sidewalk he tried to be of good cheer. When his foot slipped on the frozen walk and his skull bounced off the concrete, visions of sugar plums danced in his head. This was truly a magical season.

He decided to stay down this time, listening to the rhythm of the city. Someone stepped on his hand and he assumed that was code for "Merry Christmas." It was going to be a long day.

"I hate Christmas," he grumbled.

"Are you all right?" a sweet voice asked. A face came into view. It was beautiful, blonde, and she had the most beautiful green eyes he'd ever seen.

"Is it me or do I just keep falling for you?"

Abbey rolled her eyes. People did that a lot around him. She offered a hand up, electricity shocked him at her touch. He was tempted to do another kip-up, but something told him the impressiveness of the move would be somewhat negated by another slip on the ice.

Abbey was not alone. There was a slightly smaller, toe-head looking girl in uniform beside her. Could have been a mini-me except for the chestnut brown eyes.

"Mister," the girl who was definitely not Abbey asked him. "Are you okay?"

The uniform was crisp and gleaming, the sash sparkled in the early morning light. Girl Scout. Dan opened his mouth to say something when he noticed they weren't alone. Five more: two brunettes, a blonde, and two girls with bouncing locks of curled black hair.

Dan adopted his patented smile, the Lady Killer 9000, junior edition. Everyone was staring at him. He leaned over to Abbey, "Don't look now, Abs, but I think we're surrounded."

"They get a merit badge for assisting people," Abbey replied.

"Do they often travel in packs?" Was packs the right word? Herd? Flock?

Gaggle, said a little voice in his head.

"Good grief," Dan said aloud, "It's a gaggle of girl scouts. Ladies, your help is much appreciated. Happy holidays, season's greetings. Happy Kwanza and Hanukah. Merry Christmas and Festivus for all the rest of us."

Dan turned to Abbey, "Did I leave anything out?"

The girls stared at him blankly. They all had clear eyes with remarkably neutral expressions. It was starting to give him the creeps.

"Do you need us to take you to the hospital?" one of the brunettes asked.

"Do you drive?" he asked.

"Dan..." Abbey warned.

"What? It's a fair question. After all, you barely drive. So what do you think? Does one do the steering while the other presses the gas?"

They gave him the look. It shouldn't have surprised him that girls this young could give a man the look. It was probably genetic.

He liked to interpret it as "How can such a handsome man be such an idiot?" At least when it came from legal aged women. Not so much from these Cupie doll pre-teens.

"My mom's right there," the other brunette said, pointing down the street to a nicely dressed woman talking on her cell, oblivious to the fact that her scout troop was talking to a strange man. She was just the sort of middle class white female who normally hired Dan to snoop in her husband's business.

She was probably calling the police, he realized. It was time to leave.

"I'll be fine," Dan said backing away slowly. "Thank you very much, I appreciate the assistance. Come along Abbinator."

As he neared the corner he gave a little wave, fighting the urge to run. The red horizon caught his eye.

"Yep," he told his newest friend, "it's going to be a long day."

Despite the ominous skyline, warm feelings inexorably flowed through his body. It was scary how good he felt. He was definitely experiencing a lightness of being, and possibly nausea. Was this the spirit of Christmas, he wondered? Or was it the head injury? Probably the head injury.

Obviously, the little voice spoke again, the cute blonde staring with such concern has nothing to do with it.

Nothing whatsoever, Dan thought back.

"I thought I dropped you off at the front door?" He asked.

"I wanted to score some cookies. They're doing holiday themed thin mints. Peppermint cookies!" She held up a box.

"Truly, we live in miraculous times."

They set off for work in search of coffee, aspirin, and the milk of human kindness. The humiliation of this morning's events was worth it just to hear her laugh.

Work was Murphy's Department store, his current job was Loss Prevention, LP for short. Normally he worked as a private investigator, specializing in cheating spouses. Everyone had their niche and Dan had long ago found his.

The job had landed him the friendship and smiling face of Bernice Agnes Smith, better known as Abbey, who was on her way to becoming Doctor Bernice Agnes Smith, PhD. As thrilling as being a paid snoop was, the holiday season was a bad time for a hired detective. It took an extremely lousy person to cheat at Christmas. Dan's clientele was only in the mostly lousy.

Thanks to a well-timed phone call, he was collecting a paycheck as a wage slave at Murphy's Department Store, one of the largest shops in town. He had made sure Abbey got a job there too. He needed the company, she needed the money. She made this bleak world a little brighter. He owed her.

It was probably just the Christmas spirit working on his cold heart, but Dan was glad Abbey had a chance to earn a few bucks while on break from her dissertation research. In this dog eat dog world, Abbey-Wan Kenobi was a Yorkshire Terrier.

This town was cold. The temperature was low, the people uncaring, and the gray buildings stood in bleak contrast against the whitish snow. Or, what amounted to snow. The latest snowfall had turned into slush; a dismal off-white flurry that only succeeded in creating frozen patches on the roads and sidewalks.

No one ever sang, "I'm dreaming of an off-white Christmas." And, Dan noted bleakly as he carefully made his way to work, the street corner Santa wasn't even at his usual post. Kind of day when even Father Christmas stayed home. The guy probably wanted to sleep in or he'd taken one look outside and decided to ring his bell in Hawaii.

The sight of a Santa or two calling out to the passersby, waving cheerfully, would have been welcome at this point. Those street corner Santas' ringing away for some charity made him believe, for a moment, that people weren't always as terrible as he believed.

Except, Santa or not, there was definitely a ringing in Dan's ear. He stopped, Abbey spinning on one heel to face him. Leaning against a brick wall, Dan waited for the ground to stop spinning. Even the building felt cold and heartless. He reflected yet again on the magic of the season. Looking back, if he squinted really hard, the four story garage where he parked was almost visible.

The stupid store made him walk two blocks, just so parking at this bastion of capitalism could be reserved for paying customers. He put a lid on his rage. He needed the money and it was only for a few more days. After that, he could go back to playing his usual game of "Snooping for dollars."

That and Mama Landis had always taught him not to gripe, to take the lemons life gave you and make lemonade. Only right now Dan felt like taking the lemons, grabbing some vodka, and having a party.

"Are you alright?" Abbey asked.

"Fine," he waved her off, "What's your opinion of a Tom Collins?"

"His work with Ronny Milsap was amazing!" She began singing at the top of her lungs. Something about not missing it for the world. She had many positive qualities. The ability to carry a tune wasn't one. He wrapped an arm around her and led the cheery human jukebox to work.

He stopped at the employees' entrance to brush the snow off his black pants. He checked to make sure there was no mud on his scuffed black dress shoes. His uniform was a red vest and clip-on tie. His boss, Mr. Peters, insisted he dress "nice".

Since he had no clue what "nice" meant, Dan just wore his usual ensemble, but with dress shoes instead of sneakers.

Dan's black jacket went well with his black silk shirt. The crimson tie was clip-on, because he was a rebel. He also wore Day-Glo socks. Nothing said "personality" like neon green.

Murphy's was too warm for Dan's taste. He had grown up just outside Pittsburgh. Anything above zero was shorts weather. He slipped off the jacket, ready to ditch it in his locker. He had an unabashed love for jackets of all types. A black bomber jacket was second only to a duster in coolness. Too bad coolness didn't factor into a place like Murphy's.

The store's bright lights were a bit too dazzling. Dan almost regretted not wearing sunglasses. Black sunglasses would have been pushing it. There was a fine line between "Cool man in black" and "Goober trying too hard."

Abbey woke up two hours early to be ready. She was probably born ready. She breezed to her locker, threw in that oversized pink purse of hers, and walked away, beaming as she walked.

Blinded by the light of that smile, Dan made his way toward the locker room. His locker was in the third row across, fourth one down. As he opened the door, he caught a glimpse in the mirror.

Bloodshot blue eyes stared back at him. At least the pupils weren't dilated. So, hopefully no concussion. Turning left then right, he checked his face. A clean shaven, twenty-something stared back at him. He smiled and checked his hair, the jet black mane was still in its carefully ruffled state.

Bed head, his stylist called it. Dan had laughed, but Alfonzo was right, it worked for him. Glancing around, he adjusted an errant strand for the perfect effect. Lady killer, Maggie used to call him. Dan winked at his reflection.

He glanced from the mirror to the picture he kept in his locker. The three of the most important women in his life. Dan's sister, Julianne looked so much like him they could be twins even if she was four years older. The biggest difference in their features were their eyes. Hers were gray, almost translucent.

Next to Jules was Bernie, with her tight dreadlocks and devil may care smile. Bernie had one arm around Abbey, who looked surprised to find herself the center of attention. Surprised and a bit terrified.

Danny's Angels, Bernie had scribbled in that weird handwriting that was required for all doctors. The four of them had gone out to celebrate Abbey being ABD (All but Dissertation, in deference to her grad status). Dr. Bernie Wilkins, M.D. insisted on calling Abbey "Doc Smith" all night.

Except, Dan thought with a smirk, there was only one Doc. Professor Leroy "Doc" Brown. He had bought the whole bar a round that night. It was good to see everyone so happy.

Dan sighed, looking down from those three smiling faces to a waving snowman. It was a postcard from Maggie. She had bought it for them, their first Christmas. Sammy the Snowman, always worth a smile. The idea of putting up with eight hours at this job made his smile melt away.

"Craptastic day," Dan grumbled.

There was a polite cough behind him. He had learned to despise that cough. His brightest, most professional smile gleamed back from the mirror. Turning on one heel brought him face to face with his boss; Mr. Peters. Or, the Prince of Dorkness as Dan called him. Not to his face of course, because that would be rude.

"Mr. Landis," Mr. Peters began, "we do frown on profanity here at Murphy's Department Store."

"Absolutely Sir," Dan nodded. When in doubt, be agreeable. "Thank you for reminding me Sir." You could never use 'Sir' too much with Mr. Peters.

"Of course, Mr. Landis," Mr. Peters nodded agreeably in return. "You have your duties to get to. Please, don't let me detain you." With one parting glance, Mr. Peters walked away.

The man never moves his arms, Dan realized. That's it, that is what was so annoying about Mr. Peters. Although, being a pretentious efficiency Nazi with no sense of humor whatsoever didn't help either.

It was like the man worked at being unlikable. The three strand comb-over, horn rimmed glasses, and sweater vest with bow tie ensemble sure didn't help any. It was kind of sad, Dan thought, because I could almost feel sorry for the little man. If only he wasn't such an obnoxious little piss ant, we might even be friends. I am going to buy Mr. Peters some Day-Glo socks for Christmas, he decided.

He slipped on the red vest, the one he refused to wear outside of work. At least he didn't have to wear the red sport coat required of all the other helper-monkeys. Why, Dan wondered, did Mr. Peters only address folks by Mr. and Ms.? Dan wondered. He didn't even know Mr. Peters' first name. Maybe, he considered, the man doesn't have a first name. Maybe Mister was his first name. That elicited a chuckle, and Dan felt a little bit better. It was good to laugh. Laughter kept him from going crazy. For now anyway.

"Thanks Mr. Peters," he called out, stepping onto the floor. His eyes adjusted to the harsh glare of the fluorescents.

Years of living by his wits had given Dan a sixth sense for trouble. It was the same instinct that kept cops and school teachers alive.

Someone was watching him.

Dan glanced around. It didn't take but a minute, she wasn't hard to find. The floor should have been empty; the store had barely been open five minutes. She stood over by the unattended jewelry display, smiling. Her flaming locks of auburn hair shone like a beacon, splashing brightly against the green of her sweater.

It was a Christmas tree sweater, complete with ornaments and lights. The lights even blinked synchronously, probably to O Tannenbaum. Her smile was dazzling.

Dan had learned the hard way, never to trust a smiling face. Particularly a smile attached to a gorgeous redhead, one with the air of someone who knew exactly how attractive she was. The redhead in question held up a bottle of perfume, the really expensive stuff a pretty but vacant woman would spray directly into your eyes.

Her emerald eyes twinkled with laughter. She winked at him. The perfume bottle slipped before his very eyes into her giant

matching green knitted purse. And then she bolted, that purse
flopping from side to side as it bounced off her hip.

Of course, Dan thought, a supremely attractive shoplifter
would choose first thing in the morning to play cat and mouse. It
was just his luck. He took off after her. The lady could move.

Dan had a lot of experience running, mostly from other
people, but this cutie was booking it. Right for the emergency exit.
He picked up speed, ignoring the sheer agony of the blood
pounding inside his bruised head. He had picked the wrong day to
quit sniffing glue.

The redhead hit the emergency exit a beat ahead of Dan
and the heavy door was just closing when he flung it wide open.
Part of him noted on a subconscious level that the fire alarm hadn't
gone off. That could be a problem. On the bright side, it wasn't his
problem. A sexy thief was his problem.

Thank God for small favors.

The crisp morning air hit him like a hammer; the sunrise
was bright, almost blinding. Dan hated how blistering cold was
always so bright and sunny. It was such a tease. With a shock he
realized the alley was empty.

Dan listened. There were no running footsteps and the alley
had a good 50 yards of space in either direction. No one here
except for Dan, some dumpsters, and a whole lot of nothing. He

sighed. She was probably in one of the dumpsters. Maybe behind one of them. On a whim he looked up.

No green eyes were staring impishly down at him from the roof. Of course, there was no ladder nearby, but Dan wouldn't have been surprised if she could fly. She'd had that magical, "I can do anything I want" look about her. He glanced down seeing no manholes, open or otherwise, within sight.

Resigned, he headed toward the nearest dumpster. "How come I always end up in a dumpster?" He asked no one in particular.

The dumpster didn't answer, instead it just looked nasty, tetanus filled, and generally uninviting.

"These pants are dry clean only!" Dan yelled, lashing out with one foot.

It wasn't until his foot connected with the somehow surprisingly solid dumpster that he remembered he was wearing dress shoes, not work boots. As his foot thumped against the metal, pain shot up his leg.

Dan hopped up and down, holding his foot.

"Funky butt loving...!" he howled.

Then he saw the dead Santa Claus stuffed behind the dumpster.

"Oh," he said more calmly, still holding his foot. "That's not good."

Chapter 2

"Yep," Dan told no one in particular, "This is bad."

A dead body stuffed behind a dumpster was never a good thing. A body dressed as Santa Claus just a few days before Christmas, was really bad. All the gin joints in the all the world, Santa had to get stuffed here. He gingerly put down his foot, the pain in it now secondary, and leaned in for a closer look. He was no pathologist, but the body definitely looked dead. Color, position, plus a creepy lifeless stare. It was no gaggle of girl scouts staring at him creepy, but creepy nonetheless.

"Probably dead," he declared to no one in particular. The silence was beginning to bother him. It was possible Santa had died of natural causes. Reindeer and/or lactose related. And somehow became wedged behind the dumpster. However, bodies weren't normally stuffed like towels in a linen closet. Or, Santa was playing Zombie hide and seek.

"Olly olly oxen free?" Dan called out, just in case.

The dead Santa didn't move. Well, the red suited, white bearded, fat white corpse didn't move. Which was good because Dan was not prepared to deal with Zombie Santa.

Which Santa is this? Was this? It was hard to tell. Murphy's had a Santa; a pretty authentic looking one at that. There were two within a couple of blocks, working the street corner like a season specific bearded lady of the night.

The silence was starting to weigh heavy on Dan. No bells were ringing, anywhere. Their absence was deafening, weighing against his chest. He looked closer at Santa, trying to tell.

Is this the street corner Santa from just to the right of their store? Maybe. The dead man definitely resembled the Santa from that street corner. Maybe it was the one from three blocks down. The problem was: all Santa's looked alike to him. When you've seen one bearded man in a red suit, you've seen them all.

Dan walked back to the emergency exit, trying hard not to disturb the crime scene. Contrary to what Hollywood wanted you to think, crime scenes were for trained professionals. Not private investigators.

From his perch near the door, Dan could see the red hat lying off to one side, near the white haired head. He leaned against the exit door and sighed, grateful for the low temperatures. Santa could have been ripe had it been above freezing. He looked around; the area was deserted, which was a relief. Last thing he needed was for someone to come by and start jumping to conclusions.

The door burst open cracking Dan in the back, the hard metal radiating cold through Dan's thin shirt. He gave a high-pitched squeal and whipped around.

"Mr. Landis, what are you doing out here?" The beginnings of a lecture faded quickly. "What on earth?" Mr. Peters yelped.

Dan stared wordlessly at him. He thought about saying, "It wasn't me," then figured that would be pointless.

"Hello Sir," Dan said instead, trying to keep his voice level. It was always important to remember courtesy, even at the worst of times. "As you can see, we have a problem. With your permission Sir, I'd like to call 911," he suggested, using his most professional voice.

"Absolutely not, I will not have The Season disrupted," Mr. Peters attempted to maintain control of the situation.

It was always "The Season" for Mr. Peters. Never Christmas, the Holidays, or even Festivus. Calling it "The Season" made Dan think a rampaging hunt was going on.

He glanced around the empty alleyway. Still deserted. He fought down the impulse to beat Mr. Peters senseless. While it would make him feel better, it probably wouldn't accomplish anything. Instead, he tried the reasonable approach.

"Mr. Peters," Dan used the calm and reassuring voice that always worked its magic on soon to be divorcees. "I assure you I will be discreet. If we don't report this body and someone else does, we lose the opportunity to seize the momentum. It's all about spin control." Dan's fists itched, desperate to pummel.

Mr. Peters stared at him and then, slowly, he sighed. It was the first human thing Dan had seen the man do, even if it was a bit theatrical. "Of course, Mr. Landis. Please perform your official duty as a representative for this store." Mr. Peters waved a hand dismissively.

Dan watched the man turn to leave, pausing for a moment mid-turn. Mr. Peters looked toward the heavens for strength.

"Mr. Landis," Mr. Peters started, staring at the sky, "Please inform the police there are no security cameras in this area. This is a mistake I will remedy immediately." He left, the door slamming shut behind him.

Dan exhaled. He glanced at the dead Santa. "Just between you and me pal," he told the body, "that guy's getting on my nerves."

Dan didn't add that Mr. Peters had hit on something with the cameras or lack thereof. He hadn't even noticed their absence; he'd been too busy looking for that shoplifter. He squinted, trying to remember her face. There was a hint of red hair. Mostly, he remembered that green sweater. No one would commit a murder wearing something so memorable. He wondered if the red and green wunderkind had any connection to Santa.

Maybe she was his elf? Dan decided it was time to call the police. Fortunately, he had them on speed dial. One of them anyway. He dialed. The line was busy.

"Crap," He hadn't anticipated Gary not being readily available. Of course, he hadn't expected to find Santa Corpse, either. He tried again.

"Who are you talking to at nine in the morning?" Dan screamed at the phone while the voicemail version of Gary blathered monotonously about leaving a message. He bit his tongue. Drawing attention was the last thing he needed. He put his phone away, and took a breath. He almost gagged.

Deep breaths were never a good idea around evacuated bowels. He leaned his head against the door, staring at the sky, and taking shallow breaths. The smells of the city wafted down the alley. Exhaust fumes mixed with industrial salts, the press of people, and the far off smell of something deep fried. Dan felt himself relaxing. This city was insane, but it was home.

The diner across the street was serving a brisk breakfast crowd. He wondered if they'd seen anything. From this viewpoint he could see clear across the street to the busy sidewalk.

Closing his eyes, Dan mentally walked out onto the street. He had passed this alley a hundred times; from the parking garage to the store, and back. He had ambled past this morning, in fact.

There was a wall. A wall that hid the dumpsters from view. It wouldn't have surprised him if that was Mr. Peters' idea, to keep any hint of garbage from view. But, the left hand side where he stood was visible. That probably didn't help much, unless Santa and his assailant brawled across the alley. Doubtful. Dan was about to lash out with his foot and kick a can, when he stopped.

Almost forgot where I was he mused, tossing a glance over his shoulder at the unmoving black boots. Given his luck, the can he kicked would have been filled with concrete.

Dan tried calling again. The number was Gary's work number, his direct desk line. He also had the big man's cell, except this was business. Business meant you used the business phone. And when you found the body of Father Christmas, you didn't just call 911, you called the best cop on the force.

He glanced at the dumpster again. Santa still hadn't moved, which was good. The minute he did, the Guinness people had better be there because Dan was prepared to set a land speed record. He pressed redial, listening to the voicemail that said Detective Jones was on the other line. Leave a message, take two aspirin, and call in the morning.

Something was missing from the alley. He flipped his phone shut and looked around. The entire city was speckled in white, but the alley was untouched by the off-white slush. Looking up, he noted the massive overhang and gutter system.

Well, that was no help, Dan thought. Snow would have meant shoe tracks, telltale mud, maybe someone's name written out in red or yellow. He lashed backward with his foot against the door.

The thump of the metal fired a synapse, and Dan realized with a shock he was locked out. Except the Lord of the Dorkocalypse had gotten back in. There was no handle on this side of the metal security door. Dan ran his fingers along the edge, tracing the frame. He felt his fingers slip into the groove and he pulled. The door came forward easily. That was interesting.

"Very interesting," he muttered to himself. The door should be locked from the outside. He shut it, and then opened it again to make sure it wasn't a fluke.

Dan decided to file this little tidbit under 'To check out later.' He swung the door back and forth, breathing in the store's recycled air.

It was hot and slightly sickening, still it beat the dead body smell. Dan stepped back into the cool air of the alley, and tried to think.

Other than Gary, he didn't know any cops. He corrected himself, he didn't know any he could trust. He stared at the phone and dialed again. No answer. He wondered if he should call 911. Glancing at the time, Dan put his phone away. He'd give it another minute. Dan was reasonably sure Santa still hadn't moved.

"You wouldn't want to fill me in, would you?" he asked the body. "You can tell me, trust me. I'm good at believing people." Santa didn't answer. "It was the Easter Bunny wasn't it? All those people biting chocolate bunny heads off finally got to him. The

Tooth Fairy's next. I'll probably have to break out The Holy Hand Grenade."

Dan was grateful no one could see him. Talking to a corpse was only cool on TV and if you were Jennifer Love Hewitt. Actually, anything you did was cool if you were Jennifer Love Hewitt.

Why are you so certain you're alone? The little voice in Dan's head asked. Shivers ran up his spine. Every great detective needed a little voice in their head. For Dan, it was his partner Maggie's voice. At least he wasn't seeing her ghost anymore.

"Thanks," Dan replied. Keeping his feet firmly planted, he leaned left, trying to see the other end of the alley. "Hello?" he called out. No one answered. "Free beer!" Nothing. No one here but Santa and us chickens, he hoped. He checked the time. His minute was up. Dan pulled out his phone, his thumb hovering over redial. He leaned against the door.

"So Gary," Dan rehearsed, "There's a dead Santa in the alleyway. Don't worry, just the one. My prime suspect is the Easter Bunny. You may want to put out an APB. Big white guy, long ears, carries eggs." He sighed, "Yeah, that can't possibly sound crazy."

He glanced over at the body, just in case. Yep, still there.

"Why can't you be Zombie Santa?" He asked, fairly certain that was the first time that question had ever been asked. Santa was still there and still dead. Dan had no choice. He thumbed the line. The phone rang. He heard a click, and then a deep voice answered.

"This is Detective Jones" it said.

Dan couldn't help but smile at the familiar grumpy voice. It was like a warm blanket of reality.

"Hi Gary," he said.

Chapter 3

It had been a long morning for Sergeant Gary Jones. For some reason the closer they got to the holidays, the hotter everyone's tempers. Unfortunately, arguments escalated. Sometimes they got out of hand. And then, on tragic occasions, they ended in murder.

Since he had clocked in at seven this morning, Gary had already handled three dispatches. And he wasn't expected to get off until eleven tonight. This close to Christmas everyone worked double-shifts. Gary had been tapped as the senior watch officer for the morning shift.

His desk was located in the far corner of the Homicide department, at the coveted spot near the vending machine. Seniority had certain perks. The big room was painted in muted earth tones in an effort to feel warm, and there was always a constant undercurrent of noise. Phones ringing, copiers humming, keyboards clicking, and idle chit chat, added to the office symphony.

Gary hated the cacophony of sound, the idle chit chat of vending machine conversation, the walls that were slowly closing in. He was a beat cop, through and through. Gary loved the open sky, the fresh air, and the exercise that came with walking a beat. Life was so much simpler then. You found a crime, you solved the crime, and you moved on to the next crime. Sometimes the criminals ran, and then you chased them. Sometimes, they chased you.

Unfortunately, those days were behind him. Onward and upward, through the departments and the ranks Officer Jones had risen. Now, here he was, trapped by his own success. Thanks to the twisted logic of bureaucracy, Gary, who had scratched out a career as a beat cop, was best suited for desk work.

As one of the most seasoned and experienced officers, he was invaluable to the department. So they told him. He not only offered the experience and instincts of a street monster, he also had the maturity and level headedness of a seasoned professional. His nose for trouble, and the ability to talk that very trouble down were qualities that seemed to elude most of his fellow officers.

Everyone seemed to forget that a calm voice and a cool head did more than a gun ever could. With success came enemies, some great, most of them small. Gary sighed, leaning back in his chair. He rubbed his aching neck. Heavy was the crown.

Gary stared at the reports on his desk, kicked up the chain from anyone and everyone. Anything that required even a modicum of reasoning and thought went straight to Gary. Good old Gary. Reliable Gary. Gary the desk jockey. The black phone on his desk burred. He glared at it, but his hand automatically reached out to answer.

"This is Detective Jones." His rank was technically Sergeant, however, he was first and foremost a Detective. Gary knew Captain Meyers tolerated this small indulgence, and Meyers' was the only opinion Gary cared about. Besides his beautiful wife.

"Hi Gary," said the familiar voice on the line.

"Hello Dan…" he hated getting this call, hated that artificially happy little voice. Whenever the kid called, it meant trouble. Gary knew Dan only called this line when it was trouble. He stifled a smile. Escape from the office danced before his eyes.

As he listened, one hand reached to his chest, feeling for the bulletproof vest he always wore beneath his shirt in the field. He didn't blame the kid, but Gary still felt the twinge of pain from the first time they met, the first time he was ever shot in the line of duty. On the upside, life with Daniel Gertrude Landis was never boring.

"I told you to stop calling this line," Gary aimed for low and slow, the better to temper a hotheaded youth. "If this is an emergency, call 911 like normal people."

"Why can't this be a social call?" Gary sighed. Right now Dan was probably giving his usual movie star smile. The detective was under no illusions about his brother-in-law's good looks and natural charm. The man had a little black book thicker than the

Manhattan white pages. He stayed perpetually upbeat too. He was always so happy, so chipper. It was scary.

"Dan…" Gary began to protest, "I'm looking at an inbox that is almost, almost mind you, as high as I'm going to shove my foot up…"

"I got a dead Santa," Dan interrupted.

"Did you kill him?" Gary asked carefully.

"No!" Dan responded, his voice cracking, "Why do you always think..."

"Gertie," Gary dropped the hammer. Dan's middle name was an apparent peace offering to his paternal grandmother. It was like an off-switch for the kid, and he knew to use it sparingly. "Tell me what happened."

As the young man began talking, Gary listened carefully. He took careful notes. Accurate note taking was a lesson he tried to impart on his fellow officers. No detail was ever insignificant. If you wanted proof, look at how many cases Gary's wife had won.

Julianne Jones née Landis was the city's foremost criminal defense attorney. Too many cases were thrown out due to technicalities, overlooked details, or the always dreaded discrepancy. And Julianne knew every one of them. She could rip a case apart in the blink of an eye, embarrass you in front of the court, and look great doing it. Many a seasoned officer thought he could skim over a minor detail, only to find out the little punk had hired Julianne "Boom-Boom" Jones. She was merciless in the courtroom and was paid handsomely for it.

The fear of her knowing smile made many a vice cop lose sleep. She also motivated Gary to be a better policeman. For the sake of their marriage, the two had never met in court.

"Gary, I promised Mr. Peters I'd be discreet," Dan reasoned, his tone getting dangerously close to a whine.

Gary felt a swell of pride that Dan was taking this job seriously. He knew the kid needed the money, and Gary still had his fingers crossed that maybe, one day, he would wake up and seize the chance for respectable work. Dan deserved some stability. Not that Gary would ever tell him that.

"Dan, I'll meet you at Murphy's."

"Thanks…Should I call 911 too?"

No one really asked advice anymore, especially know-it-all private detectives with a modicum of success under their belts. He wiped the smile off his face, lest it translate over the phone. "No, I can call dispatch," Gary assured him. He glanced at his watch. "All right, I'll try to be there in ten, fifteen on the outside."

"Thanks boss," the relief was palatable.

Gary hung up. He stared at the phone, feeling that thrill he got when a new case landed in his lap. This could be nothing, a mugging gone wrong or, it could be the tip of an iceberg. You just never knew.

He rubbed his face, feeling the leftover stubble he'd missed. Early mornings always made shaving difficult, and no one had been there to give him a goodbye kiss. He cleared that thought from his mind and stood up, stretching.

At six feet four inches, he was the tallest officer on the force, something he still got teased about. The cookie cutter furniture was agony, with a constant need to contort his legs in order to fit them beneath his desk. Yet another reason to miss being on the beat. He opened his desk, pulled out his service holster, and carefully checked his revolver. It was the same model his father had carried, a Colt Official Police Revolver.

So far in his career Gary had never needed to draw his weapon in the line of duty. Still, he went to the range once a week. He was still a crack shot, second best on the force. The holster went around his shoulders; the revolver nestled in his armpit. Bending down, he pulled up his pant leg. With his free hand, he reached into his desk's bottom drawer and pulled out his back up revolver. He slid that into his ankle holster, completely hidden by his pants leg.

As he stood, he could hear the various creaks and pops. I'm getting old, he thought. He'd caught a glimpse in the mirror this morning, and concluded he would have to either start dyeing his hair or accept the encroaching gray. Gary stretched out his arms, and then pulled his old brown trench coat off his chair. Julianne always fussed that he let it get so wrinkled. Julie just didn't understand it was part of the coat's charm. Not that they'd talked about it recently. Or anything at all recently for that matter. Gary sighed. Success had taken a heavy toll on their marriage.

With coat in hand, he turned to leave. Time to find out what trouble Dan Landis had gotten himself into this time. But first he had to stop by his locker. He couldn't see Dan without proper protection.

Chapter 4

The minutes crawled by and Dan tried not to panic. After he got off the phone with Gary, he'd called Mr. Peters' office. It seemed the right thing to do.

"Mr. Peters?" Dan asked, redundantly. Who else would answer the man's phone?

"Mr. Landis," Mr. Peters confirmed needlessly. It wasn't a question. Questions weren't efficient. Apparently neither was a polite "Hello."

"I wanted to inform you that a senior officer with the police force is on his way, Sir. He's promised to be as discreet as possible under the circumstances."

"Under no circumstances can we allow The Season to be disrupted." You could feel his pencil thin mustache bristling over the phone.

"I absolutely agree, Sir," he rolled his eyes. "And you should know, I've volunteered to act as liaison between the store and the police force to minimize the employees' exposure to the case."

"That would probably be for the best," Mr. Peters almost sounded like he approved. "Any official statements to the outside will need to be cleared by me."

"Absolutely Sir."

"And Mr. Landis," Mr. Peters added, "while I appreciate your enthusiasm, please refrain from making decisions on behalf of Murphy's Department store without first consulting me." There was a click. It was most uncheerful.

Dan pressed the end button, and carefully put away his phone. "Jerk." He debated hanging around the alley's entrance, then decided against it. No one was going to come into this alley without a reason, and hanging around the entrance would just attract unwanted attention. He decided to stay by the emergency exit, leaning against the door.

He propped a foot against the metal. His perch was probably a fire hazard, but he had no interest in going back inside. Plus, from this vantage point, he could still see the alley's entrance. And even better, no one could sneak up on him from the other end. The metal door thumped against his back again and he jumped.

The face was haloed by strawberry-blonde hair. "Oh it's you." Abbey didn't seem surprised to see him. "What are you doing out here?"

"Smoke break," Dan flipped back offhandedly. "Aren't you supposed to be working?"

"Shouldn't you?"

"I am at work."

"Well, I'm on break," Abbey stepped out, closing the door behind her. She crossed her arms and leaned against the metal mimicking his previous pose. She sighed.

"And you didn't want to use the normal exit?"

"This is the special exit. Everyone knows that." She pointed to the nonfunctional latch on the door.

Dan fought the urge to throw up his hands. Who didn't know about the disabled lock and lack of cameras out this way? "I didn't think you got a break this early."

"It was sort of involuntary." Her shoulders slumped. "So, I'm thinking of going back home."

"Really? I'm thinking of going back to England."

"You've been to England?"

"Yep. Twice with Doc, once to surprise Bernie on her birthday. Needless to say she was shocked." Dan smiled. It faded when he caught her expression.

"That's nice," Abbey released a low sigh. "I'd like to leave the country. Maybe live under an assumed name."

Dan didn't stare. He could feel the undercurrent of emotion rippling out from her. She was good at hiding her feelings, but he knew her too well.

"Want to talk about it?"

"There's nothing to talk about."

"No? Okay, want to hear what I just…"

"I got fired."

Dan did a double take. Abbey was a model employee. She was fast, efficient, hardworking, and easy on the eyes. Granted, she had all the people skills of a spork, but that was hardly her fault. She was an Art History major, a field that rarely bred social acumen.

"How?" he stuttered, "I thought you were doing great in Wrapping. You're the poster girl for adorable gift wrapping."

"Thanks," Abbey glanced at her feet. "I bumped into Mr. Peters this morning. By the time I got to my station it had already been decided. Mr. Alejandro told me I was terminated before I picked up my first roll of paper."

Dan almost asked if Mr. Alejandro had used an Austrian accent, but realized Abbey had probably never seen a Schwarzenegger movie. She would never catch the obtuse reference.

"When you say, 'bumped into Mr. Peters'…"

"I mean I sort of…bowled him over," she used one hand to knock another over, "I helped him up, helped pick up his things. He never seemed angry. He didn't say anything."

"That's why we call you Grace."

"No one has ever called me that."

"Well, I'm going to start," he countered with a smile. There was the faintest hint of a grin on her face. It was like a ray of sunshine peeking through the clouds.

"Thanks."

"No problem Grace," Dan smiled back. "As soon as Gary gets here, I'll go talk to Mr. Peters. Might even take Big G with me as backup."

"No!" she shouted, and then blushed. She froze, her head cocked to one side. She glanced at Dan, her eyes lighting with curiosity. "Why's Gary coming over? What, what are you up to now?"

"Me? Nothing," he shook his head.

She raised an eyebrow.

"I might have found a body though." He nodded toward the dumpster.

"Is that why it smells like poo?" Abbey asked, staring intently. She took a step forward and Dan gently took her arm.

Her skin was cold beneath the silk blouse Jules had bought her as an early Christmas present. The poor kid didn't have any decent work clothes.

"Gary gets very touchy about disturbed crime scenes."

"And you're definitely sure it's a dead body?"

"Well, I'm pretty sure he's not alive."

"Could it be a mannequin?"

"Yes, it could be. If it is, I will gladly apologize to Gary for wasting his time."

He didn't add that Dan had seen enough death in his time to know exactly what it looked like. No point in frightening her.

"No," Abbey's train of thought was more suggestion then anything else. "Don't talk to Mr. Peters. I'd rather just go home. Promise me you won't cajole Mr. Peters into giving me my job back."

"Well," Dan began.

She glared at him,

"Fine, I promise. If you'll wait, I will gladly drive you home."

She smiled, "That's sweet, but I actually meant home-home. As in Connecticut. It's been a while, and Father isn't getting any younger."

He had a vision of Abbey and her elderly father sitting around a roaring fire, sipping cider and having a riveting discussion about Keats. Or knitting. Or whatever two people did in the complete absence of a TV.

"Thank you," she said quietly.

"No problem. It'd be nice for you, going home, seeing family." Except Abbey was family. She was his Nakama, his friend. He didn't have many. Apparently, she didn't feel the same.

"Sure. You know, there will be other jobs."

He didn't answer the girl who hoarded fast food ketchup packets for cheap tomato soup. He liked saving his packets to add to her store of strange booty. Instead he asked, "Bus?"

"Oh," she responded flatly, not meeting his gaze. "I know someone who's going to Connecticut. I can catch a ride."

You're a lousy liar, he thought, making a mental note to hop online at lunch and get her a bus ticket.

"Well," Dan nodded toward the diner across the street. "When this is all finished how about I buy you breakfast? They do a Southwest Omelet that's to die for."

"Thanks," Abbey said, "But, I had a big breakfast this morning."

"Sure you did. But, I haven't. So you can sit and watch me eat, and then I can drive you back to campus. Because, between the Girl Scouts, and my falling for you, and mysterious shoplifters it's been a weird day."

"You think a Girl Scout killed Santa?" she asked with a grin. Abbey had a great smile.

"I won't know anything until Gary gets here. Just stick close by, please? Eat a cookie. It'll make you feel better."

She sighed dramatically. Given that she was a classically trained theater geek, it almost looked natural. "All right, you win. I'll wait for you to take me out to breakfast. We can talk about the case and then you can drive me home. Campus home, obviously."

"Obviously," Dan pulled the door open.

Abbey stepped inside, then turned on one heel.

"Don't think you can talk me into staying," she said, "I'm onto your little games."

Dan didn't bother replying. He was too busy laughing at her serious expression.

The door closed with a heavy thud.

Dan was good at staying put. He'd made a career out of parking in one spot and waiting for people to come to him. He was intimately familiar with every cheap no-tell motel in this town. He'd seen a lot of rendezvous. By-the-hour hotels, restaurants, even an occasional car wash. Been there, done that, got the t-shirt.

At least when he was in the car waiting he had a radio to keep him company. He had a spectacularly eclectic music collection. And, if the would-be Romeos, or in rare cases Juliets, picked the right spot, Dan could even get a pizza delivered to his car. Once he'd sent one to a room, in the case of an admirably enthusiastic couple. By his reckoning, they'd needed the fuel.

Dan had long ago developed the ability to sleep anywhere. Even standing up. In the P.I. business it was a survival trick because you never knew when you'd get to sleep next. Leaning his head against the cool metal of the door, hoping no one else would open it, he dozed off.

It was the sound of footsteps that woke him. Plodding boots, heavy, size 14 police issue. Dan didn't even bother opening his eyes.

"Hi Gary."

"Hiya Landis," a snide nasally voice shot back.

Dan's head shot up so fast, he heard his neck pop. There was Gary all right, and there was Bill Kelly, Gary's partner. The guy moved like a cat. An evil cat.

"Billy," Dan greeted him without much enthusiasm, "I thought you were on vacation."

"Yeah right," Billy sneered. "Us get Christmas off? Not hardly. We can't all be lollygagging around corralling shoplifters. Some of us have to catch real crooks."

"Dan…" Gary warned, gesturing with a thumb, "A word." He headed for the end of the alley.

As he followed Gary, Dan glanced back. Bill Kelly was eyeing the body. Billy was in his thirties. Older than Dan, younger than Gary, and short. Well, shorter than Dan who was a hairsbreadth under five ten, six feet in heels; everyone was shorter than Gary. Except maybe Godzilla.

Billy wore raggedy jeans, because someone once told him they looked cool, and a buttoned shirt with the top button always open. A thick rug peaked out over his white tank top. Billy had curly black hair, a permanent five o'clock shadow, and enough ego for ten men. Dan always wondered why Billy hated him so much. He knew better than to ask.

"Why not," the man would have answered with his predictable sneer.

As a private investigator, Dan always made it a point to never deliberately antagonize the police. The little man was a bottle of rage just waiting for a chance to unload. Then again...

Dan had once caught Billy cheating. That was Dan's job. Though sending them that pizza probably hadn't been a good idea. What he considered more important than any slight was the fact that he hadn't told anyone. Not on the force anyway. He had to tell Billy's wife. Obviously. She'd hired Dan.

But he had never told Billy how he'd happened to be there that night, never even hinted at it. If there was one thing Daniel G. Landis was good at, it was keeping secrets. He had gotten a lot of practice.

"Why'd you come out here?" Gary asked.

"Needed some fresh air," Dan lied.

Gary stared at him, and then looked back at the crime scene.

"Mr. Peters wanted me to tell you, there are no cameras out here." Dan explained. "Specifically, no helpful camera over the emergency exit."

"So I noticed," Gary didn't look at Dan. He was busy taking in the scene. "Why make it easy on us?"

Dan noticed how exhausted his friend looked. Even his mustache was droopy. Burn out was never pretty to watch.

Gary's slacks and white button-down shirt were as wrinkled as his coat. Even his black tie was crooked. The normally well-ordered, crisply pressed man looked hassled. Dan felt bad for calling the poor guy out here.

"Sorry," he offered lamely. Gary stared at him. "For calling."

"Never apologize for doing the right thing."

Dan leaned in and whispered, "What's up?"

Gary stared at the ground and whispered back, "Just doing my job, Gertie."

The slam of a car door made them both turn around. It was the Crime Scene Unit which amounted to a black SUV, a couple of college grads who had watched too much TV, and the Coroner's truck following close behind. Dan wondered if he should whistle *Who Are You*. He was surprised the crime scene van was available; Gary had been complaining single cops kept borrowing it to pick up chicks.

Gary turned back to face his brother-in-law, nodding in the direction of the body.

"Leave him alone," Gary said.

"Santa? Absolutely. I have no plans for messing with the dead."

"Kelly," Gary said, his voice taking on a strange tone. "He's having a tough time and I don't want you antagonizing him."

Dan was surprised at the tone in Gary's voice. It sounded so un-Gary like. What was it he heard? Sympathy? Empathy?

"Thank you," Gary said, walking away.

Dan resisted calling out to him. It didn't sound like the big man was up for the usual Landis shenanigans or to hear about Abbey being fired. And he probably could use a hug. Crime scenes were no place for hugs. Dan fought back his natural curiosity. The Jones' both had stressful careers; but as far as Dan knew, Gary and Julianne loved each other dearly.

Still, his little voice whispered, something's going on. Dan nodded to himself, then put it aside. Gary had a mystery to solve and it was best to just get out of his way while he did it.

He decided to go back inside. He felt chilly, and it really had nothing to do with temperature. The alley was giving off some bad mojo and he couldn't shake the image of Santa's body from his mind. He needed a change of scenery. He wondered where Abbey had gone, hopefully to the break room. Nodding cordially at Billy, he opened the metal door.

The crush of humanity was a welcome respite from the lonely emptiness of the crime scene. Dan even found the warm temperature a relief. Normally the great mass of unwashed shoppers gave him the creeps. He had had no idea he was demophobic until he started working at Murphy's. He got all of two steps inside the store when he was accosted. A helper-monkey bedecked in a crimson sport coat was standing there, arms crossed. Dan tried to recall the kid's name. Dave? George? Ralph? Dan looked at the nametag: Waldorf. Poor kid.

"Mr. Landis," Waldorf raised his chin and smoothed his coat. "Mr. Peters wants to see you in his office at your earliest convenience."

Dan nodded. This kid had to have been home schooled, private at least. No public school graduate ever used "At your earliest convenience" in normal conversation.

Waldorf left before Dan could ask where Statler was, which was disappointing. He loved those heckling Muppets. "Earliest convenience," Dan mumbled with a snort and decided to go check on Abbey first.

The sparkles of different bits of merchandise created a vast undulating sea of twinkling lights in the hands of shoppers fighting one another over last minute deals. The inordinate amount of sparkle might have had something to do with the gender of most of the shoppers. There were far more men here than normal, and the closer to Christmas it got, the more husbands started appearing, frantically trying to buy something perfect for their "lucky" ladies.

Suckers, Dan thought. He had done his Christmas shopping in June. Of course, it didn't hurt that he only had five real friends to buy for. He started checking off his few near and dear: Doc's getting a bottle of Scotch, Bernie didn't want anything so she's getting Saltwater Taffy, Gary's getting a signed copy of *Tuesdays with Morrie*, and Abbey's getting a brick. The girl loved bricks. She had a weird obsession with the art of masonry. Of course, it wasn't just any brick. It was a chunk of the Berlin Wall if the internet could be believed.

Hang on, Dan realized, that was four. He was forgetting someone. Jules! His sister was the hardest person in the world to buy for. Mainly because she was picky. Also, because she was rich. She was the most successful defense attorney in the City, maybe even the State.

"Crap," he glanced around to make sure Mr. Peters wasn't going to chastise him for swearing. The little bastard. He thought about wandering over to the toy department. She was a sucker for a stuffed animal. Maybe a Build-A-Bear? There was a workshop in the mall. Dan shuddered at the idea of facing the mall during Christmas. He decided to set that aside for now, leave it until later. He had time. He headed to the break room in search of coffee, Abbey, or preferably both.

The break room was empty. It wasn't anything extravagant, just a couple of tables, a microwave, a refrigerator and the two vending machines. But, there were no customers, and you could sit in peace. Some unused napkins were on the table.

Dan headed for the coffee machine. He hated this machine. He fancied himself a coffee connoisseur and had begged Mr. Peters to let him bring in a coffee maker. Just something small that he could set up on the counter. And, as the first one in, Dan could bring in the grounds. He had a Jamaican blend that was heaven in bean form. He was more than willing.

"That isn't very efficient," Mr. Peters had told him. Efficient. Dan had never realized how hateful that word could be.

Three counter girls walked in laughing. Two brunettes and a bleached blonde. They were giggling amongst themselves and paused when they saw Dan. He gave a wink and a smile.

"What's happening wage slaves?" Dan turned on the charm.

"Did you hear about your little friend?" The blonde asked, not even bothering to feign real regret.

"You'll have to be a bit more specific," Dan replied with a shrug, "I got lots of friends."

"Miss I-can-wrap-the-fastest-and-everyone-loves-me!" the blonde aped a Valley girl accent complete with hair flips.

Dan had to remind himself it was impolite to punch a girl. "What happened," Dan asked, turning to the coffee machine. He hit the button for the strongest coffee the machine made. Black, strong, and bitter, just like Gary. That made him chuckle.

"I heard she tried to put the moves on Mr. Peters," the blonde said, venom dripping from her tongue, "And she got canned." Her eyes narrowed. "Maybe she wasn't quite as good as he had hoped."

Dan put the coffee to his lips and took a long sip. He headed for the door.

"Where are you off to?"

"Oh, Mr. Peters office. He promised if I tapped into the employees' rumor mill to see if anyone knew what was really going on, he'd give Abbey the Wrapping Manager's job. Apparently Mr. Alejandro just can't satisfy him anymore."

The break room was dead silent as the door closed behind him.

Chapter 5

While Dan strolled across the main floor, he made a mental note to thank Gary for this wonderful job with such good hearted people. It was sometimes hard, when the cynicism well ran dry. A place like Murphy's was perfect for filling it back up. As he sipped his coffee, his eyes drifted from one face to another. All ages, all types, all with the same predatory expression. The customers of Murphy's Department store took shopping very seriously. Naturally, the Loss Prevention department, LP for short, took security equally serious. Cameras monitored every move while helper-monkeys in crimson sport coats browsed amicably amongst the shoppers. This whole fiasco had started with a phone call.

"What are you doing for Christmas?" Gary had asked. No greeting, just straight to the point.

Dan had glanced at his calendar, it was September. "What are *you* doing for Christmas?"

He heard Gary sigh, visualized him shaking his head. The big guy did it so often around Dan that by now he could do a dead-on impersonation. Not one for wasting time, Gary came straight to the point: Murphy's Department store was hiring. Would Dan be interested in picking up some LP work? An endorsement from a senior police officer like Sgt. Gary Jones went a long way. Of course Dan had said yes. He was going to have work during his slowest season. He even did a happy dance. He wasn't dancing anymore.

Someone coughed behind him. Dan turned around. Several women were glaring at him. Apparently, he had stopped walking and was holding up the line at the makeup counter. Dan had enough sense not to poke this particular dragon, so he stepped to one side with as sincere an apology as he could muster.

One middle aged woman in line kept staring at him as he walked by. A former client? Maybe.

Dan smiled at her.

The woman glared back.

Yep, definitely a client.

Memories started flooding back. Dan walked away slowly, still smiling at the customer. He tried not to run. He suddenly remembered that this client owned a pair of fuzzy handcuffs. He should probably mail them back to her.

He headed for the Security office. Mr. Peters could wait. Around the corner and past the Men's Dressing Room. Up the hidden stairwell, walking four flights, six landings, and seventy-two steps. Turn left at the exit, and you're at Security. Dan could do it blindfolded. The problem is, he mused, I'm too good at this job. As a member of Loss Prevention, his job was to ensure that all merchandise leaving the store was paid for first. Which was fine, except no respectable thief came into Murphy's. Dan had asked them politely not to come.

Now he was left watching the customers, all the time, waiting for them to steal something. From early in the morning until late in the evening. Seven days a week. It was as fun as it sounded. He tossed his now empty coffee cup into the trash can next to the elevator. Any trained monkey could do this job, Dan mused, and I hate being someone else's monkey. As he walked through the open door his eyes found the organ grinder who made the monkeys dance.

The man was big, bald, and wore thick glasses that gave his brown peepers that lovable bug-eyed expression. His name tag said Mr. Anderson. Dan called him Karl. He had tried calling him "Mr. Anderson," but it kept coming out slow and sarcastic. Sarcasm was forbidden at Murphy's.

Plus, Dan genuinely liked the guy. Sure Karl was king of his little hill, stood no chance of promotion, and smelled like moldy cheese. The big man was also quiet, unassuming, and kept a large dish of candies on his desk. The heavy bags beneath Karl's eyes, and a generally hang dog expression made Dan think of Droopy the Dog. Karl spent his entire workday sitting in the office, watching the huge bank of monitors. Dan hated those monitors.

As a private investigator, watching people was part of the job. In fact, he enjoyed people watching. As individuals, they were fascinating. But as a great pressing throng they gave him the willies. He had two options: walk the floor or sit in this room and listen to Karl's heavy breathing. At least there was candy.

With the strategically placed cameras, inconspicuous so as not to spoil the shopping experience, you could monitor the entire store.

The monitors allowed a bird's eye view of the store; it always felt like he was looking down on the common folk. The black and white screens gave Dan vertigo.

"Problem is, I am common folk," he told the room. He liked being common folk.

Karl continued observing the monitors. The big man tended to ignore Dan's random outbursts. Karl had on his standard off-white shirt, black slacks and black suspenders. He could never tell if the man changed clothes, or just wore the same thing continuously.

Stealing a toffee candy, Dan unwrapped and popped it in his mouth. He tossed the wrapper in the garbage. Karl was fastidious about office cleanliness. Dan turned to watch a master at work. Karl had the job down to a science. Like a skilled poker player, Karl simply had to watch for a shoplifter's tells. It was all in the body language. The bobbing head, the shifting gaze, the awkward stance. The shoulders would tense up, and the hands would fidget.

The real give away was the eyes. If you looked close enough you could always spot the hopeful thief eyeing the nearest employee, before they even pocketed an item.

Half the time, Dan never saw the actual theft take place. Not that it mattered. Karl saw; he saw everything. He would spot the shoplifter, lift up his walkie-talkie, and call in his minions. A polite young man bedecked in a crimson sport coat, would walk up to the offender. Congenial words would be exchanged; the trained monkey would carefully avoid making a scene. Some excuse would be given, such as a car's lights being on or that they won the 1000th customer prize. Karl probably had a list called "A hundred things to tell the Customer." The thief would be escorted into a nearby office, and the door would shut. A few minutes later, the unfortunate soul would be discretely escorted off the premises. Mr. Peters took theft seriously.

Of course, Dan thought with a smile, Mr. Peters probably took tying his shoes seriously. For his place in all this, Dan just tried to keep out of trouble, quietly spinning his wheels. He had no idea how Karl could stand this room. All four walls were painted a dull pea green, illuminated only by the bank of monitors. He supposed painted walls were a concession, as plain white was more efficient.

Someone, probably Mr. Peters, had hung up a cheerful motivational poster to boost morale. Odd since only Karl used the office regularly. The poster had a kitten hanging onto a branch, with a caption that read "Hang in there!" The kitten was adorable. The affect on Karl seemed negligible. Dan hated that poster.

When the day came that he finally snapped, Dan was going to tear down that poster. Probably replace it with a humorous demotivational poster. He had one picked out. Swapping them was Dan's safety valve. In case of insanity, break glass.

So far he hadn't, but that day was approaching fast. He could feel it every time he was forced to speak to Mr. Peters. The problem is, Dan thought, I'm trapped. The security office only needed one man to run it, and he was too qualified to be a helper-monkey on the floor. I am now, he reminded himself, frustrated with his big mouth.

On day one he'd been given his crimson sport coat and wore it without objection. Then he'd seen something he couldn't ignore.

"Mr. Anderson," Dan had said to Karl innocently enough. "You should probably keep an eye on Tex."

Karl had glanced sideways at the young man and grunted. It had taken half a dozen one-sided conversations for Dan to realize Karl didn't speak. He grunted. The man was capable of speech, but he used the minimum amount of words as a rule. It reminded Dan of his Dad. Maybe that was what he liked most about Karl. The big butterball.

"There's a big guy," Dan had said, putting on his most helpful smile. He even pointed the guy out on the screen, "Jewelry section. Big blond fellow, relaxed expression. He's casing the place."

Karl had stared at the fresh faced new kid. Dan was painfully aware that the loose crimson sport coat, his inability to grow facial hair, and baby face made him look all of twelve. Karl turned back to the monitor. The man never asked why Dan was not on the floor. Dan never forgot that Karl took him at his word.

"There," Dan pointed out again, though it was a bit unnecessary at that point. Tex, with the ten gallon hat, flowing duster jacket, and pacing of a barracuda stood out in the crowd. Once he'd been pointed out there was no losing him.

After a moment, Karl picked up the phone. Not the walkie-talkie, the telephone. Tex was still eyeing the display cases, carefully noting employee movements.

It was like watching a lion singling out a gazelle. Karl had grunted, and then dialed a number. Dan was proud of his contribution. The problem was he had helped all right, a little too well. Mr. Peters was very pleased. As it turned out, Tex had been planning a robbery for rush hour later that day. He would have cleaned out the register, the jewelry counter, and most of the customers.

Worst of all, crimson sports coats weren't designed to stop bullets. Tex always carried his signature weapon, twin six-shooters with pearl handles. The police had the sense to handle the man with care. He was as dangerous as a tiger when cornered. Dan had always tried to avoid dealing with Tex, and fortunately their paths had never officially crossed. He knew enough about him to know the guy was bad news, not afraid to get dirty. Also, his real name was Mortimer Hasselberg. With a name like that, Dan would call himself Tex too.

Now the urban cowboy was in jail, Mr. Peters was happy, and Karl seemed to tolerate Dan's presence. He had worried that Karl might feel threatened, that the young upstart was poaching on the big dog's turf. As it turned out, there was no need to worry. Karl was a professional, and his grunts toward Dan had taken on a friendlier tone. At least it made hanging out in Security easier. He was now free to walk the store at his leisure and Karl even compromised on the sport coat. Show the colors without attracting attention. Incognito was the word Mr. Peters had used.

Dan knew that meant 'blend and play nice' in the Boss' mind, and knew better than to argue. His new responsibilities were to smile a lot, keep an eye on the customers, and look out for any bad guys. Or attractive shoplifters. Funny thing was, he couldn't remember what she looked like. Dan wondered if Karl could make a tape of that girl. Which reminded him of why he was here.

"So," Dan said, "I sort of found a body in the alley behind the store." Silence. "Mr. Peters probably told you that, huh?" Karl stared at the monitors. "On the upside Gary, uh Sergeant Jones, is on the case."

"Good man," Karl grunted.

Dan wasn't surprised. Karl and Gary probably hung out on the weekends at the Quiet Contemplative Detectives Club.

"Cold outside, huh?" Dan asked. "Was traffic bad when you came in? Because it was a madhouse over on Blakely."

Karl didn't respond, just reached into his candy dish and extracted a peppermint. He unwrapped it one handed, popped the candy in his mouth, and tossed the balled up paper in the can. Karl's eyes never left the screen, it was a well-rehearsed symphony of movements.

"Any thoughts on who might have done it? The dead body I mean. I'm pretty sure the traffic was just road construction. Though, the two could have had something to do with one another." Karl turned, raising one eyebrow. "Right. I'm gonna go find Mr. Peters."

Karl turned back to face the monitors.

On his way out, Dan stole two butterscotches. They were Abbey's favorites.

Chapter 6

As Dan ambled around the corner, he was nearly run over by a jogging Santa. He bounced off the soft belly, falling on his butt. Santa blushed scarlet, as red as his suit.

"Oh I am so sorry young man," the jolly elf reached down for him.

"I'm sorry about that." Dan replied, as he took one black gloved hand.

Santa picked Dan up one-handed, setting him on his feet. Apparently Father Christmas worked out. "Nonsense," he said, not even winded. "I'm a silly old fool, and should certainly watch where I'm going." Santa eyed him carefully, a sincere smile on his face. He was the most authentic looking Santa this side of 34th Street. Rosy cheeks, twinkly eyes, and a full fluffy beard. Even the belly looked perfect for shaking like a bowl full of jelly.

"Santa?" Dan asked, blinking with a loopy smile on his face.

"Yes," Santa smiled back.

"I'm…just really glad to see you alive," Dan scooted around the big man.

"Thank you," Santa bobbed his head at him. "You're Daniel Landis, correct?"

"Um, yes?" Dan wasn't sure how to reply. "How did you…"

Santa just tapped the side of his head. As he left, Dan tried not to run. He had the impression that this Santa knew exactly how naughty he had been. That wasn't good.

"I hope you're not going to be talking to Mr. Peters about me," Santa called out, a smile in his voice.

Dan stopped, staring at Santa. "Well, um, no." He stuttered, unable to find the right words. "You're not the Santa he's worried about. Completely different Santa, no relation I'm sure."

"Ah my boy," Santa drew himself up and rested his hands on his belly, "Aren't we all united by the great spirit of giving; the true meaning of The Season. Aren't all Santas, in fact, one Santa?" Dan blinked, uncertain what to say. With a grin and a nod Santa strolled away. Apparently Santa was also a philosopher.

Dan watched him jog away. It was part skipping, part waddle, and all too authentic. Santa stopped at the corner, theatrically looking around it to check for oncoming traffic. He turned back, staring directly into Dan's eyes.

"Merry Christmas," Santa said with a knowing grin.

"Merry Christmas," Dan replied automatically. Santa continued on his merry way.

"He's good," Dan mumbled under his breath, staring at the departing St. Nick.

"Oh yeah," Abbey's familiar voice agreed, "And really friendly too."

Dan spun around, finding himself inches from the Abbinator. He'd been too busy staring at Santa. She bit her lip, shuffled her feet.

"What are you doing here?" He assumed she was up to something.

"Waiting on you?"

"How'd you know I was going to be here?"

"Because you promised that you wouldn't coerce Mr. Peters into giving me the job back. I'm here to make sure you keep that promise."

"Would I go back on my promise?" Dan asked.

Abbey raised an eyebrow.

"Would I lie to you?"

She raised the other eyebrow.

"All right," he admitted with a chuckle, "stop with the third degree. I promise, I won't try to convince Mr. Peters to give you the wrapping job back."

"Or Mr. Alejandro's Managerial position," she said. Dan's face must have given his shock away, because she smiled demurely and pointed back the way he came, "I'd been hiding in

Karl's office this entire time. I only left when you came by. Thank you for sticking up for me in the break room."

"Two things," he said. "One, you're my friend, and I'll always stick up for you. And B), I will never turn down an opportunity to stick it to the man. Or woman." He wrapped one arm around her shoulder, giving her a quick side-hug and squeeze. "Wait for me in Security, okay? And stop lip-reading, it scares me when you do that."

As Dan walked down the hall, headed for Mr. Peters office, he felt good. Between Santa and Abbey, it was hard to stay angry. He started whistling *God Rest Ye Merry Gentlemen*.

Mr. Peters was standing at his desk, his back to the door, when Dan knocked on the doorframe.

The door itself was open, as Mr. Peters always encouraged an open door policy. Dan hated open door policies, they were condescending. It just meant the person with the open door was better at hiding things. As he walked in, he noted that Mr. Peters was staring at the bank of monitors, twins of the ones in the Security office. Plus one. Dan's eye was drawn to Abbey, grabbing a seat beside Karl. She didn't talk, just stared at the monitors. The pair of them looked adorably antisocial.

Mr. Peters cleared his throat. Dan held his peace. He stared at the back of the man's balding head as he watched the screens in front of him. Despite Santa and Abbey's calming influences from earlier, he still wasn't sure what the first words would be out of his mouth. It might involve too much snark to be polite.

Mr. Peters remained silent. Dan wondered if this was one of those stupid power games. He hated games; well, power games. He loved Monopoly.

"I wonder, Mr. Landis," Mr. Peters spoke without turning around. "If your skills are benefitting us here."

Well Abbey, Dan thought, you win. It looks like I'm going to have to keep that promise.

"I thought I was benefitting you, Sir," he kept his voice even, "Until now," he decided not to add.

Turning around, Mr. Peters switched topics. "What have the authorities discovered thus far?"

Dan was shocked by his boss' change in appearance. Mr. Peters' looked tired; his face was pale, his shoulders drooped, there was even a shadow under his eyes. It never crossed his mind that Mr. Peters might be having a hard time with this situation, though a dead Santa outside your door would be a challenge for the best of them. Dan had assumed Mr. Peters didn't feel human emotions.

The strain wouldn't be noticeable to a casual observer, but then again, Dan Landis was no casual observer. Reading people came with the job description.

"The police are investigating," Dan assured him, "And I know the officers involved personally. Their investigation will be thorough, and definitely discreet."

Mr. Peters pursed his lips and nodded curtly before turning back to the monitors.

They both waited out the next minute, Dan was uncertain if he was dismissed.

"Mr. Anderson speaks highly of you, Mr. Landis." Mr. Peters finally said. It seemed he wasn't finished yet. Dan wasn't sure how to react to that, or where this new line was leading. It was definitely the strangest way he'd been fired.

Well, that's what you get for fraternizing with the hired help, Dan's little voice chided. Yeah, Dan thought, but fraternizing is what I do. Isn't it just, the little voice shot back with a smile.

"In your outside position," Mr. Peters broke into Dan's inner monologue, "What sort of duties do you typically perform for your clients?"

Dan blinked rapidly. That question was a loaded one. The answer depended on how you defined duties. Exactly what was Mr. Peters proposing? And why, oh why, Dan thought, do I now have the mental image of Mr. Peters proposing to me? He tried not to shudder.

"You mean as a private investigator?" Dan asked, hopeful.

"Of course Mr. Landis," Mr. Peters said with the hint of a sneer.

"Oh, a variety of things," Dan said, sighing in relief, "Process serving, private security, background checks…"

Like the background of a cheap motel room, he thought. Dan figured Mr. Peters didn't need that kind of clarification. He would probably think that it was distasteful. Probably right, too.

"You said private security," Mr. Peters spoke to the monitors, "Would that include acting as a bodyguard?"

Dan's brain was racing, Mr. Peters had his curiosity piqued. Where was this going? "Of course," Dan smelled money on the horizon. "I've done a variety of private security and bodyguard work. In fact, I'm licensed to carry a concealed weapon." Mr. Peters mouth dropped open in horror. Dan quickly added, "But out of respect for the company and the safety of my fellow employees, I have never carried a weapon on the premises." And, he didn't mention, the gun he carried only fired blanks. He didn't like to advertise that fact.

Mr. Peters still seemed shocked. Dan decided to sit down. It helped diffuse the situation, made him less intimidating, and helped ease the obviously uncomfortable Mr. Peters. He sank down in the chair, Mr. Peters elevated high above him in his strategically larger chair. Mr. Peters closed his mouth, his beady eyes locked onto Dan. He decided to adopt what he called his

"Client Voice." Calm, reassuring, and most importantly a voice you'd be willing to trust with your money.

"Mr. Peters," he began, staring openly up at the man. "I have an excellent track record as an investigator. I've been trained in counter-surveillance, evasion techniques, and am on excellent terms with the local and state authorities."

"Well," Mr. Peters said cautiously, steadying his trembling hands on the desk, "I wonder if you would be interested in taking on some extra responsibilities, in addition to your current duties here at Murphy's Department Store."

"Certainly Sir," Dan nodded, struggling to keep the grin off his face. More money came with more responsibility. "I assure you, you will find yourself in good hands."

"Excellent," Mr. Peters said, "please meet with our store's Santa after we close tonight."

Dan blinked. "I'm sorry, what?"

"Someone has killed an individual dressed as Santa Claus right outside our store." Mr. Peters said, matter-of-factly. "I would like to retain your services. To, for lack of a better word, protect our store's investment, i.e. Santa Claus."

Dan tried hard not to laugh at the thought of Santa as a tradable commodity. Mr. Peters was obviously waiting for a response. Choking back his laughter, he cleared his throat and resumed his professional tone. "Of course, Sir. But, you should know, as a private investigator, my rate is significantly higher than my current wage."

"Naturally," Mr. Peters waved a hand dismissively, "Murphy's Department Store would retain your services as a freelance contractor. Please submit an invoice to our accounting department."

Dan tried to discretely check to make sure his mouth was closed. He nodded slowly. "I can do that Sir." Mr. Peters hadn't even flinched. For Dan, Christmas had come a few days early. Mr. Peters nodded signaling their conversation had come to an end and Dan shot to his feet. His boss seemed briefly startled by the sudden movement, but quickly regained his composure.

"As I said, please meet our Santa at closing. Your new duties will begin then."

"Hopefully, this whole fiasco will blow over with only this one unfortunate incident." Mr. Peters picked up a pen and turned it in his hands, "At any event, our Santa's contract ends with The Season. Thus, this will not be our problem for much longer."

There it was, that irritating Season talk again, Dan blew a mental gasket. He found it was a little easier to tolerate with a few zeros behind it.

"Don't let me detain you," Mr. Peters put the pen down on his desk, arranging it just so before turning back to the bank of monitors.

Dan paused, a marvelously evil thought occurring to him. "Sir," he said, trying not to grin, "I wonder if I might make a suggestion, pertaining to bodyguard duties."

"Yes?" Mr. Peters rotated back, his pinched face suspicious.

"Yes Sir," Dan said, "whoever killed Santa may try something inside the store."

"My word," Mr. Peters blanched. He slowly sank down, melting into his seat. "Do you think so?"

Dan leaned in, careful not to put his hands on the desk. That would only offend Mr. Peters, and take away his momentum. "It's possible," he said quietly. "So, with your permission and as part of my bodyguard services, I would like to put one of my associates in close proximity to Santa, during the day at least."

"I had hoped you would remain close," Mr. Peters bobbed his head.

"Absolutely. I will definitely be keeping a very close eye on Santa and will make sure to get him home safely each night. But, it occurs to me there's a way to get even closer than standard surveillance." Dan gestured with one thumb at the monitors. A pair of Elves was talking to the parents, entertaining them until Santa came back from his break.

"I assume you do not refer to yourself for this costumed role?" Mr. Peters asked, no hint of humor in his voice. The man probably had his funny bone surgically removed for lack of efficiency, Dan mused.

"No Sir. But, I do have a trusted associate who would blend in perfectly."

"Whatever you think is best," Mr. Peters again waved his hand.

Victorious, Dan straightened and headed for the door. "She'll be in tomorrow morning," he called over his shoulder. Mr. Peters nodded. "And I'll meet Mr. Claus at the employee locker room tonight," Dan said, "After his shift ends."

Mr. Peters once again turned his back on Dan. He continued his careful observance of the various monitors. As he left, Dan tried not to skip. There were worse jobs than being Santa's bodyguard. He couldn't wait to tell Abbey, she was going to be thrilled.

She wasn't.

Chapter 7

"Are you out of your mind?" Abbey shouted. It wasn't exactly the reaction Dan had hoped for.

"No," he felt his smile fading, "I thought you'd be happy."

"You lied to me!" She was flush with rage and more than likely a healthy dose of indignation.

"Yes…no, wait, I did not."

"I told you not to…"

"You made me promise not to get your old job as a wrapper or Alejandro's job."

"Exactly."

Dan glanced around. Karl was staring at the monitors.

"Can we not argue in front of the kids?" Dan leaned in and whispered. "It bothers him."

Abbey ignored his attempt at levity. "So, anytime I make you promise something, I am supposed to eliminate any possible loopholes?" she asked, her green eyes blazing.

"No," Dan said, a little hurt, "You just have to trust me."

"How can I trust you if you always lie to me?"

"Well you can trust that I will always lie. And keep life interesting." He offered his most genuine grin.

Karl snorted. It was very close to a laugh. Dan glared at him. The big man continued to stare at the monitors with his back to his visitors.

"Anyway," Dan decided to cut his losses, "You'll be working for me." He rolled his eyes up and made a circular gesture with his hand. "For Murphy's through me. Through LP through Karl, on behalf of Murphy's through me." He worried his attempt to clarify possibly was doing the opposite. Abbey threw her hands up in the air and stormed off. Dan glanced at Karl's wide back. "Any advice?" Karl stared at his monitors. "Right," Dan watched the monolith of a man maintain his silence, realizing how much Karl reminded him of his Dad. "You're right, I could have broken it to her easier. All right, I'll go apologize."

He stepped out the open door, heading for the stairs. Abbey was at the balcony looking down on the teeming masses. "Two psychics bump into each other. The first one says, 'Well you're fine, but how am I?'"

Abbey turned around, "What?"

"Joke," he smiled uncertainly, "Break the tension."

"I hate when you lie to me."

"Yes, but I do it so artfully. It's my shtick."

"Well I'm tired of your shtick. I want to go home. Homesick is my shtick." She frowned, becoming predictably sidetracked. "Actually, accents are my shtick. That and juggling. And wearing funny hats."

"Can you juggle while wearing a funny hat?"

"Not really." The corner of her mouth tugged up.

Dan felt his shoulders relax. "Why not?"

"The hat keeps getting in the way." Abbey eased onto an elbow on the balcony railing.

Dan knew he was forgiven. Then he held his breath for the next part, wondering how long the forgiveness would last. "There's a costume with the job, possibly a funny hat."

"Yes," she pointed at an elf, "That costume specifically. I did reason that part out."

The Elves were managing the crowd flow expertly, shifting the parents and kids every few seconds in a synchronized effort. Santa was holding court in his little section of Murphy's. The two of them watched for a minute. The business of bringing cheer went like clockwork.

"I hate crowds," she said backing away, "it was fine when I had a counter between us and them."

"Demophobia," he said knowingly, taking a step closer to her. "I looked it up; I feel the same way about crowds of people."

"I'm agoraphobic."

"I thought that's open spaces."

"Yes, and fear of crowds of people. It's complicated. I also don't like open closet doors right before I go to sleep."

"Afraid a monster's going to come out and get you?"

"No, I'm afraid my clothes are going to strangle me in my sleep." She gave him one of her smiles.

He turned to stare at her.

She mistook his focus on her and grew uncomfortable. "I just want to go home," she glanced down again to watch Santa's village, "Be around completely normal people. Like Papa."

"You don't have to…I'm not forcing you to stay."

"I know," Abbey said, distracted.

Hoping to keep her with him by his usual method of dragging her along, Dan waved a hand. "Let's go get breakfast and I can plan. I can't think on an empty stomach." He headed toward the stairwell, pausing when Abbey didn't follow. "Abs, you coming?"

"Yes, I just, I was looking at Santa."

He glanced back. Right at that moment Santa looked up at them and waved. Dan and Abbey waved back.

"He kind of weird's me out," she confessed.

"That's okay," he said with a smile and a wave, "he scares the crap out of me."

"After we eat," she turned, her face oddly flushed, "Can you take me back to campus?"

"Yes," he studied her expression curiously.

"I'm sorry for getting angry."

"That's okay, you're kind of cute when you get angry."

"Thank you," she blinked, considering his words.

"I bet you'd look downright fashionable dressed like a little elf," he added.

"No." Dan glared at him. "And those aren't elves. At best they're gnomes, though given the mythology, they're more like brownies than anything else."

"What?" Dan found himself overtaxed, a common side effect of hanging out with someone significantly smarter than him.

"Nothing, just forget I said that," Abbey shook her head. "Just take me back to campus, I need to pack."

Dan sighed. He knew better than to push the issue. When Abbey started quoting mythology she was really mad.

"All right," he wisely agreed, "Let me just check in with Gary, find out what's going on with the body. Want to meet me out front?" He checked the time on his phone, "Say, fifteen minutes?"

Abbey nodded. He watched her walk away, exhaling. She could be stubborn. And had a cute butt. A cute stubborn butt. Now what? His little voice asked. "Gary," he said aloud. When in doubt, talk to Gary. The big man was a fountain of good advice.

A sense of loyalty gave him pause and he decided to tell Karl he was bailing for a bit. Karl didn't care. So long as Dan didn't cause trouble for the big man, he was given free rein to do things his way. Apparently it was a perk of being known for getting good results.

On his way back to Security, he was tying himself in knots. He was supposed to be good with people. Always had been, with his little black book as exhibit A. They said he was good. Abbey was more difficult to get a bead on. He couldn't be sure from moment to moment where he stood with her. Maybe that was what he liked about her.

Just when he thought he had her all figured out, she threw him a curve ball. Sometimes he thought she was contrary just to prove a point. Abbey was stubborn and had her dignity to consider. Though, if their situations were reversed, Dan knew he'd have jumped at the opportunity to infiltrate the capitalist establishment's seasonal facade. Apparently, Abbey didn't have Dan's burning anarchistic tendencies. On the upside, he had a real job for once and was taking it seriously.

That he had neglected to inform Mr. Peters that he'd never actually worked as a bodyguard didn't bother his questionable morality. It wasn't that he didn't know how, he had merely never gotten the opportunity. Dan had told the truth about his training though. He had learned from the best. That was qualifier enough by his reasoning.

Yet, for some reason no one wanted to put their lives in the hands of Dan Landis. Mr. Peters would be the first. Just not his own life. The poor man had to be really desperate, or cheap, probably cheap. Maybe things are finally starting to look up, Dan thought. He would have been more excited at the prospect of such lucrative work except other questions kept nibbling at his consciousness, whispering in the back part of his brain. He stopped, thinking.

For starters, why didn't the emergency exit alarm go off? That was a pretty important security feature. Even if the smokers had disabled it, wouldn't the store fix it? Why did everyone but security know about it? And speaking of security, the door should have been locked from the outside. That was pretty universal for security systems. Yet, Abbey had gone out the door. She wasn't a smoker and she knew. How? And how had he forgotten to mention it afterwards to Gary? The whole 'Dead Santa' thing was more distracting than he'd given it credit for.

That returning quandary brought with it another forgotten question. What ever happened to that one thief? Dan paused. He remembered a goofy green sweater, with twinkling lights. He stuck his hands in his pockets. This could get ugly and he'd drawn Abbey in deep.

Dan's finger played with the butterscotch candy in his pocket. Abbey liked butterscotches. Maybe he could ask Karl for advice about Abbey? No, that idea died on the vine. Karl just didn't seem the type that went anywhere near women. Except maybe online.

But, Karl did need to know about the fire alarm. That was probably important. That and he definitely needed to tell him about the lock on the door. The likelihood that the two were connected was high. Maybe, Dan hoped, he would luck out and Karl would have captured that mysterious thief on video. It would be nice to put a face with a sweater.

Arriving, he glanced at the Security door. It was closed which meant Karl was out. The gray door automatically locked upon closing and only Karl had the key. Dan knocked on the door, just in case. There was no answer. If you were going to break into a room, it was important that the room be empty. He turned his back to the door, facing the hallway. With one hand he pulled his lock pick kit out of his back pocket. He loved that little kit.

Letting his free hand move across the rows of picks, Dan's fingertips searched for just the right tool. The right tool for the right job he always said.

The Security door's lock was a standard Corporate R91: self-locking, stainless steel, and mighty intimidating. His personal best on this particular lock was nine seconds, and that was with Dobermans chasing him. He leaned against the door, resting his head on the cool metal. This should be a piece of cake.

He had to resist whistling while working the lock. That would probably be overdoing the whole image of nonchalance. Instead, he studied the framed picture of flowers hanging on the wall across from him. He supposed the bowl of tulips was supposed to inspire some sort of sense of well-being.

An amateur would have bent down, not bothering to think about appearances when breaking and entering. A real pro always left a way out, in case someone walked by. Also, there was a camera in this hallway, which meant he needed to be as inconspicuous as possible.

Footsteps rang faintly against the linoleum. Fairly light, intentionally quiet. Probably Mr. Peters. Which meant he wasn't in his office monitoring this hallway.

The lock clicked.

Dan slipped inside, quietly closing the door behind him. He hated attracting attention on a job. Feeling the door's lock click back into place, securing it, Dan turned around and searched the monitors for the hallway camera.

There.

Dan smiled at the image of Mr. Peters approaching the Security door. His boss paused to pull out his keys and Dan slipped into his usual chair, stealing a peppermint from Karl's dish. He decided against propping his feet up on the desk. Instead he opted for mildly interested.

The door opened, and Dan stood up, smiling politely. "Hello again, Mr. Peters Sir," he said, feigning surprise.

"Mr. Landis," Mr. Peters was once again unflappable. He seemed to have recovered his composure from the last time they had spoken.

Dan was glad. It was almost sad to see the Prince of Dorkness lose his cool. Well, not cool, but at least less shaken.

"Anything I can assist you with Sir?" Dan asked benignly.

"No," Mr. Peters replied, equally bland. "I was looking for Mr. Anderson."

Dan dutifully looked around the small room. "I'm afraid he isn't here Sir," he raised his eyebrows. "I was going to wait for him to come back. You're welcome to join me if you'd like." Dan continued to smile politely at the man, daring him to ask how he got in here. He had to know where Karl was. Mr. Peters knew everything. He probably assumed Karl gave Dan a key.

Technically that was allowed since Security was entirely Karl's domain. However, duplicating a key had not been officially approved by Mr. Peters. Everything had to be approved by Mr. Peters.

Dan wasn't worried. Karl was too valuable to be fired over something as trivial as a key, and Mr. Peters was too proper to reprimand him. Besides, Dan would be gone by January. So even if it wasn't acceptable, at least it wasn't a misstep that called for action. Especially for Karl, the big old Jelly Belly. Dan was starting to understand the appeal mind games had for people like Mr. Peters. They allowed for a brief distraction in an otherwise painfully dull life.

Footsteps shook him from his thoughts. Big, heavy, stomping footsteps; belonging to someone who didn't care about the linoleum. It was either Karl, or an elephant was loose in the hall.

"I believe that's him now Mr. Peters," Dan offered. He gave his biggest, cheesiest grin, and opened the door. Karl was indeed coming towards them, key in hand. His shirt, possibly white in another life, was stained gray from external as well as internal sources of oil and other fluids. He was breathing heavy and covered in sweat. Dan grimaced, fearing his comrade would not make it.

Mr. Peters always made the big man take the stairs. Something about fitness goals. Evil came in many different packages.

Karl finally reached them and grunted, standing outside the door. Dan continued to smile. Mr. Peters sniffed.

Dan couldn't understand his boss' attitude toward the big man. Karl was great at his job, and yet Mr. Peters still treated him like dirt. Just another reason to get out as soon as this was done. He had a vacation with Doc planned. Two swinging bachelors tearing up Warrenton, VA. An exhausted Karl plopped down in his seat, looking from Dan to Mr. Peters and back. He stared with bloodshot eyes at Dan.

Karl knew exactly how Dan had gotten in, and as always his face was unreadable. Dan felt a cold feeling in the pit of his stomach. He hoped that Karl wasn't angry with him.

"Police looking for you," Karl wheezed.

Dan nodded. The "Get out" was left unsaid. There was the faintest hint of a spark in Karl's eyes, the tiniest ghost of a smile. Dan felt his spirits lift. Somewhere in that chubby little cubby all stuffed with fluff, Karl was a rebel at heart.

"I was hoping to speak with you, Mr. Anderson," Mr. Peters said to Karl. The "In private" was also left unspoken. While louder, it was far less effective than Karl's dismissal.

Dan turned to leave. "Karl," he called back, "remind me to ask you about something later." Karl grunted. The grunt was smug, slightly satisfied. "Be seeing you Mr. Peters, Sir."

Mr. Peters was too busy frowning down at his other employee. He didn't even acknowledge Dan's goodbye. Dan was in the hall when the office phone rang. It was a sharp, distinctive ring that reminded Dan of the Batphone. He paused, his curiosity getting the better of him, and he slipped against the wall, out of sight from the door. Peeking in, he was only able to see Karl. Mr. Peters was further in. Karl answered the phone with one beefy hand and pointed to a monitor with a pinky. Dan saw himself in the hallway.

The big man rolled his eyes.

Dan was getting sloppy. Maybe it was time to hang it up before he hurt himself. He hoped Mr. Peters wasn't watching the monitors too.

"Security," Karl answered. There was muted conversation on the other end, and then Karl nodded. "I'll send the tapes along shortly." Karl hung up and Dan waited. "Police. They want security tapes sent over." He cleared his throat, glancing in Dan's directions. Dan nodded at the camera, and then walked quickly away. Time to leave.

Security tapes? That's interesting.

Especially, his little voice pointed out, since there were no cameras at the Emergency exit.

Jinkies, Dan thought, I smell a mystery! As he headed for the stairwell door, he wondered how all these events were connected. He'd been in the business too long to believe they were coincidences. A dead Santa, stuffed behind a dumpster, alarms that didn't sound, exit doors that weren't locked, and now the police were requesting useless video footage. Maybe they were just being thorough? Maybe. Gary was nothing, if not thorough. Dan loved that about him. That and the mustache. Gary had an awesome mustache.

The hallway came out by Sporting Goods. Golf, baseball, basketball, hunting. All the comforts of home. Dan closed the door, hearing it snap shut, the lock clicking in place. The snap sparked something in his mind. Something he had been thinking about since he first closed the Security Office's door. The emergency exit had never snapped shut. The lock hadn't just failed to engage, it hadn't clicked into place at all. Those kinds of doors, generally, were meant to be locked from the outside. So either the door was unlocked which they'd all assumed, or someone had gummed the works.

All right, he thought, who would want to jam the lock?

The murderer? His little voice suggested sarcastically.

"I almost forgot," Dan said to the ether. He hated murder mysteries even more than unfaithful spouses. Why couldn't he ever get fun cases? Like someone digging a giant tunnel from a pawn broker's to a bank? Better tell Gary. The man devoured mystery novels and always figured out the ending halfway through. He was a natural detective besides being one by vocation.

Dan, on the other hand, usually flipped to the last page to find out who did it and then gave up the book halfway through.

With that realization, he figured out another. That call for video wasn't for footage, it was for him. Gary told Karl he was looking for Dan, and he told him to be quiet about it. Which put

Dan on alert. Gary wasn't one to waste time nor be secretive if he didn't have to be.

They were on the dreaded 48 hour crime clock. If a case wasn't solved within the first 48, statistics said it was likely to remain unsolved. Unsolved mysteries gave Gary ulcers.

Dan paused mid-step, his Spidey-sense tingling. Someone was watching him, he could feel it. He turned around, eyes scanning the crowded store. No sign of a green sweater, six foot tall cowboy, or anyone wielding a knife, rope or smoking gun. But he could tell, someone did have their eyes on him. He'd have put money on it. Past the racks of clothing and aisles of merchandise, Santa was still holding court. The man really had his Father Christmas act down to a science, he had the rapt attention of every child. Even the mothers were being civil.

That wasn't what had tweaked Dan's senses. He realized that in between talking to the kids Santa kept looking directly at him. A chill ran up his spine.

The look on Santa's face, the steady, piercing gaze Dan saw even from this distance, left no doubt that this man didn't have to check his list twice. He knew exactly who had been naughty and nice. And unless Dan was mistaken, Santa was smiling at him.

He wasn't sure how to react to that smile; it was a bit too knowing for Dan's taste. That and the fact that there was no small amount of amusement in Santa's smile.

He suddenly had a burning desire to escape: the crowds, the slightly unnerving manic Christmas music, and the big elf. Especially Santa. He could feel the man's eyes fixed on him. It felt like he was an open book, his deeds written clearly for the man to peruse. Dan sensed that Santa could see through all of his silly, witty masks. And he wasn't entirely pleased with what was being read on those pages.

The holly jolly season was too intense for him, and he dashed inside the employee locker room. Thankfully, it was deserted. Dan opened his locker and grabbed his jacket, tossing in the red vest. He slipped on the jacket, took a moment to orient himself, and made for the exit.

It was 125 steps from the locker room to the emergency exit. Closely examining the red painted front, Dan saw the expected posted notice: 'Alarm will sound if opened.'

"Thought so," he muttered. He pushed on the door slightly, the door swinging open smoothly. He waited for the alarm.

Nothing. The heavy door swung shut, Dan heard no telltale click. The lock was definitely off. Shrugging, he slammed the door open. There was a thump as it hit something solid.

Dan rushed out; horrified at the idea that he hit someone. The last thing he saw was a fist rushing toward his face.

Chapter 8

Dan's head snapped back, rolling with the punch. He felt the familiar tingle in his jaw, the old rush of adrenaline. His body moved instinctively. Legs automatically spread apart, bending at the knees, his feet flattened to hug the ground. The muscle memory moved automatically, fists launching out. His right moved, catching just below the eye, the left went in for the kill. Dan's fist connected below and to one side of his attacker's jaw, his muscles tightening at the last possible second. He felt the impact shoot up his arm, heard the body go down with a satisfying thud. When he looked down, he knew he was in trouble.

Billy Kelly lay flat on his back and glared up at him, murder in his eyes.

"Knock it off you two," Gary bellowed as he ran over.

With a steel grip, Gary yanked Dan away, holding out a hand to keep Billy at a distance. The man didn't look to be in a hurry to stand up.

Kelly rubbed his jaw, enjoying the sight of Dan in trouble.

Good old southpaw, Dan thought, trying not to smirk. Be glad I pulled that second punch. Otherwise you wouldn't be conscious. Gary yanked Dan away, leading him to the street end of the alley.

I'm in trouble, Dan snapped back to reality. Gary's going to kill me, I'm going to get arrested, and Julianne is going to dig up my body and kill me all over again. Gary was so angry he wasn't even speaking, just making splutters. If it weren't for his ebony skin tone, Dan was sure Gary would be cherry red. Dan didn't have to be told how serious this was. This was assault on an officer. Gary had done a lot of things for his idiot brother-in-law, but lying would never be one of them.

"You..." Gary stammered, at a loss for words. "What?"

Dan's mind raced. Billy had started it of course, but that wouldn't fly. Even though the man was notorious for starting fights, he was a cop. A cop who had many forced 'vacations'.

"I'm sorry Gary," he said, meaning it. "I was an idiot. I opened the door too fast. It must have struck Officer Kelly, and in my haste to assist him in getting up, we must have gotten all tangled up. It was entirely my fault."

Gary stared at Dan. Dan decided to adopt his most humble expression. Gary didn't buy it for a second, and Dan knew it. Worse, Gary knew that Dan knew it. But, they both knew Billy couldn't get suspended again. The man was on his last legs, legally speaking. Billy had as much reason to keep this quiet as Dan. More importantly for Dan, Julianne wouldn't hear about this little incident. Jules had a scary temper.

"Be more careful…we don't want you opening the wrong door," Gary said flatly.

"Absolutely. You never know what could be behind it."

"Dan?"

"Yes G-Man?"

"Good hit. Now stop pushing your luck." There was a slight smile on his face. He turned his back on Dan, watching the cars pass.

Dan stared at the back of the big man's head, wondering how many of those gray hairs he had caused. "So, you wanted to see me?" Gary didn't answer right away. With a sigh, he turned back around, and stared over Dan's head. Dan turned back, following Gary's lead. The body was long gone and Billy was standing by the dumpster, talking on his phone.

Hopefully talking to his court appointed psychiatrist. The man had anger management issues.

"What are you doing right now?" Gary asked, still not looking at Dan.

"Trying to stay out of trouble."

Dan heard the heavy footsteps shuffle toward him to stop at Dan's side, towering above the young man.

"I need to go over your statement," Gary sounded tired.

"Really?"

"We're opening an investigation."

Which meant murder, Dan realized with a sinking feeling. A murdered Santa two days before Christmas. Seasons greetings, everyone.

"The Coroner's initial theory is intracranial bleeding due to violent head trauma," Gary said, reading Dan's mind. "They're scheduling an autopsy for later today."

Dan nodded. He had a bad feeling about this.

"Call me crazy," Dan began, "But hear me out."

"I'm listening."

"Any chance this was a mugging gone wrong?"

Gary said nothing. Dan took his silence as an opening.

"I'm no expert in anatomy." He ignored Billy's distant snort and lowered his voice. "But, I know the skull can be pretty fragile. Especially the back," he rested a hand at the point where spine met skull on himself as a point of reference. "So," Dan continued, "Let's say some stupid schmoe jumps Santa, he wants the change bucket or something. He hits him on the head with a plank or a brick, or I don't know, an anvil. Our mugger makes off with the money and Mrs. Claus is a widow."

"That's an interesting theory," Gary said, "except for one thing."

"What's that?"

"We found the bucket. It was stashed behind the body. Must have hit him at the end of his rounds. Had close to a hundred bucks in change."

"Whoa, I'm in the wrong racket."

Gary spun his head and glared at him.

"I meant Santa. I should be a Santa next Christmas. Raise money for the 'Dan Landis Needs a Vacation Fund.'"

Gary sighed again. He did that a lot around Dan.

"This place has a Santa right?"

"Yep. He's very authentic."

"I thought so, Gale took her kids to see him." Gale was Gary's older sister, and Dan's favorite of the Jones siblings.

"Really?" he asked, "I didn't see her."

"Right."

Dan was sure the kids mentioned it the second they saw Gary. They loved Dan. Who wouldn't, he almost said aloud then cast a backward glance at the dumpster. "Speaking of, Abbey's still up in the air about coming to dinner. You never told me what you want me to bring."

"What?" Gary stared blankly at the younger man.

"Christmas Dinner?" Dan lifted a brow, "Big meal the family eats on Christmas? Gale brings pie, Georgia brings biscuits, Gabriella brings her new boyfriend?"

"Dan," Gary warned his tone going cold and hard.

"Sorry."

"We're not having dinner at my house this year; everyone is going to Mom's."

Dan's face lit up, "We're eating at Mama Jones'? Please tell me she'll make sweet potato soufflé?" Dan rocked on his heels in anticipation.

"I'm not going Dan." Those brown eyes wouldn't look at him.

Dan slowly deflated. He kept a halfhearted smile plastered on his face. "What? Why?"

"This case, this time of the year. Everyone's on overtime."

Dan blinked, and leaned in close to Gary's profile.

"What about Jules?" he asked, his voice barely a whisper. Julianne got along fairly well with her in-laws. They were all successful women, and she was naturally a people person. Dan had a bad feeling. Gary's answer didn't help.

"Julie," Gary began, and then paused. Dan wished the sick feeling in the pit of his stomach would go away. "Julie is busy. She's got a heavy workload right now, a lot going on."

You're hiding something, Dan thought. You're trying to lie to me, and I'm an expert at lying. I'm the grand champion of lying. I even have a trophy, right next to my Procrastinators Anonymous Participation Medal.

"It's not what I wanted," Gary stared toward the crime scene. "It just happened this way."

"Right," Dan nodded, and intently studied the rusty dumpster.

"Dan, do me a favor. Stay out of trouble?"

"Always," he said with a smile.

"I'm serious."

"You usually are." That got through. There was the faintest hint of a smile. A spark of life in the eyes.

"Right."

"Oh, any I.D. on Santa yet?" Dan asked as the thought crossed his mind.

Gary looked down at his notes.

"Yeah," he looked up at Dan, and then shrugged. "David Barr. Do you know him?"

"No," he lied, "I was just curious."

Gary raised an eyebrow.

"All right, if it's the same Barr I'm thinking of," Dan admitted, "He works at the halfway house on 3rd."

"Any family?"

"Not that I know of, though Mr. Ortez is the Director. He'll probably be able to identify the body." Dan tugged on his earlobe. Something was rotten in the state of Denmark.

"You have a strange rolodex."

"Hey, what can I say? I'm a people person. Speaking of people, I've got to pick up Abbey. She got fired today."

"Really?"

"Yeah. I think she's going home."

"I see," Gary sounded bone tired, "It's good to have a home to go to."

"We'll see. Listen Gary, if you want to grab a beer sometime, talk about things…"

"Maybe when this is over. No promises. Now, let's get your official statement." It took Dan about ten minutes to carefully recount everything; he knew Gary was a stickler for detail.

"I'll have you sign this later. I think you have someone waiting on you."

Dan smiled, and headed down the sidewalk. It took a moment before he realized he was going the wrong way. The front entrance was to the right. Dan had automatically gone left, heading for the big parking garage. His stomach grumbled. He headed for the front entrance, worried about Abbey, Gary, and Santa's everywhere. The fresh air felt good, and it was nice to take a beautiful woman out to eat and not have to listen to her sob story. Abbey wasn't one to sob and he already knew her story.

Walking toward his regular haunt for home cooked hash, he glanced about for her. Her curly hair was a beacon, the winter sun catching it just right and making the strawberry-blonde hair glow. Dan walked toward her with a spring in his step.

"How you doing Grace?" he used her new moniker to poke. She glared at him, wrapping her coat around her lithe body. Her teeth were chattering.

"Where's your car?" she asked, her cheeks flushed with a combination of indignation and cold. "I thought you would drive in this weather."

"In the garage. I figured we'd eat somewhere close and then go get it. Right now I'm starving."

"As long as it's warm I'll go anywhere."

Dan chivalrously offered his arm and she looped hers around it, snuggling close for warmth. Together, they set off across the street.

Just as they got to the other sidewalk, Abbey's feet slipped on the ice. Dan caught her before she fell, and helped her stay vertical.

"Thanks," she blushed and smiled.

"No problem," he said, smiling back. It was amazing how comfortable it felt to have her close.

"You can get your hand off my butt now," Abbey said, with an edge to her voice.

"Right," Dan said, removing his hand. He pointed with a thumb toward the diner. He'd stuck mostly to their breakfasts, but had heard they made a great Reuben too. They walked toward the steamy windows, the crimson OPEN sign a welcome sight. He held the door for her, feeling the blast of heated air smack him in the face. Dan blinked to wet his eyes.

"Thanks again." Abbey stepped in, past him.

Dan spotted movement against the reflected door. Gary was walking up the street. Dan shut the door, turning around to watch.

Striding down the street, like a black John Wayne, Gary headed up the opposite street, rounding the far corner. His coat billowed out in the wind like a cape. He looked badass. Dan had always resisted wearing a trench coat, just because it was such a P.I. cliché. That and no matter how hard he tried, he could never look as good as Gary in it. He resisted the urge to call out; something told him to keep quiet. Gary rounded the corner without breaking stride. Dan glanced back, checking to see that Abbey was in line to order. He pulled open the door.

"Abs," he called, pulling out his wallet.

"Yeah?" she glanced over her shoulder.

Dan tossed Abbey his wallet, "Order what you want. Just get me two eggs, some bacon, and a root beer if they have it."

She stared at him, mouth open.

"I'll be right back," he promised, leaving before she could reply.

He walked quickly up his side of the street. He was fairly familiar with the area by now. If Gary was still walking down the sidewalk, heading west, then he should be visible from the approaching corner. For better or worse, Dan was good at his job. He could wait for hours in one place, dig up dirt on anyone, and he was very good at following people undetected. He stopped at the corner. Damn, Dan thought, wish I had my binoculars. Gary was stopped about thirty yards ahead, talking to a tall woman. Body language suggested familiarity, but Dan didn't recognize the woman.

It was definitely not Jules, unless his sister had dyed her hair blonde, stuffed her bra, and was wearing platform shoes. Whoever the woman was, she stood at nearly eye level to Gary and carried herself like a model. Dan watched as Gary nodded at something the woman said; she laughed, touching his arm. He saw Gary flash a dazzling smile. The woman turned around and Gary held the door for her. They entered the store together.

Jewelry store, Dan realized. On the way over, he had reviewed his mental map of the area. Whoever Gary was talking to, correction laughing and holding doors for and talking to, had led him into a jewelry store.

Dan cursed his suspicious mind. It was the nature of a private investigator to be immediately cynical. He had a very warped view of the world and relationships. There was nothing inherently suspicious about a married man going into a jewelry store. With a beautiful woman who wasn't his wife. Not suspicious at all.

Dan rubbed his temples. Sometimes he really hated how jaded a person he had become. He leaned against the wall, waiting for the sick feeling in his stomach to go away. =Dan's cell phone was in his hand. He didn't even remember pulling it out. He looked down. Jules cell was already punched up. Well, he thought, it couldn't hurt to check. Dan pressed dial.

"Hello?" a voice asked.

"Hey."

"Hi." She said again, recognizing her brother without being more patient for him to speak.

"I have an odd question. I want to get Abbey something nice for Christmas. I wondered if you had any ideas?"

"Abbey's the little blonde, correct?" Julianne sounded stressed, "Didn't we already get her some clothes?"

"Fair enough," Dan bobbed his head, "Do you know what Gary's getting you for Christmas?"

"Nothing. We're not exchanging gifts this year."

"Oh," Dan felt his brain freeze. And his heart dropped to his stomach. At the last possible moment, he remembered he was talking to a woman who made her living being a mind-reader.

"What's wrong Gertie?" Julianne asked. There was no concern in her voice. Concern cost a grand an hour.

"Abbey doesn't want to stay for Christmas."

"You can be a bit clingy. Have you thought of buying a teddy bear?"

"I already have one. His name is Roger."

"Glad to hear it."

The phone clicked. The call had ended.

"Well, bye to you too," he muttered to the device in his hand. This situation stank. He sniffed. "Something really stinks," felt a lump in his throat. The smell was very familiar. After all, he'd smelled it earlier today. He walked forward, reluctantly following his nose. There was an alley behind the diner. As a rule, Dan tried not to investigate his favorite eateries. Ignorance was always bliss.

Something smelled bad, and Dan was starting to wish he was somewhere else. He thought about going to get Abbey, but there was no sense spoiling her appetite. It was probably just a rat. A dead rat.

It wasn't.

Dan peered around the corner into the alley, where something red caught his eye. A red sleeve ending at a black glove. It was when he saw the white beard that Dan felt his stomach drop. It was definitely dead, smelling terrible, and Santa. Another Santa. Dan bolted, running at top speed across the street. A car narrowly missed him. He didn't notice, didn't even care. A tall figure stepped out of the jewelry store, breathing in the cold air.

"Gary!" Dan screamed.

Dan ran at top speed. Gary held out his hands, stopping Dan when he reached him. Dress shoes skidded, but the older man's strong grip on the jacket kept Dan from falling.

"What's wrong?" Gary asked, his voice edged with fear.

"Another," Dan said, pointing toward the diner, "Another body. Another Santa."

Collapsing to his knees, Dan vomited into the gutter.

Chapter 9

Abbey sat alone, watching Dan's breakfast get cold. She picked at her omelet, pushing pieces from one side of the plate to the other. Her body screamed for fuel. She was lightheaded from lack of it. Tentatively, she took a small bite. The omelet wasn't bad, but it wasn't good either. She'd had better. Papa made a mean Spanish omelet and she had even tried a vegetarian omelet once when a roommate had made breakfast. Both were much better than her present meal.

But, this omelet had been paid for. She felt obligated to eat well and be grateful. Of course, if she knew anything about Dan, he was going to be reimbursed. He never paid for you unless it was a date or on an expense account, maybe both. That made her grin. After all these months, she still wasn't sure what to make of Dan Landis. He was sneaky, dishonest, and a bit of a letch. He was also smart, brave, and roguishly handsome. She never thought she'd meet someone that could be accurately described as roguishly handsome.

But, the scoundrel fit the bill. Then, Dan had shown her another side of himself. He had acquired a job, gotten her a job, and spent the last month driving her to work. Abbey sighed, taking

another bite of the mediocre omelet. Every morning Dan picked
her up at the curb just outside her dorm, every evening he dropped
her off at the same spot. He never complained about the early hour,
never made her feel like a burden. He never even asked for gas
money. He just did it. Of course most nights, he also stayed on
campus late into the night, having drinks with Professor Brown, or
'Doc' as Dan called him.

   Her cheeks flushed at the memory of Professor Brown's
rich laughter, his gentle brown eyes, and of the graceful way the
Professor moved. Abbey would always be grateful to Dan for
introducing her to the amazing and eccentric Anthropology
Professor. Not only was he warm, intelligent, and a great
storyteller; but, he had also persuaded the University to allow her
to remain on campus over the Christmas holidays, an unheard of
privilege for a student.

   Granted, Abbey had saved Professor Brown's life, after she
and Dan had found him poisoned on the kitchen floor. But, that
was a story for another time. He always made Abbey feel welcome
when she would accompany Dan for drinks, even if she couldn't
match his and Dan's eccentricities. And the stories they told!
Professor Brown had published a series of novels chronicling the
adventures they had undertaken. Crisscrossing the globe, visiting
strange places, meeting unique people, and always staying just one
step ahead of trouble.

Yes, the books Professor Brown had written were exciting, but they didn't convey half the fun and sense of adventure the two men shared. To her great joy, he had promised to take Abbey on the next adventure they went on. She sometimes dreamed about the wonderful places they might visit, the strange people they would meet. All thanks to Dan, she mused. Speak of the devil, she watched as he opened the glass door. When he spotted her, he attempted a weak smile. Abbey was shocked at how pale and shaken he looked. Cheesy Christmas played in the background. She would be happy to have the awful noise behind her after this job was finished.

"Dan?" Abbey started to get up, frowning.

"Hey," Dan was faster, falling down in the wrought iron chair, a faraway expression to his eyes. His arms hung loosely by his hips.

Abbey wondered what he'd seen, Dan looked like he was in shock. "Are you all right?" She leaned across the stained white table. "You look like you've seen a ghost." He looked up at her. His eyes were vacant, he'd dropped his attempt at a smile leaving his face eerily blank. After a moment, he finally focused on Abbey.

"Sort of, yeah," he said, nodding dumbly. He reached out for his soda, his hand shaking. He took a sip. He shuddered. "What is this?"

"Root beer." She was on the verge of panicking. This wasn't the Dan she knew.

"Oh, right." He took another sip. "Interesting. So, would it be okay if we hang out here for a few minutes?"

"Why?"

Sirens screamed in the distance, coming closer.

"No reason."

Abbey reached out, taking Dan's free hand.

"You're worrying me," she said softly.

He didn't squeeze her hand in return. "I found another body. Another Santa."

"Are you sure it wasn't the same one?" She dared ask the ridiculous, curious which would be more horrible: a body being placed around town or someone killing Santa's.

"Either that, or someone is playing 'Where's Zombie Santa?'"

It was another twenty minutes before Officer Jones came in. In the meantime, Abbey dragged the details out of Dan. They both leaned in, speaking in hushed whispers. As he told her the whole story, he devoured his eggs. Color returned to his cheeks, and the hint of a smile was on his lips by the time he'd finished. Abbey felt chills running up her arms and rubbed at them for comfort.

"Two dead Santas?" she asked.

"Exactly."

"Why?"

"That's a good question."

"You…you didn't did you?"

He nearly choked. Abbey jumped out of her seat, ready to help. That CPR class would finally come in handy. As if reading her mind, he held up one finger, and then took a long pull of his root beer. Giving one last cough, he glared at Abbey.

"Sit down," he ordered. Realizing how harsh he must have sounded, Dan's expression softened.

"Please sit down," Dan requested again, gently. "No Abbey, I didn't kill either of them. I…that's not who I am. Santa especially. Or Santa's. Or whatever you call more than one Santa. A herd?"

"That's reindeer," Abbey corrected him automatically. She leaned in, whispering. "Do you think…does this mean there's a serial killer on the loose?"

Dan shrugged, hunched over his food. He kept his eyes on the table.

"If there is, he's taking serial killing to a whole new level."

"Or she."

"She?" That made him look up.

"Women are just as good at being serial killers as men." She felt more at ease discussing something less personal and frightening. "Look at history. You have Belle Gunness, Mary Ann Cotton, Rosemary West…and don't even get me started on Countess Bathory."

"Or she," Dan conceded. Glancing over to the glass door, he called out, "What do you think Gary?"

Stepping through as the glass door swung shut behind him, Gary took off his trench coat and glared at Dan. Pulling up a chair, he gently folded his coat over the black metal back. He looked from Abbey to Dan, and ran a hand over his face. He sat down, his broad shoulders sagging.

"We'll know more when CSI gets done," Gary said, stealing a piece of Dan's bacon. Dan decided not to make the obvious pig joke. "May I make a suggestion? I'd make yourself scarce before Bill gets here," he looked Dan in the eye. "I'm putting this down as a concerned citizen, no names."

"It wasn't me," he replied. "I just found him."

"Yeah," Gary crunched on the bacon. He didn't sound convinced.

Dan glanced from Gary to Abbey, and back. "Do I give off some kind of creepy murderer vibe?"

"Not at all," Abbey reassured him. "Trouble just tends to follow you."

"Exactly," Gary agreed, swallowing. "Also," he nodded toward Abbey, "Stop telling people about ongoing investigations."

"I didn't tell anyone but Abbey," Dan shot back defensively. He squared his shoulders. "I trust her."

"Abbey's people," Gary told him pointedly.

Dan turned to Abbey. "See, you are people! Thank you so much," Dan told Gary, his voice dripping with sarcasm, "I've been trying to convince her of that forever now. She thinks she's a house cat. These kids today."

Abbey shot him a dirty look, "Who are you calling a kid? In two years I'll have a PhD."

Dan leaned back in open mouthed surprise. "Hang on, are you older than me? Gary, I think Abs is older than me. How old are you anyway?"

"Just ignore him," Gary advised.

"I try," she replied, feeling giddy from nerves.

Dan grinned, "I meant to ask, how's that going, the PhD?"

"Oh don't get me started," Abbey gave a quick laugh, "I mean, trying to find a decent translation of 15th century Italian, ha, tis to laugh! Apparently 5th Century Gaelic, turn of the century Zulu, and Sanskrit from 1200 BC are no problem! But, finding one person, just one, who can translate a letter that Brunellesci wrote to Donatello is impossible!"

She looked up. Both men were staring at her.

"What?" she huffed.

"You're adorable when you make no sense," Dan gave her a wink.

"Hush," Gary warned Dan. Turning to Abbey he said, "I'm surprised no one at the university could help you."

"I speak Klingon if it helps," Dan offered. No one responded. "Just throwing it out there." Not getting a response, he interjected again. A spoiled child when he was nervous. "And I'd like to point out I have refrained from making a Ninja Turtles joke. Admittedly, Donatello wasn't my favorite, but still." He finished off the last of his eggs and loudly crunched the last of his bacon, washing it all down with the root beer while the other two talked about possibilities for Abbey's translation woes. Gary had some translators in the office, though nothing like she needed.

"Gary," Dan said, "would you mind if I take Abs back to campus? She's had a long day and needs to go Google Babel fish for some translations. I promise to come back and go over my statement."

"As long as you promise not to find any more bodies on the way," Gary replied. "Then it's fine with me."

"I'll try to keep an eye on him," Abbey felt her grip on herself slipping. She and Dan stood up, and he again held the door for her. After she walked out of earshot as Dan was stepping through the door, Gary called out.

"Dan?"

He looked back, waiting.

"Do me a favor, and please be careful."

Dan simply nodded and let the door close between them. Abbey was waiting on the sidewalk, stomping her feet to keep the heat in her flesh. Dan threw an arm around her, needing her warmth.

"Come on Abs, let's blow this town," he tried to joke.

Neither of them laughed.

Chapter 10

Chapter 10

It was pleasant to actually drive during daylight hours. Dan rolled the window down and took a deep breath of crisp air in the relative warmth of the daytime sun. In a few hours it would be too cold to have anything but windows up and heat cranking, with more stale recycled air. To and from work it was always so dark in these short winter days. Sometimes he cursed his nocturnal hours, this town looked good in the daylight. It had a certain sort of charm. A sleazy, rustic sort of charm, but charm nonetheless.

For a town that didn't know how to deal with snow, it certainly wore it well. The white powder covered up all the blemishes, the reflected sunlight gave the city a wonderful glow. Like an expectant mother. Pregnant with promise, his little voice said. Dan's mood was holding steady. Murphy's was in his rearview mirror, a visit with Doc was ahead of him, and a beautiful woman was in the seat beside him.

Granted, she was still complaining about the deplorable lack of Italian translators, yet somehow it added to her allure.

The car turned left at the light, and headed toward the University. He knew the route by heart. Of course, he had every way to that place memorized. All roads led to Doc. And Abbey. He glanced over. She stared out of the window, watching the occasional car pass. She had gone silent.

"I got an Italian Grandmother," Dan said, "if it helps."

"Does she speak Renaissance-era Italian?" Abbey asked, without turning from the window.

"No, but she does speak a little Yiddish."

Not even a flinch. "Thanks anyway."

"Something on your mind?" He prodded, wanting to get her to turn his way.

"Did Mr. Peters really hire you to watch Santa?"

"He did. I'm supposed to keep an eye out for trouble. Be a bodyguard, if you can believe that."

"I can." Her implicit trust sent a thrill through him. "So, why me?" Still she didn't turn.

"Because I trust you. Because you need a job. And because, honestly, of the two of us you're the only one who could be convincing as an elf." Dan checked. Not a single smile.

"Why are you so set on me dressing in little shorts and stockings?" Abbey continued to stare out the window.

"Kind of a no-brainer, isn't it?"

She turned at that, staring at him. Her face scrunched up and she punched his shoulder. The lady packed a pretty mean wallop. It almost hurt. He was impressed.

"Jerk," she failed to hide her smile, "Are you serious about paying me?"

"Yes," he glanced from her to the road, "When it comes to money, I'm always serious. Money, gun safety, and comic books. Those things I take very seriously."

"I'll think about it," Abbey tossed her hair, making a bid at being coy.

"Don't think too long," Dan didn't try to hide his smile, "I've got to figure out how to sneak you in tomorrow morning."

"What do you mean sneak? I thought Mr. Peters said 'yes.'"

"He did, he just didn't say 'yes' to you specifically." Dan fidgeted.

"Dan," Abbey's voice took on a warning tone. She always sounded like that when he started skirting the rules. She wasn't a fan of him pushing the limits of the law.

"What?" He turned right at the light, pulling through the main gate. She still hadn't answered his question. He glanced her way. She was busy gathering her things, readying to leap out of the car. Dan could read body language well enough to know this conversation was over. Looking up, he saw that there was a light on in Doc's office. Right now, he wanted nothing more than to kick back, have a drink, and chat with his two dearest friends.

Except now wasn't the time. There were too many questions that needed answers. There were now two bodies, and that was two to many. Dan pulled into his usual space outside Doc's building and parked. Abbey unbuckled and then waited for Dan to do the same. When he didn't move, she opened the door and climbed out.

"Abs," he called after her.

She looked back over her shoulder.

"Be careful," Dan told her, meaning it. "Whatever you decide is fine, just let me know. I got enough travel miles, if you don't want to do this I can get you a round trip ticket on whatever. Car, bus, plane, Hogwarts Express, you name it." That got a smile. Know the audience, Dan thought.

She reached out, and he met her halfway, held her hand in his. Her skin was freezing. She squeezed, her hand dwarfed by his disproportionately big mitt. He smiled, some of the tension between them melting.

"Thank you. Either way, thank you. I'll call you," she said, letting go of his hand. She stood, slamming the door. It was a weird habit she had; always slamming doors.

"Hate to see her go, love to watch her leave," he told the empty seat next to him. Reversing, he kept an eye out for Campus

Security. The gate house had been empty; technically campus was closed to visitors. And sneaking around was what he did best.

All part of the job, said his little voice.

Chapter 11

Abbey watched Dan drive away, following the car with her eyes until it vanished around the corner. She thought about going back to her dormitory, but a pang of loneliness changed her mind. Professor Brown's light was on and Abbey could smell the hot cocoa from here. She loved his cocoa. Him too, if she was honest with herself. It felt good to have friends.

The door to the Humanities building was unlocked and Abbey let herself in. School was where she felt most comfortable. Art History was theoretically her major, but Abbey had a profound love of learning. She loved this building. Even more than the school library. She felt far more at home here than in her little dorm room. Though, if she were being honest, her real home wasn't as welcoming as campus. It could have something to do with Papa's house being a parsonage. They'd never had a real home of their own.

Abbey chastised herself for being petty. Papa tried, he really did. It was just that for him the Lord's work was the most important thing, family came second. She set that train of thought aside for later. With careful footsteps she quietly approached Professor Brown's office. She loved surprising him. Even if the door to his office had been closed, it would have been easy to pick out. The door had a beautiful replica of Da Vinci's Vitruvian Man. As she stepped closer, haunting flute music wafted down the hall. She ran a finger along the far wall, idly tracing the brick seam.

Masonry had always been an art form to her. The careful placement of each brick in perfect unity and conformity, the daring defiance of gravity, the chorus of man's handiwork and craftsmanship sang to her. Abbey was still a few paces away when a voice called out.

"Hello Abigail," Professor Brown called, his deep baritone filling the hall, bouncing down the corridor. The voice always gave her butterflies.

She smiled. Her real name was Bernice Agnes, a combination of Mama and Grammie Smith's names respectively. But, she'd been called A.B. or Abbey since she was a child. However, only Professor Brown ever called her Abigail, always making it sound so perfect. She didn't dare correct him.

"How do you always know Professor?" Abbey leaned around the doorframe.

"Elementary my dear Watson," Professor Brown said, taking a puff from his pipe. The pipe smoke gave an exotic odor to the room. "You always open the door so quietly, yet still drag your finger along the wall outside. And let's not forget the gentle waft of lilac."

Abbey blushed, impressed at his attention to detail and amazed he could hear her over the gentle music.

"Also, I saw you come in," he said, pointing at the open window.

She gaped at him and Professor Brown gave her a familiar grin. It was obvious Dan had learned from a master. He gestured with one hand, offering her the only empty seat in the room. He was sitting at his desk, sprawled out in his red overstuffed chair. His long legs were stretched out, resting on a small pile of books. The desk was crowded with books of all sizes, mountains of papers, and a vast assortment of knick-knacks. The entire office was filled with souvenirs from his journeys, cultural artifacts, and enough books to fill a decent sized library.

A small brown notebook was lying on Professor Brown's lap, a gold ballpoint pen resting inside. He set it gently on his desk. Placing his legs on the floor, he straightened up and smiled as she walked over.

Before she sat, Abbey closed in on the small copper pot near the window, grabbing a pottery mug that looked handmade. Knowing Professor Brown, it probably was. He always kept the hot plate hidden in his office, as faculty weren't supposed to cook in their offices. The fact that it was disguised as a flower pot stand was perhaps the worst kept secret at the University. The fern was resting on the floor, and would be dutifully placed back in its spot once the hot plate had cooled. Say what you will about him, at least Professor Brown pretended to follow the rules. Abbey had a sneaking suspicion that, much like his protégé, he relished his rebellious streak.

"How goes the world of retail?" Professor Brown inquired, taking another puff from his pipe.

Her shoulders drooped as she poured half a mug full of comfort, "I got fired."

"I'm so sorry," Professor Brown set his pipe aside. Abbey saw his deep brown eyes were full of sincere sympathy. He reached over, turning off the music player. The flute ceased its gentle cry. "What happened?"

"Oh it was stupid," she waved a hand dismissively, finally taking her seat. "I'm thinking of going home anyway."

"Really?" He returned the pipe to his mouth. "I thought you had planned to attend the Jones' Christmas dinner."

"I…" she stared into her cocoa before taking a sip. Its warmth made her cheeks flush. Or maybe it was his unrelenting scrutiny. "I'm not sure. It's been a while since I've seen my family."

"Of course," he nodded. One of his most endearing qualities was his sympathetic ear. One of many in her humble opinion.

"Well, here's the thing. Dan asked me for a favor. It's not that I don't mind doing a favor, I just…"

"Just?" They drank their cocoa.

"Just, that I don't think he takes me seriously," she confessed. It felt good to finally get that off of her chest. "I know, he's, that we're friends. As a friend I will gladly help him, but then he offers to pay me."

Abbey kept her eyes down in shame. "I feel like he's doing it out of pity, and not because he sees me as an equal. I know that's why he got me a job in the first place. Because he feels sorry for me." Professor Brown puffed on his pipe. "And, I will be the first to admit, I'm certainly not swimming in money. Still, I wasn't raised to be pitied." Her shoulders straightened as she had another thought. "And another thing, I've known him almost four months and he's never taken me on a stake out, never so much as asked me to help him on a case. Then, the minute I get fired, he's there, making offers," she fumed, then blushed at her outburst, "I'm sorry Professor Brown; I don't mean to burden you."

"I had no idea you wanted to be an investigator," he said, his eyes focused intently on her, seeming to peer into her soul.

"Well," she stuttered, "it's not something I'd want to make a career out of. But, you have to admit, it is exciting," she admitted. "Dan's always working on amazing cases; he always seems to be running from some trouble or other."

"That's true. Have you spoken to Daniel about this? Your wanting a more active role?"

"No...should I? I mean, I know he's being kind, and Charity is a wonderful virtue, but do you think talking about it would do any good?" Abbey asked.

"It would probably help," Professor Brown answered. He glanced at the clock before giving it a look. "Abigail, I hate to rush you out, but I have a dentist's appointment in an hour."

"Oh," Abbey's eyes went wide. She jumped to her feet. "I'm so sorry."

"Don't be," He replied with a toothy grin, "I'm just having my teeth cleaned. But...could I trouble you for a hand?" She nodded. He picked up a mug similar to hers, handed it off. "Would you mind washing these out for me? I have some thoughts I wanted to capture before I head out and I'm afraid I won't be coming back until after the New Year. I'd hate to return to an infestation of ants."

She obediently took the cup, walking across the hall to the bathroom. She rinsed both cups thoroughly, even using the hand soap to scrub out any stains. She caught a glimpse of herself in the mirror. The sunlight from the bathroom window showed just how messy her familiar rat's nest of hair had gotten, and Abbey noted how puffy and red her eyes still looked.

She took a long breath, and then closely examined each mug. Both were sparkly clean. She set them to one side and then glanced back at her reflection. She splashed some water on her face and scrubbed vigorously; color returned to her pale cheeks. On a whim, she pulled her shoulder-length hair away from her ears, wondering what they would look like pointed. She'd never been one to play dress up. Still, elf ears could be fun.

Maybe, she thought, considering the job.

When she came back to his office, Professor Brown was putting the final book into his leather satchel.

As she entered she spoke up, "I meant to say, that's beautiful music you were listening to. Not that I was trying to eavesdrop."

"Why thank you. A gift from Daniel. R. Carlos Nakai, a flautist of considerable skill. The album is called *Guadalupe, Our Lady of the Roses*. He also gave me an Arizona calendar with it. I get the feeling he's wanting me to visit Flagstaff at some point. Knowing Daniel as I do, I'm certain he's trying to connive me into taking him to the Grand Canyon. Speaking of, have you seen a small canvas bag?" Professor Brown stood, hands on his hips, looking around the office.

"Your overnight bag?" Abbey began to scan the dark, crowded room.

"Yes," he confirmed, sounding uncertain.

"I think it's in your closet," she walked over to the closed closet door, opened it, and reached up to pull the bag down. Knowing what the bag meant, she stopped. Clutching it to her chest, she turned around. "So, where are you going?"

"Oh? I'm going to spend New Year's at a small bed and breakfast near Washington, D.C. The Gray Ghost Inn, I believe it's called."

"Is Dan traveling with you?" She fought to keep her voice level.

"Yes, it was his idea. Apparently he is quite a Civil War aficionado, and wants to visit the John S. Mosby museum. I must admit, the idea of a quiet, simple excursion, peaks my interest." He paused, embarrassed. "This isn't an official, on the books, adventure."

"I didn't say it was."

"It's just a small excursion. I promise, the next adventure, you're invited." Professor Brown said.

"Of course," Abbey replied, handing over the bag. He stared at her offering. "Oh!" she jumped in place, pulling the bag back and walked over to her purse to pull out a beautifully wrapped box. She hadn't bought it at Murphy's, but she had used Murphy's wrapping paper. At this point, it probably didn't matter; it wasn't like they could fire her again for stealing their stupid paper. Good old No. 6 gold Tartan, the very best. She handed it to

Professor Brown, who was at a loss for words. "I know you're supposed to give eight of these…"

He took it gingerly and started blinking rapidly. "Abigail, I don't know what to say. Thank you, this is beautiful…Did you wrap this?"

"Yes," she felt the flush of emotions close to the surface. She set the cleaned mugs on the table, turning her back on the Professor. She didn't want to cry in front of him.

"I'm hesitant to even unwrap it," he told the back of her curly strawberry blonde head. Gently, he placed it on top of his leather satchel. "I'm afraid my own wrapping pales in comparison," he turned to the bookcase behind his desk. Reaching to the top of the shelf he took down a small package wrapped in simple brown paper.

"Merry Christmas," Professor Brown handed it to Abbey who stared at it, uncertain what to say.

Her eyes must have betrayed her eagerness. "Feel free to open it now." A knowing smile crossed his lips. She ripped it open to reveal dark brown leather. Gold letters were embossed on the cover.

"*Hound of Baskerville*…" she ran a finger along the title.

"Daniel told me you enjoy Sir Doyle's work. I have to confess this is my favorite Holmes story."

"It's gorgeous." She leapt forward, bounding around the desk separating them, and threw her arms around the Professor's neck. Hopping up, she kissed him on the cheek. "Thank you, thank you, thank you!" She finally let go, returning to flat feet once again.

He gently pulled her to arm's length, and with a shock, she realized he was blushing. It was the first time she'd seen his tanned cheeks go pink. "After all that you've done for me…for all of us, I could do no less," he said and took a deep breath. "And Abigail," he started, "If you do decide to remain in town, I would be delighted for you to join Daniel and I on our trip to Warrenton over the holiday."

"Really?" Abbey asked her eyes dancing.

"Of course. Though I can't promise that it will be exciting. And probably not much of an adventure." Professor Brown said.

She began hopping up and down, clapping her hands childishly. "Thank you!" she squealed.

"On one condition," he shook his finger.

"What? Yes, anything! What?"

"Abigail, I have never felt comfortable with you staying by yourself on campus. And, since I won't be coming back until next year, and security being so sparse, it would ease my tired soul if you would choose to spend the holidays among friends and family.

Should you decide to stay in town, is there somewhere else you could stay?"

"No," She was taken aback by his concern. She had never thought of campus as unsafe.

"Well," he seemed prepared for this condition. "Fortunately I know of at least one place with plenty of room." She paused, her heart skipping a beat. "The Jones'," he clarified, smiling at her confused expression. "I believe Julianne and Gary have offered you use of their guest room?"

"Yes," though Abbey was unsure how he would know or care. Why would Dan blather that? Certainly it didn't mean anything but inconvenience to him if she stayed at his sister's house, that wasn't worthy of discussion.

"Good," Professor Brown said, and then glanced at his watch. "I believe we have enough time for me to drop you off. As it happens, my dentist's office is near their home. And Abigail?"

"Yes?" She was pulled from her thoughts.

"Merry Christmas," he said with a warm smile.

"Happy Chanukah Professor Brown," she returned his smile.

Chapter 11

Dan hated his suspicious and cynical nature. He had stopped by the halfway house where David Barr, the first dead Santa, had been a case worker. Mr. Ortez wasn't in, and the cops hadn't come by. No one knew David was deceased and Dan wasn't about to be the one to break the news. All he'd found out was that Barr was a saint, beloved by all, and probably walked on water. And that he'd started growing his beard in September. The man lived for being Santa. He'd also died for the same insane cause. It made a grown man want to crawl in a bottle. He left the halfway house grateful to be gainfully employed. Many weren't these days.

Dan sighed as he got back in his car. It was a long shot, hoping maybe David had some kind of enemy. Maybe he died because of mistaken identity. Maybe there was a serial killer on the loose, and every Santa in a ten block radius was in danger. Without realizing what he was doing, he headed for the jewelry store. "What am I doing?" he asked his reflection.

Making a terrible decision, said the little voice of Maggie. Ever the devil on his shoulder.

"Yeah," Dan said. Gary would beat him senseless if he caught Dan investigating the dead Santa case. He probably wouldn't be all that happy to catch someone snooping into his personal life either. Yet, the thought of the Mr. and Mrs. Jones heading for divorce sent a shiver down Dan's spine. Serial killers he could handle; the dynamic duo breaking up, that was just beyond his limits.

If only it was something as simple as mistaken identity, he pleaded to anyone listening, slowing to a stop at the light. The Murphy's building caught his eye. His eyes locked on the monolithic store as he drove past. That wasn't his destination. Curiosity was never a good thing. "Well," he said again to the nebulous powers that be, "you only live once." He found a good parking spot and hopped out. The wind was picking up, and he adjusted his jacket's collar. The cold air felt good.

The jewelry store was definitely not the kind of place Dan would normally frequent. Too upscale, too pricey, and just too much. Add that to the fact that he avoided commitment like the plague. Jewelry was a serious commitment. Jewelry said either I love you or I'm sleeping with your sister, possibly both. Dan paused at the window, staring at the display case. His reflection looked back with a smirk. His thoughts ran to Abbey and the smirk melted into a quiet smile. He rubbed his face. The store was decorated for Christmas, tempting passersby with the promise of that perfect Christmas gift. He wondered if a brick was the right gift for her. Granted, it was a historical brick, but it was still a brick.

For the first time he wondered if she would prefer something sparkly. Women and Magpies loved sparkly things. Then again, she wasn't the typical girl. She wanted something sincere, deep, meaningful. He had no clue what that was.

Opening the door, he glanced around the empty store. A lone clerk was chewing gum and lounging at the display case. She was reading a magazine, not even bothering to hide it from him. He could smell the boredom from the doorway. He wasn't really surprised when she failed to look up from her reading material. This close to Christmas male shoppers were a dime a dozen. Maybe that's why I don't want to give jewelry, he thought, because it's a shallow cliché.

The clerk looked up as Dan came closer. He flipped the switch, turning on the considerable charm. He may be the millionth customer, but he was determined to be the most memorable. "You another cop?" she asked leaning back, suspicious.

"Nope," he rested one arm against the counter. He turned on Lady Killer 9000, setting it to the lowest level. No sense blasting the woman out of her socks. "Many cops been in here?"

"Pretty much a constant stream," she shrugged. "Mr. Diego's still freaking out."

Interesting, his little voice said, in the private investigative business, we would call that a clue.

"I'm a consultant for the insurance company," Dan lied confidently. "They want me to do an independent investigation." He handed her his business card.

"I just want to get things back to normal," she studied the card. It was a great looking business card, very professional. Bernie, in addition to medicine, did graphic design in her spare time. Some people were so talented it made him sick.

"I completely understand," Dan assured her, placing his warm hand over hers.She smiled up at him. He smiled back. He turned the charm up to seven. "I'm here to get your life back to normal," he told her. "Possibly to take you to dinner."

"Thank you," she leaned against the counter. "I still don't understand why he's freaking out. He's got insurance." She frowned and traced a thoughtful finger on the glass. "It's not like they stole the good stuff, just a couple of necklaces and some coins."

"Well," Dan said, resting his arm against hers on the counter. "You know how it is in the jewelry business. You have to take the job seriously, care about every detail."

"Yeah," she rolled a shoulder, uncaring, "Well, Mr. Diego is in back with a customer. Some guy who had his stuff in here for appraisal."

"That's fine with me," he gently stroked her hand with one finger, "I got something pretty valuable to appraise right here."

"Oh really?" her full lips curved up, her brown eyes sparkling.

"JANINE!"

They both jumped, straightening. He saw a heavyset man striding out from behind the beaded curtain.

Why is it, Dan wondered, fancy jewelry stores and fortunetellers have the same partitions? And pawn shops for that matter. He adopted his most professional demeanor, walked forward to meet the sweating brute, and stretched out his hand. "You must be Mr. Diego," he said, "it's a pleasure. I'm…"

"Mr. Landis?" another voice called out from behind the partition.

Dan froze mid-step, caught entirely off guard.

From behind the beads emerged the last person Dan expected to see here and now. Though if you had to pick the stereotypical coin collector, Mr. Peters was a perfect fit. He probably had them alphabetized.

"Mr. Peters," Dan shook off his shock and stepped forward. "Sir, please accept my deepest sympathies for your loss." He turned to the store owner, grasping his hand firmly. "Mr. Diego, if there's anything I can do, please let me know." He gave Diego his card, "My humblest condolences to you both."

With that Dan turned on one heel, and marched out of the store. He stopped at the door to wink at Janine; she smiled back.

You're a dog, his little voice said. He refrained from defending himself in public, since he tended to do it out loud. Opening the door, he left, trying not to run. Know your limits, Maggie had always told him. Three wild lies per group per day seemed like a good quota.

Plus, he had one question answered, never mind that two more had cropped up in its place. As he stepped into the blinding light, Dan remembered a nagging question his visit to this particular store had brought back. Who was the woman Gary had been talking to?

He didn't have to wonder long since she was walking towards him. Dan was grateful for his continued good fortune, and at the same time wondered when the other shoe would drop. Every good thing that happened to him came with a price. The universe was always looking for balance, he supposed. He hoped he'd already paid with the start of this day.

Stepping forward with his best attempt at charm, he extended a hand. He handed her his business card while making a mental note to print off a new batch of copies. The sun was catching her blond hair perfectly, it flared into a gorgeous golden halo. She was stunning.

"Pardon me ma'am," Dan said as she returned his smile, "Sergeant Gary Jones wanted me to speak with you, if you have a minute?"

Her face lit up. "You're a friend of Gary's?" her mild French accent gave her words a beautiful lilt.

She ignored the hand he'd offered and embraced Dan in a short but enthusiastic hug. He felt his ribs being crushed. "Any friend of Gary's, is a friend of mine!"

This could be fun, Dan thought as he caught his breath.

It was close enough to lunch that he offered to buy her a croissant. That earned him a coquettish giggle. Offering her an arm, which she took, they strolled to the nearby coffee shop. Not too nearby, he had decided to go at least one block away from Murphy's to reduce the chances of an accidental run-in. Sitting at the diner across the street from work would probably be pushing it, even for him.

"Gary," she resumed the conversation about their mutual acquaintance, it came out Gay-Ree, "He is a legend in the policing world. I am so grateful to be able to work with him. He was the whole reason I accepted the invitation with the officer exchange program. I heard him speak at a conference in Denver. He was wonderfully engrossing! It is so terrible what has happened to those old men, have there been any new developments?"

"Not yet," Dan wondered what kind of conference Gary had spoken at, and why he hadn't invited his brother-in-law. Usually Jules insisted he bring Mama Landis' favorite son to these sorts of things. "But it may be possible the robbery and the murders are connected."

"Really?"

"It's a theory." That I just made up, he didn't add. Even if it makes for a good excuse to talk to the beautiful woman. He found it difficult to think; her good looks and ample natural gifts displayed in her low cut blouse were a bit distracting. "It's just a hunch. You know Gary and his hunches."

"I was always told Gary disliked hunches; he says that they cloud the facts and distort the truth."

"Well, that's what he's required to say. Because no one else has Gary's razor sharp skills. He's a policing machine and has a killer gut instinct." Dan waved off her doubts. "Me, I look for patterns, weird angles; I expect the unexpected. Gary and I always come at cases from very different angles, which is probably why we work so well together. I'm the Ying to his considerable Yang. We complement each other's abilities. Did Gary tell you about the DeMarco smuggling case?"

"Not personally," she said, her voice dropping into the sultry range, "but I've heard stories."

"Well," his own voice dropped a few octaves. "I was the one who figured out how they were getting the diamonds in. Broke the case wide open."

"And you've been riding that one ever since," Gary's hand dropped heavy on Dan's shoulder.

When Dan turned his face up, he could see Gary wore a relaxed smile, yet his grip was like a vice. With his other arm, he whipped a chair up to the table. The big man exuded a coolness and danger that was normally reserved for glaciers on a midnight cruise.

"I see you've met Katherine," Gary lowered himself into his seat. He'd still not removed his iron grip. Dan was starting to lose feeling in his shoulder. "Katherine, I'm sure Dan's introduced himself properly"

"Oh yes," Katherine bobbed her head, her expression sincere and open, "He told me he's a police consultant. You've worked with him before."

"That's right," Gary nodded, "In fact, I was just coming to look for him. I could use a consultation."

I'm dead, Dan gulped. Jules was sure to take Gary's side on this one.

"Would you excuse us for just one moment Katherine?" Gary asked, standing with a smile. He yanked Dan out of his chair and out the door. He didn't stop dragging the smaller man until they were out of sight, past the glass front of the building.

"Excuse me," Dan said to her with a grin. It came out more wince than smile.

Gary pulled Dan along, only letting the younger man go once they were out of sight. He rubbed his sore shoulder.

"What do you think you're doing?" Gary hissed, bending down to stand nose to nose with his brother-in-law.

"I was looking for something nice to get Abbey and bumped into your friend. She really digs you by the way," Dan winked.

"Leave her out of this," Gary whispered harshly, baring his teeth. "Don't you have a job you should be doing?"

"Not really," Dan admitted with a shrug, "I was hired to meet Santa Claus after work tonight. Also, Mr. Peters was in the jewelry store when I went in there. He was backstage talking to the owner."

Gary relented and took a step back. "I know," he said before adding, "And this is a job for Robbery Investigations. You are not Robbery Investigations; in fact you are not even a cop. You work Loss Prevention at Murphy's Department store. I realize how you might think the concept of robbery would confuse you. You are a small fish in a small pond. You are also a private dick who is going to get fired if he doesn't go back to work in his small pond," Gary's voice quivered with rage.

"All right I'm sorry. I mean it, I'm sorry. I'll go back to work."

"Good, and before you go, there's one more thing."

Gary's shoulders drooped. His voice dropped into a whisper. "I want you to keep an eye on that department store."

"That's kind of my job," Dan grinned. "Or my pond, if we're going to keep abusing the metaphor." He stopped when Gary caught his eye. Gary looked like death warmed over. Dan wasn't sure what to think about his condition. Or if he wanted to.

"In particular, I want you to keep an eye on Santa," Gary went on. "That second body you found…it was a murder too. Someone strangled the poor guy. We think he may have been the first Santa killed." A chill danced up Dan's spine that had nothing to do with the temperature.

"That was across the street," Dan stated the obvious.

"Pretty much a straight line," Gary said, with a nod. He paused. "And just so I can keep that famous Landis curiosity in check." Gary reached into his coat pocket. He extracted a crumpled piece of paper and handed it over. Dan stared at the gift. It was the police report of the jewelry store robbery.

"They emptied the safe," Gary summarized for him, "not much, just the stuff not currently on display. A couple of the display necklaces, the petty cash, and Mr. Peters' coin collection. Your boss dropped it off earlier that day for appraisal. Whoever broke in disarmed the alarm and opened the safe." He rubbed a large hand over his face. "Whoever stole it knew the combination and the alarm code. Bypassed lots of stuff to steal a bunch of necklaces worth less than a hundred bucks and a coin collection."

"Personal?"

"Maybe. Here's the scary thing: that coin collection is worth a mint. Bunch of rare coins, all in sequence. Appraisal put it at close to a million dollars."

"Holy crap!"

"Quiet you idiot," Gary hissed. He grabbed Dan's arm, whirling him around to face the Murphy's building staring at them from the other side of the street. Gary angrily thrust one finger at the silent behemoth.

"Now," Gary spoke through tight lips, "March right back in there and keep one beady eye on Santa and the other one on Mr. Peters. Because someone has robbed the jewelry store manager right down your street and someone is killing Santa's on your doorstep. I get the distinct impression someone might have a grudge against that store."

Dan nodded.

"One more thing."

"Yo?"

"You want to find out what I'm doing, you ask," Gary put a hand on Dan's neck. It was warm, gentle; sadness crept into the big man's voice. "You don't have to investigate me, you just have to ask and I'll tell you what I can. I've never lied to you, Gertie. I won't start now. And as far as investigating goes, have your rates changed?"

Dan raised an eyebrow.

"I'm going to put you on the payroll as an actual consultant on this one," Gary said. "I know you're going to keep feeding that police consultant line to people anyway. So, I figure I might as well make it true." He sighed, "We don't have enough warm bodies to keep an eye on every Santa. It would be nice if you could watch out for the one in the store after hours since someone keeps dropping bodies around there." He patted the side of Dan's face, tossing him a tired grin. "Gale says the kids loved him. Think he's the real thing."

"He's absolutely believable," Dan concurred with Gale's opinion.

Gary nodded, "I'll fax you the paperwork."

Gary walked toward the nearest pane of glass. Dan followed. Katherine was still sitting at their table. She waved at them. They both waved back.

"She seems nice," Dan said.

"Nicely married," Gary replied.

"Never stopped me."

"I know," Gary growled. He turned to Dan and then pointed with a thumb back toward the store. "Go."

Dan winked at him then blew a kiss at Katherine. However, when he turned around, he had to stop. The view was unnerving. The violet light of the fading sun backlit Murphy's, lending the whole thing a eerily sinister air. The windows were dark gashes against the cold white stone. For the briefest of seconds, the place looked like a giant skull. A skull that was glaring down at all the little people. Suddenly this job looked a little less inviting; a little more dangerous. He felt sick to his stomach. Right now, even the idea of extra money wasn't helping to make him want to go in there.

There was trouble on the horizon, and Dan was stuck in front of the oncoming storm. Taking a deep breath, he headed to work, hoping this day would just end with no one else dying.

Chapter 12

"Are you sure you have everything?" Professor Brown asked Abbey, glancing at the passenger seat.

"Yes sir," Abbey double-checked her Hello Kitty suitcase stuffed in the back seat. She didn't own much, and all of it fit in the bright pink suitcase, borrowed from her roommate. There was enough room that Abbey had debated asking if she could take her roommate, Jennifer, as well.

She leaned back, enjoying the cool leather car seats. Professor Brown eased into traffic, keeping his distance from the cars in front of him, while keeping an eye on the ones behind them. She couldn't blame him. Doc had a gorgeous vintage car, a Packard Dan had called it, and she was always afraid she would somehow soil it unintentionally.

He drove with a relaxed professional ease, navigating smoothly and expertly. As he drove, Professor Brown chatted amicably with Abbey about her doctoral process. Disappointingly, he didn't speak the right kind of Italian, although he promised to email a friend in Florence who might be able to help.

The Professor carefully made his way down the streets, heading toward the upper-class neighborhood where Gary and

Julianne Jones lived. No one had answered the phones. Abbey felt a rising tide of panic and wanted to call off staying in an empty house. What if they were on vacation? What if they were already in bed? What would happen if she was murdered breaking into someone's home? Julianne Jones was an ace lawyer, and Detective Jones would be an expert in hiding a murder investigation. Her heart raced.

Professor Brown insisted, he was certain they wouldn't mind. Both of the Jones' had always made it abundantly clear she was welcome. That she had an open-ended invitation to drop in anytime. That and with Dan always staying over, they were probably used to impromptu guests. She swallowed what she could of her nerves.

"Is there something wrong?" She must have been unusally quiet. He was watching her with those penetrating, soulful eyes.

"No nothing," Abbey assured him with a false smile, "Just wondering if anyone's home."

"Hmm, I hadn't considered that," Professor Brown frowned.

"I mean, they gave me a key," Abbey held it up for proof. "Well, Dan made me a key. They gave him a key. And Julianne liked me enough to buy clothes…And were very welcoming, whenever I've been around. Do you think they would mind?"

"I would highly doubt it," Professor Brown sounded pensive, "I must admit, I am bemused and slightly offended. Daniel has never made me a key. Not to the Jones' anyway. His office," he clarified, when he caught her expression, "I have a key in case Daniel needs me to get into his office. In case you were wondering why the first time we met, I was in flagrante delicto."

"Oh, right." Abbey blushed at the memory of Professor Brown lying prone, poisoned on Dan's kitchen floor. At the same time, she noted, I don't have a key to his office. She tried not to read too much into the fact that Dan had a habit of outing people in little cubicles. That his friends could only gain entrance to parts of his life, not the whole.

"We're here," Professor Brown interrupted her thoughts.

Abbey turned, surprised they'd arrived so quickly. She must have been pretty deep in her own head to have zoned out so much of the drive. No shock there, she was always doing that sort of thing. Professor Brown pulled up to the front gate. Fern Meadows was a beautiful gated community surrounding a serene private lake. There were less than 30 houses in all, with the Jones house just around the bend from the gate. She could see the roof from here, and through the spaces between the houses she caught a glimpse of the lake.

Each house was painstakingly decorated, beautiful gingerbread mansions lining the lake. Their warm Christmas lights reflected against the still surface. It was like something out of a Norman Rockwell painting, if he had painted an upper-class white collar neighborhood around Christmas time. Her eyes focused back on the wrought iron bars of the gate. A sudden realization made Abbey start. "I don't have an access card," she said.

"Quite all right," Doc said, manually rolling down the window, "I've done this before."

A call box was encased in a brick enclave next to his car. From the road it was concealed by some of the giant signature ferns that gave the community its name. Professor Brown pressed four digits and Abbey heard the clicks and buzz of a phone dialing. From the center speaker came two rings, then a loud beep. The gate swung open. The car eased through the opening gates and Doc winked at her. Abbey giggled. He didn't park in the drive, instead pulling alongside the curb.

"Abigail," he started, his tone sounding too severe for the occasion.

"Yes sir?"

"I hope you'll stay here for the holidays. Even if you don't, I want you to know that the offer is still good for New Year's. If you would like to go with Dan and myself, we would be happy to have you." The edges of his lips curved into a tight smile.

"Thank you," she ignored her nerves at his guarded behavior, grinning toothily at the prospect of adventure with her hero and the most exciting man she'd ever met. She pulled out her bags and purse. On a wildly uncharacteristic impulse, she leaned over and gave Doc a peck on the cheek. Not daring to look back, she climbed out of the car.

The only downside to riding in this gorgeous car was getting in and out. Thanks to the strange combination of angles between frame and seat, it was absurdly difficult. It made a quick and graceful exit impossible and the scrunch of leather made a fart noise which caused Abbey to blush and quietly giggle everytime. She sighed as her feet finally found pavement, hating how she could never be cool. Good manners forced her to walk over to the driver's side, where Professor Brown still had his window open. She didn't dare make eye contact after her boldness.

"Thank you again. For everything." She held up the book he'd given her. Her knuckles where white with the vice grip.

"Don't mention it."

"So, I guess I'll let you know about later."

"At least tell Daniel, I would assume you will be seeing him again." It wasn't a question.

"Right," she exhaled harshly, "I'll tell Dan." Abbey stepped back and watched him drive away. She followed the car with her eyes as it went through the gate, and then merged into traffic going back around the other side of the fence.

     Stepping over the curb she headed for the empty driveway, trying to avoid the wet grass. Abbey shifted the bags in her hands awkwardly, staring at the Jones house. "What am I doing? She asked the universe at large. "Greyhound leaves in half an hour. I can call a cab, be home in time for breakfast." Papa might even make flapjacks. But flapjacks were not, in general, filled with adventure. Neither was Papa. Unless stamp collecting was considered adventurous. Still, there was a lot of love and she knew where she stood. At least she had that to go home to.

     Abbey sighed, pulling out her keys. It wasn't hard to know which one belonged to this house. It was shiny brass and twice the size of her two other keys. She rang the doorbell twice; there was no answer. The door opened without creaking, which was the first of many differences between this house and Abbey's dorm. The living room was another. Normally, the main living room was well decorated with warm and inviting color combinations.

     It was obvious, even to her untrained eye, that a professional decorator had done the interior of this house. There were always fresh flowers on the coffee table. Usually all the lights were on.

Abbey paused, the Christmas lights barely offering any illumination. She could see enough to know the room was empty of any decorations, the shades were drawn and all the lights were off in the house. Her first thought was that a surprise party was about to go off and she'd stumbled in to ruin it. Except she would have smelled cake and she hoped Dan would have warned her, maybe even invited her. Unless it was Dan's birthday. That seemed unlikely.

The light cast dark shadows in the corners of the room. Abbey felt goose bumps rise on her arm. A lamp flicked on and she stifled a scream. Julianne was sitting in the brown Barcalounger, her long black hair down over her shoulders. She was wearing a black silk robe over black pajamas. So much black made her face look pale, almost ghostly in the harshness of the single light. It took a moment for Abbey to find her voice.

"Hello," she squeaked.

"What are you doing here?" Julianne's question cut through the silence with the severity of a thin steel scalpel.

"Standing in the doorway." Abbey couldn't move.

"Sure you are."

"I'd hoped to stay here for the night, if that was okay? I tried to call." Abbey stammered.

"You're here for Gary aren't you," a bitter flame erupted in Julianne's eyes.

"I'm sorry?" Abbey glanced at the still open door behind her. Julianne blinked rapidly, as if waking up from a dream. She leaned in to look closer and her grey eyes went wide.

"Abbey?" The woman's voice a mix of surprise and a touch of pleasure.

"Hello," Abbey replied feeling her heart restarting, holding one hand up in a timid wave. She looked back longingly at the open door. A few minutes in a cab and she could be on that bus taking her to a sure thing.

"Oh Abs," Julianne sighed. She rubbed her palms against her eyes. "I must have fallen asleep. I think I was dreaming or something…"

"Or something," Abbey bobbed her head once.

"What brings you out this way?" Despite her warm tone, her gaze remained cool and piercing. Except for her eyes, she could have been a female double of Dan. Their hair, facial features, and build were amazingly similar. Except where Dan's eyes were ocean blue, Julianne had eyes that were eerily pale grey. She also had porcelain skin compared to his natural tan. Abbey had never met anyone with eyes that grey before. They were beautiful, but gave the impression she could see straight to a person's soul.

"I got fired today, Dan offered me something else I'm thinking about taking a crack at." A nervous laugh burbled up. "Kind of a quick switch, I imagine you don't see that much in your line of work, huh?" Abbey was fumbling for the elusive light switch. She looked around, trying not to reveal her nerves. No doubt Julianne already sensed them, she was like that.

"What do you know about my line of work?" The defensiveness in her voice made Abbey's skin crawl.

"You're a lawyer." Abbey offered, before adding "A very successful lawyer who helps people stick to their guns, I mean stories." And possibly crazy? That was best not to add.

Julianne leaned back into the chair. "Aren't I just?" she chuckled harshly. Abbey wasn't sure if Julianne was responding to what was said or unspoken. "The absolute best in town. What did you want to be when you were a kid Abbey?"

"Pardon?" The strain of the surreal conversation was wearing on Abbey, she leaned against the wall. A cool breeze blew on her neck through the open door.

"When you were a little girl," Julianne pressed, "What did you dream of being when you were all grown up?"

"An actor, possibly a singer," Abbey said, without thinking. She realized no one had ever asked that question. Not even when she was a little girl. It had never come up. She hoped Julianne wouldn't realize how short she had fallen from her dreams.

"I always wanted to be a firefighter," Julianne snorted. "My grandfather was a firefighter. My father was a cop. No surprise I married one. But, I always thought it would be noble to save lives, protect the innocent."

"Don't you do that as a lawyer?"

Julianne raised her face, gazing deep into Abbey's eyes. Never one to call herself an expert on the human condition, Abbey was fairly sure those were the most haunted eyes she'd ever seen.

"Sometimes." Julianne nodded, her voice hollow, "but I wonder if they are lives worth saving."

"Aren't all lives worth saving?" Abbey asked, slightly offended. This was one of those fundamental things Papa had always taught her. Life was a gift, all life was precious and to be respected. Julianne threw back her head and laughed. Abbey was struck by how similar it was to Dan's laugh. She'd never asked if the two of them were twins. Julianne always seemed older, though right now, she looked downright ancient.

Julianne was laughing so hard she started coughing. Reaching over to the side table, she picked up a glass of wine. Abbey watched as Julianne finished its contents in one long swallow, still at a loss. She began to wonder how many glasses her host had already finished.

"Sorry," Julianne offered her a half smile, "That was classic, Abs. Thank you."

"You're welcome?" Abbey responded, unsure if she meant it.

"I needed a laugh," Julianne admitted sounding only slightly less bitter. "It's been too long since I've had something to laugh about. You haven't seen Dan around have you?"

There, Abbey thought, was definitely someone who could make people laugh, or scream. The ambiguity of that last made her ears go red. "Not since earlier today. Professor Brown was the one who dropped me off."

"Doc was here?" Julianne's brows peaked, she jumped to the edge of her seat. "Is he still here? I keep forgetting to talk to him."

"No, he's gone to the dentist right now," Abbey said, "if you want I can…"

"No," Julianne sat back. "It can wait." She glanced at her watch, then held it to her ear. The watch looked expensive and big on her thin wrist. It could probably tell you the time in twenty time-zones while underwater.

Julianne paused, then stared at Abbey, confused. "Weren't you working at Murphy's with Dan? Is that who fired you?"

"I hated every minute of that job," Abbey confessed. It came out so fast, she almost bit her tongue. She'd had no intention of telling anyone, she didn't want to seem ungrateful.

"It happens," Julianne shrugged, unaffected.

Abbey sighed in relief. This woman was obviously successful, extremely driven, and surely had an amazing work ethic. And fortunately, she was also apparently not interested in passing judgment. "Dan's offered me another job," Abbey said. "Working for him."

Julianne cocked her head at that.

"He wants me to keep an eye on the store's Santa Claus. I haven't decided yet, whether I want to take it or not. It would mean having to dress up."

"Mrs. Clause?"

"Elf," Abbey replied. She didn't figure Julianne would be interested in an exact explanation of the evolutionary history of Santa's elves from classic house spirits. She really looked like she needed a hug more than anything else.

"Ah," Julianne smiled and nodded. "That sounds more like our Dan."

"Do you think I should?" It felt good having a woman to ask advice from.

"Is he really going to pay you?"

"Yes. Actually, now that I come to think about it, the store probably will be paying me through him." Abbey tapped her chin with one finger.

"Wait," Julianne's forehead creased, "the store that fired you, that employed you in the job you hated, would be where you are planning on doing this elf masquerade?"

"Well, that wouldn't be how I would have phrased it, but yes. Essentially."

Julianne got a wicked smile. It looked particularly evil with the harsh shadows the lamp cast over her face. "Hell yeah kid," she said, "stick it to them where it hurts."

"Really?"

"Look Abs," Julianne said, with a world weary sigh, "We can all tell you what we think, but, ultimately, it's up to you." She ran a hand down her hair, pulling it to the side. "However," Julianne continued with a shrug, "If you can make a buck in life and spit in the face of the people that hurt you at the same time, well, I'm all for it." Julianne's rapid mood changes were making Abbey's head spin. She couldn't think of an appropriate response.

"Anyway," Julianne said with a wave toward the second floor, "clean sheets on the guest bed. Changed them myself the other day…" She picked up an almost empty bottle and poured some more wine into her glass.

"Are you sure I'm not an inconvenience?" Abbey wondered if Julianne was on something and mixing medications with alcohol.

"It's my house," Julianne said, her voice hardened in a blink. "I can have whoever I want staying over whenever I want."

Abbey locked the door, feeling oddly trapped when the bolt slid into place with a thud. "Thank you very much," she smiled weakly. "I really don't know how to repay you."

"Sweetie," Julianne's tone was almost normal, "You made me laugh, and you offer some much needed sunshine in this place. That's payment enough."

Abbey smiled and then turned toward the stairs. Impulsive for the second time tonight, she let go of the oversized suitcase. Running over, she flopped onto her knees, and threw her arms around a very surprised Julianne.

Not even waiting for a response, Abbey leapt to her feet and ran back to grab the Hello, Kitty suitcase. Taking the stairs two at a time, she raced upwards. As she ascended she heard a click and the living room below became dark again. Fortunately, a night light was plugged in at the top of the stairwell, keeping her from tripping over her luggage.

The window shades upstairs were drawn and Abbey felt a cold chill when she entered the prematurely darkened platform. She shivered from more than the temperature shift. The guest bedroom was to her right. When Abbey got inside, she closed the door. Leaning against the wooden barrier, she took a deep breath to steady herself.

First she had kissed Doc, and then hugged Julianne. She didn't know what had gotten into her, she never did anything without thinking it through. Her heart pounded like a race horse after the Derby. She took slow measured breaths, fighting to bring down her heart rate. Seeking distraction from what was going on inside of her, she examined the room that would, in all likelihood, be her home for the next few days.

The room was painted sky blue with white trim. The four poster bed dressed in blue and white toile had turned down covers and giant fluffy pillows. There was a single dresser, a closet, and white carpet that was probably a nightmare to keep clean. As a consideration to a guest's comfort, someone, Julianne probably, had brought in a space heater. Abbey walked over and leaned down, clicking it on. Even if it was only for tonight, Abbey thought, she might as well not freeze to death. The space heater quickly warmed up, and she could soon feel the tendrils of heat stroking her legs. She slipped out of her shoes, feeling the soft carpet with her toes. It was therapeutic on her sore feet.

She really had hated that job. The long hours standing, the never-ending people, the demanding customers, and the ungrateful coworkers. Just thinking about it made her head hurt. She sat on the edge of the bed, sinking into the feather soft mattress. "Wow," she breathed. The bed felt really comfortable. She scooted back and sank fully into its soft embrace. She hadn't considered how tired she was, or how little sleep she had been able to get lately. Working days at Murphy's, late nights split between research on

157 | The Five Santas

her thesis and visiting with Professor Brown, and early alarm clocks were all cashing in their markers.

All at once Abbey felt it all crashing in on her, lying on this wonderful bed. Bone tired, as her father would say. Her phone buzzed, and Abbey flipped it open.

"Can you be ready a few minutes early tomorrow?" Dan asked.

"Sure," she answered him drowsily.

"Okay, good," he hung up abruptly.

Abbey stared at the phone. She hated getting random phone calls, but that was perfect Dan. Randomness personified. Abbey raised an eyebrow at her suitcase. It had enough clothes for a few days, including the variety of quality work outfits Julianne had gotten Abbey. An early Christmas present, she had called the little spending spree. She had enough clothes to get through Christmas without needing to wash anything. And if she stayed longer, they had a washing machine.

Julianne is really something, Abbey thought to herself. She flashed back on the strange performance downstairs, comparing it with the kindhearted woman who usually greeted Abbey so differently. "Sure is," Abbey said out loud. She realized it was probably crazy to start talking to herself. However, since the only other person in the house was, at this moment, sitting downstairs in the dark, alone and dreaming of people coming for her husband; well, crazy was no problem.

    Abbey closed her eyes and felt the welcome fuzzy warmth of sleep coming for her hours before she would normally allow. She didn't even remember getting up to change into her Renaissance themed pajamas, climbing back beneath the covers, or turning off the lights for that matter. The next time she opened her eyes, an intruder was in her room.

    Abbey screamed.

Chapter 13

Murphy's was as busy as ever. Dan Landis strolled across the main floor, headed for security. Santa was still holding court at his little makeshift village, and Dan could just as easily keep an eye on him from Security as on the floor. Plus, he really wanted to get away from the crowds. The shoppers got more tense and desperate the closer it got to Christmas.

Hopefully, Karl would be able to talk about what he knew regarding the jewelry store heist; it was possible he might even have a theory on the whole thing. He somehow knew all the goings on in this corner of retail nirvana. However, when Dan arrived, Karl was in the far corner of the office watching prerecorded security footage.

Dan ignored the candy dish; all the bodies piling up around here had stolen his appetite for sweets. Instead he plopped down in his usual spot at the desk next to the lord of the manor. He settled comfortably into his seat and turned to watch the monitors.

Dan was able to hold out for at least twenty minutes before he felt his eyes glazing over. Needing a break from the monotony, he glanced around Karl's workspace, snooping. A romance novel was sitting there pretty as you please. It was so completely unexpected that Dan couldn't help himself. He had to look. Double-checking that Karl remained absorbed in the video monitors, Dan craned his neck forward to check the title.

Untamed Hearts. Well, he thought, that's a bit disappointing. It wasn't nearly as racy as he had hoped. The man looked sufficiently beefy and handsome, and the woman was typically busty and gorgeous as she swooned over him. Dan wondered if he had time to search for any of the naughty passages before Karl broke concentration.

Probably not. Karl looked like he was in the process of wrapping up with the footage. He hit a few keystrokes on the keyboard, pulled out a blank DVD from a giant stack of discs, and popped it into the computer. Karl glanced back at Dan and grunted. Dan nodded back. After a few moments of whirring, the computer spit out the now burned DVD.

The big man carefully labeled the disc with a magic marker and then slid it into a white paper sleeve. He slipped the DVD into his breast pocket. Probably a copy for the police. Dan leaned back into his chair. "So," Dan finally said, "Did you know the jewelry store got robbed?"

"Old man Diego's place," Karl was predictably dialed in.

"Right," Dan wasn't surprised. "I had no idea, which just goes to show how much I pay attention." Karl grunted, and then turned back to the monitors. Dan hated those monitors. "Mr. Peters asked me to keep an eye on the store Santa."

Karl cast a wary eye Dan's way and then turned back to the monitors. "Because of all the dead bodies. You probably know about those too, huh?"

"Shame," Karl said.

The big man rolled his neck, blew out expressively, and then looked at his watch. Dan checked the time on his phone. Almost closing time. "You need me for closing tonight?" Dan asked.

"No."

"Want me to bring you something for supper?"

"No."

"Okay, I'll go wait for Santa then." Dan stood. Karl grunted. Dan slapped the big man on the shoulder. "Keep 'em straight up here." Karl snorted. For some reason it made Dan chuckle. He glanced back to see Karl was still observing the monitors.

Dan gave a mild shudder as he headed out of security. He suddenly hated that place. He couldn't wait to put this store, Santa, and Mr. Peters behind him. Speak of the devil, as he turned the corner the man himself rounded the opposite corner. He was walking with head down, eyes on the floor, obviously deep in thought. His arms still weren't swinging.

"Mr. Peters," Dan called out. The man looked up, and again Dan was struck with how tired he looked.

"Mr. Landis," Mr. Peters exhaled dramatically, "I'm quite busy."

"I understand completely," he replied faking empathy for his despised boss, "I wanted to thank you for the trust you've put in me with this assignment."

"What…?" Mr. Peters frowned, then nodded comprehension, "Of course."

"I also wanted to tell you," Dan added, struggling to phrase his next statement perfectly. "I've experienced firsthand the emotional difficulties that come with the theft of one's belongings. I want you to know that I understand, the loss is much greater than just physical." Mr. Peters stared at him, mouth hanging open. "What I mean is," he added quickly, "if you need someone to talk to, I can recommend several professionals who specialize in these sorts of things."

"Oh," Mr. Peters closed his mouth with an audible snap, "Oh yes, thank you Mr. Landis. Please see to your duties." He waved one bony hand in dismissal and walked on.

Dan watched the man round the corner. Probably off to count beans, or whatever he does to relieve stress. He stopped himself from going too far down that road. The boss had suffered a loss and was having a hard time obviously. Poor guy, he thought with a flash of sympathy. He had told the truth, for once. He had done quite a few insurance investigations, discovering it was hard on people when they'd been the victim of theft. But, it was often difficult to talk about those things. He should give the man a little peace, even if he didn't really deserve it.

Before he took two steps the other way, Dan realized Mr. Peters was most likely going to pick up Karl's DVD. The one Dan had assumed was for the police. Of course, Mr. Peters would want to be the one to take it to the police. Total power play. The knowledge bothered Dan that Mr. Peters would again diminish Karl's significance in the investigation, yet there was nothing he could do. With a sigh, he resumed his pilgrimage to resume Santa duty.

The man in red was working his magic, talking to a slowly dwindling line of children. Dan noticed how efficient the Elves were at keeping the line moving. He made a mental note to point it out to Abbey, have her study it. If Abbey did end up being Santa's Elf, he was going to have to speak to her supervisor...and teach the girl how to work a crowd. He also still needed to pick up her costume. He wondered where they kept the spares.

Dan laughed at a vision of Abbey, poor, painfully shy Abbey, trying to control these little monsters. The parents were worse. Well, if anyone could rise to the challenge, it was her. That was part of the reason he'd wanted to bring her in on this job. She needed a challenge, a nice, softball, confidence boost. Man, he thought, I hope she stays.

Maggie, his former partner, had taken a chance on him. Picked him up out of the gutter, let him try his wings as an investigator. Maggie could talk anyone around to anything. He suddenly felt like he was out of his depth and had the urge to run. To leave all these yahoos to their Christmas, and let the masses deal with Santas dropping like flies. He was never going to be able to manage all these angles.

An announcement came over the P.A. system. "Greetings Murphy's customers, the store will be closing in ten minutes. Please make your way to the nearest register to make your purchases. We will be open again tomorrow from 7a.m. to 7p.m. We look forward to serving you in the future."

You don't have to go home but you can't stay here, Dan mentally added with a snort. For some reason Dan liked his version better. He leaned against one wall, watching the slow shuffle of the crowd toward the exit. No one in Santa's line showed any intention of leaving, he got a chuckle out of that. These people took their Santa experience seriously, they wouldn't be denied.

Since they weren't spending money, Dan wondered if Mr. Peters lost sleep over the inefficiency of allowing children to see Santa after close. Maybe he saw it as an investment so long as they asked for something lining Murphy's shelves. After twenty agonizing minutes, the last child, a little girl decked out in Princess Pink, got to tell Santa what she wanted for Christmas. Dan breathed a heavy breath. It was close, but he hadn't gone around the bend yet.

He put his hands in his pants pockets, breathing deeply. Dan felt a piece of candy and pulled it out. In one smooth motion, Dan unwrapped it and popped it into his mouth. His tongue savored the bittersweet taste of butterscotch. It was Abbey's favorite. The worst part of Christmas was how melancholy it made him feel. And alone. Santa stood up and stretched.

Dan didn't want to imagine what it felt like having to sit in one spot for hours at a time while child after child sat in your lap. He would have snapped. And possibly killed other Santa's. Well, that's a cheery thought.

The elves were talking amongst themselves. Dan decided to wait for Santa to head for the employee break room before speaking to him. He was shocked when Santa started walking directly toward him.

Dan gave Santa a head start, letting the older man get halfway, before setting out to meet him. However, Dan was shocked at how quickly Santa crossed the floor. He moved fast for an old man.

"Hello Santa," Dan grinned in spite of his misgivings about the big elf.

Santa smiled back, "Good evening Mr. Landis. I understand you will be my guardian for the rest of the Season?"

"Something like that," he replied, "Do you need to change?" He gave a once over to the red velvet suit, white fur trim, and patent leather belt. The man looked so natural in that suit; Dan couldn't imagine him wearing anything else. Changing into street clothes would have been more bizarre than seeing this man walking the avenue like this.

"Not at all," Santa ran a hand down the line of white fur in the center of his chest, "I rather like this suit. I only get to wear for a few precious weeks, I'd like to keep it on if you don't mind." He held up a hand and tapped it on the end of his button nose. "There is one quick thing." He gestured for one of the elves. She walked over.

"Yes, Santa?" the elf asked.

"Sandy," Santa gestured as he spoke by way of introduction, "this is Mr. Landis. Mr. Peters has asked him to provide us with an extra elf, for security reasons."

"You're Dan Landis?" Sandy asked, a suspicious look crossing her features.

"As far as I know," Dan responded with a smile meant to impress.

"Heard about you," she said with sparkling eyes and an interested smile. It had worked.

He relaxed, taking a step closer, "Only half of its true."

"You're going to be a tough fit." She snapped the top of her green hose.

"Oh it's not for me, I'll have one of my associates, Abbey, be the elf. She's much better looking as an elf."

"Abbey," Sandy rolled her eyes up, searching her memory. "Oh, the little wrapping girl?" the elf asked. "She's about my height, thin as a stick?"

"That's the one," Dan fought the urge to point out she wasn't thin as a stick. Thin sure, but he could think of plenty of other flattering comparisons.

"Yeah, I've got a spare costume that'll fit just fine. Wait right here and I'll bring it out." Sandy turned and sauntered off, unhurried. She had presence. So did her saunter. Dan watched her go.

Dan turned to Santa. "Right, so? Do you have a car, or will you be using eight tiny reindeer."

"Ho ho ho!" Santa laughed, his hands going to the sides of his generous midsection. "I normally take the bus…the reindeer are terrible in traffic." Dan couldn't help but smile, the guy was good at his job. "Well, if you don't mind, my car is out front," Dan pointed to the customer parking lot. "I'd rather drive, easier to keep you safe in there than on a city bus."

He'd snuck back to the jewelry store parking lot for his car. Gary was long gone by the time Dan passed by.

"Thank you very much Mr. Landis."

"Dan. Please call me Dan, or Daniel, if you want to be formal. Mr. Landis is my father's name. What should I call you? I mean, besides Santa. Do you have a first name?"

"Chris," Santa replied.

"Chris?" Dan said, "You're last name isn't Kringle by any chance is it?"

Santa laughed again, that rich hearty belly laugh. He has a wonderful laugh, Dan thought, very infectious. I wonder if it comes naturally, or if he has to practice it in front of the mirror. There were worse jobs than being Santa's bodyguard.

Chapter 14

Santa Claus was good company, no hint of the schlock Dan had expected. And very polite, he noted, as Santa held the door for him. Dan thanked him and walked ahead, trying to find his car. The parking lot was completely packed. He remembered having to park sort of far back, but couldn't remember where. Santa cheerfully followed as they looked for his Geo.

"I was always a VW man," Santa remarked.

"You have a car?" Dan couldn't picture the big man driving anything but a sleigh.

"For the weekends," Santa shrugged, "I can hardly take the reindeer on a Sunday drive." That set him off laughing again. Santa laughed a lot. It was endearing. They finally found his car near the parking lot exit, the easiest place to get out of. Dan unlocked the door for Santa and then came around to the driver's side. He felt a rumble in his stomach and wondered how long it had been since Santa ate. Sliding into his seat, he turned to the buckling Santa.

"You wouldn't be hungry by any chance, would you?" Dan asked.

"Of course," Santa nodded, "but please, no cookies and milk. The Elves have put me on a strict diet until the big day." That set Santa off on another deep belly laugh. Dan tore himself away from the sight of the laughing fat man whose belly really did shake like a bowl full of jelly. He cranked the car.

Well, he told himself, the man was not going to break character. A method actor, through and through. His mind flashed back to David Barr, the street corner Santa who someone had killed. Not for the money. Then why? That sweet old man started growing his beard in September and apparently cherished his store bought costume. It wasn't as good as the crushed velvet that this Santa wore, but it kept the draft out and looked real enough.

The cleaning lady, at the halfway house where David volunteered, confessed that she'd heard a rumor that he had once tried to buy a reindeer. It was always the good ones.

"Where you headed?" Dan asked Santa, Chris, as the traffic light turned red.

"I have a room at the Green Leaf Extended Stay…"

"Over on Queen Street?"

"Yes, do you know it?"

"I've worked over there a few times. That, that's a bit low rent isn't it?" Dan asked.

"Well," Santa confessed with a slightly sad smile, "You don't become Santa Claus for the money. You do it for the

children, for their smiling faces, and the small joy you can bring to
their lives."

"That's sweet, but seriously, as authentic as you look,
surely you're pulling down some serious bank."

"No, and don't call me Shirley," Santa tried to be serious
and, failing, threw back his head laughing at his own joke. The
Airplane reference caught Dan completely off guard. He nearly ran
off the road laughing at this strange old man. They drove on,
cackling together like maniacs.

Thanks to his intimate knowledge of every sleazy motel
and no-tell hotel in town, Dan also had a pretty good bead on every
nearby restaurant, bar and grill. Dan decided to treat Santa to
calzones. There was a great little spot within spitting distance of
the Green Leaf. The little restaurant's big glass window would
allow Dan to keep an eye on traffic as well.

No cars seemed to be slowing down and no pedestrians
looked interested in them as they passed by. The twilight sky was
dusky and gray, casting dark shadows over everything. This time,
the time between day and night, was the worst for a human's
vision. As the light faded completely and his eyes adjusted, Dan
began to relax. He could handle the darkness. He liked the night.

No one batted an eye when the two of them got out of the
car and walked in. This part of town had seen everything. Except
Santa was really something, Dan would have been shocked to walk

by and spotted him sitting there, eating a veggie calzone. Apparently Santa was a vegetarian.

"So," Santa said as he munched cheerfully on a chunk of broccoli, "What is it you do, Dan? When you're not taking care of Christmas that is."

"I'm a private investigator," he replied automatically, taking a bite of his Philly Cheese Steak Calzone. The sweet caramelized onion mixed with the fat and salt of the beef, it tasted magnificent. "Murphy's hired me to work Loss Prevention, they like to add on staff for the busy season. A cop friend got me the job." He didn't mention Gary's name or their relationship. "Mr. Peters has me keeping an eye out for thieves and such. We've had some trouble outside the store, so the boss asked if I wouldn't mind keeping an eye on you until your contract is up. We've had some muggings in the area, just some local punks, and you are a prized investment." He tried not to pour it on too thick.

"Ahhh," Santa drew out his response, nodding.

Dan got the sneaking suspicion that Santa knew he was lying. And that Santa knew what the real truth was. Is Santa a mind reader? Probably, Dan realized. How else would he know when I'm sleeping and when I'm awake?

"Do you enjoy it?"

"It has its moments. I mean, the hours are long, but I enjoy the independence."

"I see. That, is one of the best aspects in my line of work also. The independence. The spirit of freedom."

"Really? I imagine you put in some long hours though. That can't be all that great or freeing."

"Well, my time constraints are for only a very short window. The rest of the year is mine to do with as I like. In fact, I'm debating writing my memoirs."

"Get out of town!" Dan leaned in eagerly, "What's the title?"

"*Beneath The Beard.*" His eyes twinkled merrily.

Dan sat back and laughed.

They stayed there for over an hour, laughing and talking shop. Santa shared stories about malls around America, the children he'd met, and the strange parents who brought them. Dan shared stories about run-ins with spouses, endless stakeouts, and his misadventures with Doc Brown.

"This Professor Brown," Santa asked slowly, "would this be Leroy Brown, the travelogue writer?"

"You've heard of him?"

"I adore him," Santa admitted, his eyes twinkling. "I thought I was the only one who knew about that little valley in the Andes."

"You've been to Peru?"

"I would gladly retire in Peru, though I doubt I'll ever truly stop being Santa. That is until my time comes to a close. Do you know, Machu Pichu has the most beautiful view I've ever seen," Santa's blue eyes grew misty.

"I've never been," Dan admitted quietly. "When Doc went I had some… personal matters." He stopped, fighting to keep his composure.

"I see," Santa didn't press. "Well, if you ever have the opportunity, I recommend you go. There may be taller mountains, wider vistas, but for me, it will always be the most beautiful. Of course, I'm prejudiced, because that's where I asked Mrs. Claus to marry me."

Dan noted those twinkling eyes had a faraway look to them. He imagined that was what true love looked like. Santa smiled quietly at some secret memory. There was a shift behind his eyes, and he turned to Dan with laser point focus.

"So tell me young man, what do you want for Christmas?" the phrase was well rehearsed, yet came out with sounding perfectly natural.

"World peace." He grinned, not quite back to himself.

Santa chewed, waiting patiently, seeing through the façade.

"I can't say…" he began genuinely this time, embarrassed at first and then realized he could say it. Santa had the kind of face you could tell anything to. "I just want to be done with Christmas." Dan sighed. It felt good to tell someone that.

Santa leaned back, "I thought you might. I could tell from the first moment I met you."

"What do you mean?" Dan asked, shocked that he'd been transparent. He was good at hiding himself.

"You dislike Christmas," Santa restated. It wasn't an accusation, merely a statement. The older man's voice certainly wasn't offended, only sad.

"Please don't take it personally," Dan said hurriedly, not wanting to offend this sweet old man.

"Of course not, young man." Santa favored him with a warm look.

"I just…well, it's you. Offending you would be like kicking a puppy."

"You don't strike me as the puppy kicking type. Want to tell me about it?"

No, Dan thought. "It's complicated," he said out loud.

Twinkling eyes offered quiet sympathy.

"I lost someone. Since then, it's been hard to get into the Christmas spirit."

"I'm sorry."

"Not your fault," Dan replied evenly. He hated when people said they were sorry. That and he needed to get through this quickly. "Her name was Maggie. She was mugged, and even though she did the smart thing and gave up her purse, the guy must have gotten spooked. He shot her. She didn't make it through the night." And I went after the guy, Dan left out. That's how I met Gary. And how Gary met Julianne, his little voice added. Some good had come from that night even if he didn't want to admit it.

Santa stared at him, and Dan again wondered if the man could read minds. "It's just always been hard," Dan said softly, "Winter was her Season. And, Christmas was a big deal to her. It was kind of her holiday, you know?"

Santa nodded, "I understand." He yawned, covering his mouth partway through in scarlet faced embarrassment. "I'm so sorry Dan! Please don't take that as boredom."

"Come on Santa," Dan said with a smile, "it's been a long day, let's get you to bed."

"Thank you Dan, I'm usually more of a night owl, but it has been an exhausting few weeks." Dan nodded, holding the door for Santa. They walked to his car, enjoying the cool, clear night. He drove across the street and dropped Santa off at his hotel room.

"Now," Dan was in professional mode, "What time do you need to be at work?"

"Oh posh, I can take the bus."

"No, it's my job to keep you safe. Now, what time should I be here to pick you up?"

Santa smiled, "Mr. Peters likes for me to be ready to receive visitors at opening. I try to be there at least half an hour beforehand."

Dan nodded. That was no earlier than Abbey usually had to be there. He felt a guilty pang, he'd meant to check on her tonight. She'd been down and her mentioning going home had him worried.

"One second, I have to check on something."

Dan punched #3 for Abbey's speed dial, and heard it ring twice.

"Hello," she said her voice groggy.

"Can you be ready a few minutes early tomorrow?" Dan asked.

"Sure," was her sleepy response. Santa was climbing out of the car.

"Okay, good," he said hurriedly, hanging up as he rushed to get in front of the spry old man. He scanned the streets. Again, no one as far as the eye could see. No heads in parked cars caught his attention, no pedestrians were walking by. Dan's senses told him it was all clear. As far as he could tell, they were alone.

"All right," he said, "You go inside and lock the door, please. Do you need ice? Drinks? Anything like that?"

"No," Santa chuckled at the attention.

"Right," Dan was more serious, "I'll be here, say quarter after?"

Santa nodded, "That's fine."

"Good. Now, do me a favor? Stay inside, lock the door, and don't go out. We need you safe."

"Dan," Santa said with good humor, "I appreciate the concern. How about this: I will only answer the door to the barber's knock."

"Right," Dan said, trying to remember what that was.

Santa reached over to a wooden post, rapping his knuckles against it. Tap-tappity-tap-tap. Shave and a haircut. "Two bits," Santa added after a pause. With a wink, he walked to his door. Dan watched him cross to the door, stopping to pull a room key from a pocket hidden by the top of his coat, and unlock the door.

"Santa has pockets," Dan laughed to himself. He wasn't sure why that discovery surprised him, but it did. He spun on one heel, walking back towards the car. Once inside, he kept an eye on the room's door hanging open with the lights flicking on to illuminate the round man inside. Santa theatrically looked around his hotel room, then behind the door, and turned back. He waved the all clear, and Dan waved back. Santa shut the door.

Cranking his car, he felt some weight falling off his shoulders. At least this Santa was safe. And so far, no more dead bodies. He pulled out of the parking lot, glancing around automatically. Still nothing. Dan pulled up to the red light and debated where to go. His office was across town and he had a cot and a pile of bad movies to look forward to.

Or, a few miles away was Jules' house. She had a really comfortable couch in the basement. Dan even had a key.

With a shrug, Dan turned left. He was off to see his sister. The roads were crowded. Tons of shoppers, some going home, some searching out deals to be had at the all-night stores. Suckers all of them, falling into this idea that you had to buy a gift for everyone you knew, that material possessions could make up for a year's worth of neglect. Money equals love.

The gate was closing when Dan pulled up. Someone had just come or gone. He pulled out his wallet, extracting the pass key. Waving the pass key in the general direction of the sensor, he anxiously waited for the buzz. It gave off its distinctive warble and the gate opened with a groan. He pulled forward, heading for the Jones'.

The neighborhood was lit up with white lights. Every house on the block had been carefully decorated. The community had a list of Christmas lighting professionals that you could select from. After Thanksgiving, a fleet of white vans arrived, carefully placing environmentally friendly LED lights on each and every property willing to participate. And, in a neighborhood such as this, every house would participate. The suggestion was mandatory. Each house was tastefully decorated, each display stunning. And if any of the twinkling lights burned out, a polite technician would be out to repair it the same day. For this kind of money, you only got the best service.

From his car, Dan stared at the neat rows of houses. They looked like gingerbread mansions. The sheer absence of originality was sickening. It didn't take much for him to hate Christmas these days. Cookie-cutter decorations, crowded stores, and dead Santas. Dan figured he wasn't alone. At least one other person felt the same about Christmas.

He parked in the street in front of the Jones house, carefully avoiding blocking the driveway. Jules always fussed when Dan blocked her in. Plus, it annoyed the neighbors to have a cheap piece of crap car out on the curb, which made Dan's day. The homeowners association might even send a note. Sicking the wrath of Julianne "Boom-Boom" Jones on some busybody put a smile on his face. This much homogeny needed a little ugly thrown in, for color.

He walked across the grass, glowering at the perfectly spaced lights. If it weren't so disgustingly controlled and arranged, it might almost have been beautiful. Dan was grateful the sprinklers weren't on. Out of habit, his hand went to his back pocket for the lock pick kit. He remembered that Gary had made him promise not to break into his house anymore. Dan used a key like a normal, boring, person. Gary was such a sourpuss. The door opened, and Dan had the good sense to wipe his feet. As funny as it was to see Jules mad at other people, he had no interest in being her target. He locked the door behind him.

The house was dark, but unless someone had rearranged the furniture, it really didn't matter. Dan had the layout memorized. He headed downstairs. Through the living room and toward the kitchen he went, twenty-seven steps. He felt a little sad as he passed the vacant spot where the Christmas tree would normally stand. If it wasn't up by now, it wasn't going up. Dan had misplaced the small Charlie Brown-esque tree he kept in his office. Maggie had loved it.

Julianne had a very lifelike faux fir tree and a hand painted nativity scene. As he looked around, he realized there were no decorations. Not even the goofy Advent calendar he'd bought the two of them their first Christmas as a married couple. There was a stairwell off to one side of the kitchen, hidden behind a door. He headed downstairs. Twelve steps down to the basement. Four steps to the couch.

The basement was huge, bigger than Dan's whole apartment/office. The TV, a monster wide-screen, was on, showing some cooking show. Dan sighed quietly. Jules was on the couch, fast asleep. He rarely saw her anymore. Seeing her this way, asleep and unguarded, Dan was struck by how thin and frail she looked. Not at all the strong and vibrant woman he'd grown up with.

Too much work Jules, he scolded, you need a vacation. He walked over to the basement closet, pulling out a blanket and pillow. The blanket went over her, while he slipped the pillow behind her head, gently moving her raven hair out of the way. Dan knew this couch could cause a serious crick in the neck if you weren't careful. Of course, it was also incredibly comfortable for everything else.

Oh well, there's always the guest room. He hated sleeping there. The bed was too soft and he felt like it should be reserved for invited guests. He always thought of himself more as a gatecrasher.

Or trouble, his little voice said.

That's me, he agreed. Trouble, and no one wants trouble.

He walked back to the closet, searching in the flickering TV light for the pajamas he kept down here.

Jules had gotten tired of walking in on Dan asleep in his boxers, and bought him silk pajamas last year. Black, naturally.

Not wanting to come back down later, Dan grabbed clothes for tomorrow too. The flicker of an idea sparked across his sleepy brain, and he rummaged through the closet. It was in here somewhere. His hand touched something soft and fuzzy. Just what he needed. Hiding behind a box of junk in the closet's top shelf,

Dan found the goofy Christmas sweater. The one Jules had given to him years ago, and Dan wouldn't have been caught dead wearing it. Trying not to snicker at the look it was sure to draw from his sister, he put the sweater on the pile of his clothes. He'd finally found a use for the stupid thing.

Change of clothes and pajamas in hand, Dan headed for the stairs. He paused to turn off the TV and kiss his sister on the forehead.

"Merry Christmas kid," he whispered. She didn't stir.

He trudged upstairs and slipped out of his shoes as he went, bending down to pick them up with two fingers. He turned the corner in the kitchen, heading for the second floor stairwell. Dan unbuttoned his shirt and rolled his head around to loosen his neck. The tension of this day was starting to get to him. It had been bad, and he really hoped it would just end without further incident. No more bodies, he pleaded with an eye roll upward. He went into the guest room and hung his clothes on the closet door knob. He almost tripped over something and swore. Someone in the bed jumped up and screamed. Dan screamed then hit the light switch. Sleepy green eyes blinked rapidly at him.

"Abs?"

"Dan?" Abbey clutched her heaving chest.

"What are you doing here?" they asked simultaneously.

"I just got off work."

"Professor Brown dropped me off."

"Doc's..."

"No. He's gone, won't be back until after Christmas."

"Right." He took a steadying breath. His heart was pounding like he'd run a mile. "So, are you comfortable?"

"Yes, thank you. A little startled, but otherwise yes."

He looked around, taking in the oversized Hello, Kitty staring back at him. "Well, I'll be downstairs if you need anything."

"Great," she smiled politely, still blinking sleepily at him.

Dan spun around, walking out the door. He stopped and turned, adding quietly. "Have a good night Abs."

"Thanks Dan. Good night."

Dan shut off the light. Abbey started to lie back down. She stopped, sensing she wasn't alone.

"Dan?" Abbey called out.

"Yes?" He sounded like he was still in the doorway.

"What are you doing?"

"Just wondering how heavily you sleep," his wicked grin was audible.

"Goodnight Dan," Abbey said, an edge to her voice.

"Good night Abs."

This time he shut the door and headed downstairs. After several deep breaths his heart finally stopped jumping and he could get his mind off how adorable Abbey looked all mussed and sleepy. Long day, he thought. Here's hoping tomorrow will be better.

It wasn't.

Chapter 15

Abbey ran hard. Her legs fought the ground for purchase, clawing for traction. She felt her chest constricting as she struggled to breathe. She could hear her pursuer following, wheezing and shuffling his feet. No matter how hard she ran he stayed right behind her.

He was catching up. Abbey glanced over her shoulder. His leering grin mocked her. His clothing was blood red. He reached out for her with the black gloved hand that offered only death.

"I'm coming for you Abbey," Santa said, his voice a rattling echo. Abbey ran faster, looking around for an escape.

"Abbey," the voice called. "Aaabbbeeeyyyyy..."

She felt her legs slowing down, could almost feel Santa's hot breath on her neck. It felt like she was running through molasses, fighting for each agonizing step. Abbey pulled hard. She smelled something sweet, incredibly aromatic. Was she swimming through sugar?

"Abbey," a softer voice called.

Dan, Abbey recognized his voice. He could help, if she could just find him. She reached out, trying to find him with her hands. If he was close, maybe he could pull her out. And the smell! The smell was driving her insane.

"Abbey," Dan called again, he was close.

The sweet scent combined with something familiar, the smell of Dan's deodorant. The aromas pulled at her. She continued to look; why couldn't she see him? A gray cloud clogged her vision. She felt herself being pulled away, out of her pursuers reach. She looked down; Santa was waving his arms, gnashing his teeth in frustration. He hadn't caught her this time. They were flying now. She had no idea Dan could fly.

She opened her eyes expecting to see him above her, peering down. Her stomach flipped at the idea. There was no face smiling down. She turned following the symphony of smells that had drawn her from her nightmare; Dan was in bed with her.

"What are you doing?" she squeaked.

"Hello to you too," He held out a steaming cup of coffee. Abbey recognized the aroma from her dream. It smelled of sugar, with a slight hint of cinnamon. She sat up, and then leaned back against the headrest.

"You're a heavy sleeper," Dan smiled.

"You are an idiot," Abbey took a sip of the coffee.

"Figured this beat an alarm clock."

"Is this what you do with all your friends?"

"Jules is a light sleeper. Gary's a cuddler. Doc's asked me to stop," Dan said, "but Bernie loves it."

"I bet," Abbey rolled her eyes at the name. That one was a no brainer. Of course Dan would get in bed with Bernie. Who wouldn't? Smart, sexy, confident, and the right kind of doctor to boot.

"Sleep well?" Dan propped his head on one arm, giving Abbey dangerous bedroom eyes. She took a sip. The coffee was sweet, with an exotic twist. Abbey wasn't normally a coffee drinker, but this tasted wonderful.

"I can make a decent cup," he confessed, seeing her pleasure.

She nodded approval, "What time is it?"

"Early. Wanted to ask you something before I went to work."

"And you thought climbing into bed was the best way to ask?"

"Always worked for me before."

Abbey didn't comment.

"Want to play dress-up?" Dan asked, with that lascivious grin. Abbey raised one eyebrow. "Because, I've got a short skirt, stockings, and a cute hat hanging up in the closet."

"Business or personal?"

"A little bit of column A, little bit of column B."

"All right, but are you sure you'll fit in something like that?"

Dan laughed. He had a charming laugh. She caught herself staring.

"Want to work this case with me?" he asked, his eyes softening.

"The Santa case?" she asked, sitting up.

"None other." He rested his elbow against the pillow, laying his face in hand. "I need someone I can count on. And, I would like to point out that I avoided being sarcastic just now." That earned him a raised eyebrow. "Just saying. Really, I need you to keep an eye on Santa for me." He took the coffee cup from her hands and sipped again. "I am good by the way. At coffee, and other things." His finger played with a string on the fluffy pillow. "We've got time if you want a demonstration."

"No thanks Champ," Abbey noted the way her breath came a little faster and an image popped into her mind. Clearing her throat, she tried to hide her reaction. "I'll take your word for it. So, while I'm hanging out in a short skirt with Santa, what exactly will you be doing?"

"Keeping an eye on you." She took the cup back, taking another sip of coffee. The sweetened liquid warmed her throat. "You're the only one who could pull it off. I can't be everywhere, or watch out for everything. And of the two of us, you'd make the most convincing elf."

"Probably." She pictured Dan in a skirt.

"Afterwards," he stared at the pillow, "you can get on with your merry life." Adding hurriedly, "I can pay you. I'll double what you were making as a wrapper."

"It's always about money with you," she took another sip.

"Not always…"

"I want double my entire salary."

"Deal."

"For the whole time I worked there."

"Absolutely, I'd love to work with you."

"You're a tough negotiator."

"So I've been told," Dan winked at her.

"Do I still have to wear the costume?" Abbey asked.

"Yes."

"I'm in."

"Excellent," he said, spinning out of bed and landing on his feet.

"Are you always this quick to jump out of bed?"

"You're just lucky I didn't jump out the window. Again. Not my proudest moment," he grimaced, walking around to her side and knelt to her eye level. "Thank you." The unusual sincerity was shocking.

"You're welcome?"

He took her hand, her skin cold against the warmth he radiated, and pressed his lips against her knuckles. "I owe you."

Her skin warmed. "I know."

"Okay," he stood and stretched his arms over his head, "as I said, we have time, so whenever you're ready. There are sticky buns downstairs if you want one." He gave Abbey an affectionate pat on the leg and headed for the door. It was the jingling that made her take a long look. She finally noticed what he was wearing. It was so un-Dan.

"Dan," she asked, "what do you have on?"

Dan looked down. It was a hunter green sweater with a smiling reindeer, red nose and all, embroidered on the front. Little silver bells hung on the antlers, jingling when he walked. "It's festive," he shrugged and flicked one of the bells, making it ring.

"Ah, oh," she wasn't certain how to react. He closed the door quietly behind him. Alone, she took another sip and set her coffee down on the bedside table. She stretched her arms out, feeling well rested. She massaged her neck, working the cricks out. A splash of color caught her eye. Something was hanging on the closet door. The costume. It had to be.

Abbey flipped her phone open to check the time. Dan was right, it was early. Very early. Yet, somehow she wasn't tired. Maybe it was the bed, which had given Abbey the best rest she'd had in a long time. Or maybe it was the coffee, now starting to give her a welcome buzz.

Or maybe, something inside her pointed out, it was that Dan woke you up instead of an alarm. "No chance." She thrust the thought aside. There was no taming Dan, and Abbey wasn't interested in a fling.

She stared at the costume for a moment longer. The monstrosity was emerald and alabaster, with a vaguely Dutch design.

With a sigh, Abbey accepted the inevitable. In what should have been one smooth motion, she threw back the covers. Unaccustomed as she was to the excessive bedding, the sheet ended up tangled around her arm and she had to shake it loose. Already contorted, Abbey spun her legs around and nearly fell off the bed. Thankfully her arm shot out in time to keep from landing head first.

Dan heard a thump from above as he made his way downstairs, decorative bells jingling. He grinned, imagining Abbey stomping around up above, mildly annoyed at his intrusion. The kitchen light was on, so at least Julianne hadn't left yet. He was glad. Putting on his brightest smile, he stepped around the corner. "Morning Champ."

"Hi," Julianne responded flatly, without looking up from the paper.

"Thanks for making sticky buns," Dan tried to draw her out.

"Eh," she replied, distracted. She shifted her weight slightly, examining the paper closer. He slid into his seat at the table, reaching out to take a bun. Biting into it, he watched Julianne doing the crosswords. In pen. She was a beast.

Dan had long ago come to terms with the fact that Julianne was a genius. It was still annoying when she rubbed it in his face. Well, at least he could whistle. "How's it going?"

She finally looked up, raising an eyebrow. "It's going. How are things with you?"

"Pretty good," he shrugged.

"Are you…" she did a double take, her eyes going wide. "Are you wearing my sweater?"

"The one you gave me?"

"No, the one Gary gave me."

"I thought you bought it for me, for Christmas."

"No, Gary gave it to me, but it was too big for me. That and reindeer aren't really my thing. Really not my thing. I thought I'd already put it in the charity box."

"You didn't get me a sweater?" He felt a little hurt.

"Gertie, when have you ever worn a sweater?" her face twisted in confusion at his reaction. She tried a different tact, "Besides, you look like a dork in a sweater."

"What about now?" Dan asked, holding the bottom of the sweater out so she got the full effect of the reindeer. He jingled the bells on the antlers. In answer she went back to her crossword puzzle. The sounds of footsteps pounding down the stairs, made Dan turn around in his chair. Abbey jumped the last step, holding her arms outstretched.

"Ta da!" She declared, a big smile on her face. She was wearing the costume.

"You look adorable," Dan declared.

"Thanks," she curtsied. "Hello Julianne."

There was an almost imperceptible sigh, and then Jules looked up again, effectively giving up on her crossword. "Hello Abbey," she said, pausing, leaning back to take in the Abbinator's "elfness." "What an absolutely adorable costume," she added, seconding Dan's opinion.

"Thank you," Abbey said brightly. The costume really was kind of fun and here, with these two, she wasn't embarrassed. Out in public, that would be another story. "I really appreciate you saying that!" She breathed in heartfelt relief. "I'm just glad it fits."

"So you decided to help Dan with the case?" Julianne asked.

"I did. Only because he asked nicely," Abbey raised her chin.

"In bed," Dan added.

They ignored him. Abbey more pointedly.

"That's kind of you. Dan told me about the case just this morning." She gestured toward the table. "Grab a seat, we have buns."

"Don't mind if I do," Abbey smiled, and turned around in search of a napkin. Julianne went back to her puzzle and Dan munched on his bun while staring at Abbey. She pretended not to notice as she walked around, searching the kitchen for napkins.

"Is Gary up yet?" she asked, still looking around. It was impossible to imagine not noticing the big man if he was, though it was early for him to be gone. Gary always had breakfast with Julianne. No one said anything. Dan coughed into his hand and took a sip of his coffee before stuffing the rest of his bun in his mouth.

"Would you look at the time," he mumbled barely comprehensible, mouth full of sticky bun. "Come on Abs, we have to get you to work." Abbey gingerly took her bun in hand, picking up a napkin with her free hand. Dan swallowed, and then grabbed another one for the road. "Bye," he waved with his bun.

Julianne waved back without looking up from her puzzle.

Dan's car was still out front. So far no one had called a tow truck on him. Yet. You just couldn't trust these rich snooty types. He held the door for Abbey. She smiled up at him, shivering in the cold. He leaned over her, cranking up the car. He turned the heat up to full blast. "Be right back," he leaned over and kissed her cheek, leaving a sugary smear. He headed inside, but paused in mid-step to add with a wink, "Don't steal my sweet ride."

Abbey gave him the smile he was expecting and watched as he tore across the lawn to duck inside. She used one of the napkins to wipe off her cheek. She tried to eat the sticky bun with the minimum amount of mess while adjusting the heat vent away from her face. After a few seconds of fumbled bumping with her elbow, hot air began blasting her legs. Much better, she thought.

The house door opened and Dan appeared again carrying a wool pea coat. It was black, and looked very expensive. He was also carrying a purse. It was small, sleek, and also black. Abbey was fairly certain both belonged to Julianne; not only were they definitely way outside Dan's price range, they were women's.

Abbey glanced scornfully down at her mismatched pink polka dotted purse laying at her feet. The only nice things she had were gifts. Oh well, that was the price she paid for years spent educating herself; zero pocket change for fashion. Dan walked to the driver's side and opened his door. He threw the coat over Abbey's legs and then tossed the black purse into the back seat.

She shifted her legs, putting the coat in a more comfortable position. Abbey put the remainder of the sticky bun in her mouth, and then carefully wiped her hands clean with a napkin. Once all the sugar was off her hands, she buckled in. The used napkin was

197 | T h e   F i v e   S a n t a s

strategically placed at her feet, tucked under her purse to avoid accidentally brushing against the edge of the fine coat in her lap.

"Comfortable?" Dan asked, his hand on the gear shift.

She chewed the remainder of her sticky bun and swallowed in a rush. "Yes, I am," she replied, "Thank you very much." She patted the coat.

"No problem." Slipping on his seat belt, he checked the mirrors. It was still dark, but street lights illuminated the area nicely. There were no obvious watchers, and he decided there was only one thing you could do about the invisible ones. Dan popped the car into drive and floored it.

Abbey felt the acceleration press her into the seat. "In a hurry?"

"Kind of. Got to go pick up Santa."

"Oh. Doesn't he have his own transportation?"

"The reindeer are at the vet."

"Ah," she said, as the car whipped around a corner.

After a few minutes' silence she asked, "So why are we picking up Santa?"

"Well," he glanced sideways at her, "I was trying to figure out what to get Julianne and Gary for Christmas, and it hit me. Why not a Santa? They'll be the envy of the neighborhood."

She sighed, "If you're going to be snarky, then never mind."

"All right," he said, "I figure it would be safer for Chris if we drive him to and from work."

"Chris?"

"Santa's real name is Chris."

"Is his last name Kringle?"

"You know, I asked the same thing." Dan waved a hand. "He never said."

"He gives me the creeps." Abbey admitted.

"Me too."

"Really?"

"Oh yeah, since like Day One. I mean, I don't want someone to know when I've been bad and good, sleeping or awake."

"I just don't trust people with beards."

"You're afraid of beards?"

"They make me think they're hiding something. Even Abe Lincoln seemed a little less honest with his."

"Really?"

"No, not really. But speaking of beards, did you know Grizzly Adams had a bear named Benjamin Franklin?"

"No."

The drive was uneventful, except for Dan speeding like a maniac. He didn't cut his speed until he whipped into the hotel parking lot and slammed on his brakes. The car skidded to a stop in front of the two story building. A well-maintained car was important for a private investigator.

Abbey looked over, her fingers white as they gripped the seat. "You're enjoying this aren't you?"

"Not at all," Dan said, not bothering to hide his smile.

Abbey watched him get out, glancing from side to side. He walked quickly to the door, his head and eyes constantly on the move. Once he got to the door, he paused. It took him a minute to remember the sequence. Reaching out, he gave the barber's knock. The door opened immediately.

"Hello Dan," Santa greeted him with a laugh. "You're punctual, an admirable quality." The round man looked as resplendent as ever in his red suit.

"I try," Dan bobbed his head. "Your sleigh awaits," he gestured towards his careworn car. His eyes continued to scan the area. No one out and about on this cool morning. Just how he liked it. As Santa walked toward the car, he looked back at Dan. "That is a lovely sweater you have on," he said, eyes twinkling, "My wife has one just like it."

"I wore it just for you."

"For that, I am grateful," Santa replied.

Stepping up to beat him to it, Dan opened and held the back door for Santa. Once Chris was inside, Dan shut the door and hopped into the driver's seat.

Abbey leaned over. "I don't like this," she hissed.

"Like what?"

"Like Santa carpooling with us." She tried to bottle her panic. "He never takes that suit off, it's weird."

"Oh," he said flatly, his eyes on the move, searching for threats.

"Are you sure we can trust him?" Abbey asked, her voice cracking slightly. She kept sneaking glances back at the red suited figure staring blissfully unaware out the window.

"Yeah, but look at him," he whispered with a sly smile, "I mean, he's fluffy and squishy like a teddy bear. How could you not trust someone that huggable?"

"Just not too hard. I tend to squeak," Santa said.

Abbey and Dan both turned to look at Santa. He smiled at them, holding one black gloved hand up in a wave.

"Shall we go?" Santa asked, adjusting his seat belt over his big belly. Dan popped the car into reverse, flooring it back. Santa flopped in his seat. "Wahoo," he clapped enthusiastically.

Dan flipped the gear into drive and punched the gas. Chunks of loose gravel spat against the car's metal sides. Abbey felt herself pushed into the seat by the sudden acceleration.

"Next time I'm driving," she said, bracing her legs against the dash.

"You don't even have a license," he shot back, "But if you ask Santa, he might bring you a new car for Christmas." He caught Santa rolling his eyes and shaking his head. People tended to do that a lot around him. Dan glanced at his blind spot, before whipping into traffic, quickly changing lanes. He double-checked his mirrors, necessary at these speeds. But he wasn't taking any chances, someone would be very obvious tailing him driving like this.

The car sped along the minimally traveled street, jumping across a lane, and making a sharp right turn. A horn honked angrily behind them. Dan paid the horn no attention, never slowing down. The wheels bounced as the car hit a pot hole. He kept an eye on his mirrors, no one seemed to be following.

"Dan!" Abbey shouted.

The car screeched to a halt at a stop sign he hadn't seen. All three flopped forward and back.

"Thanks Abs," Dan offered.

"Do you normally travel this fast?" Santa asked, adjusting his hat.

Dan didn't answer. Instead, he leaned forward, checking for traffic. No one was coming so he eased the car across the road and then floored it, the tires squealing with the rapid acceleration. Two more hairpin turns, one U-Turn, and a red light later, they arrived at Murphy's.

Dan slowed as he neared the parking lot, and then pulled into the customer parking lot. He found the closest non-handicapped space and pulled in. It was easy, the lot was completely deserted.

"Everyone ready?" he asked, turning off the ignition.

"We're parking here?" Abbey had been a store employee, she knew the rules.

"Why yes, yes we are," Dan responded. They were five feet from the door without a soul in sight. Not even the early birds had arrived yet.

"Won't we get in trouble?" Abbey could see Mr. Peters' disapproval already.

"Hopefully," he turned to Santa. "I was just teasing Abbey. My primary concern is keeping you safe, and I doubt anyone will know whose car this is. Santa, I promise I'm not normally a trouble maker."

"Quite alright." Something in his twinkling eyes indicated his disbelief in Dan's last statement. "You do what you must for security's sake."

"See," Dan turned to Abbey, "Santa approves. That has to account for something. Come on."

As everyone got out, Abbey slammed her door. Dan winced, but didn't say anything. There was no sense antagonizing her and she wasn't likely to stop slamming car doors like a rampaging gorilla anytime soon. Before Dan shut his door, he grabbed the purse out of the back seat. An actor always needs his props. I'd kill for a snapshot of this, he thought, leading the way. The three of them must be some kind of sight.

Santa, a hot elf, and a dork in a reindeer sweater; fighting crime and bringing cheer to the world one store at a time. Dan chuckled to himself as he stopped at the glass doors. They were locked this early and he bent down to pick the door's lock.

"Really?" Abbey covered herself in the pea coat.

"I'll lock it back up," he promised. "But, I don't want to risk bringing Santa around to the employee entrance. Someone would be more likely to be watching that one."

She scowled at him, not entirely believing in his purity of cause.

"It's all in the name of security," Dan reassured her, "tell her Santa."

"Leave me out of this," Santa laughed. Santa's infectious chuckle must have affected Abbey, because her dour expression began to melt. Dan smiled up at her.

"You walk a fine line Daniel Landis," she warned softly, a smile threatening to break through.

"And I look fine doing it," Dan added with a wink. He held the door for her and Santa, who nodded at the courtesy with a warm expression on his face.

Dan shook his head. The man was good. Yet, there's just something unsettling about him, he admitted to himself. I just can't put my finger on what. As he watched Abbey and Santa walk toward Santa's station to get ready for their day, Dan ducked toward the bathroom. He needed to decompress for a few minutes and a locked stall was about the only place he could be guaranteed privacy as everyone started arriving. It was going to be a long day.

Chapter 16

There was a carefully cultivated assembly line at Santa's Village. When one set of parent and child were close enough, an elf would step forward, greeting them both with a million dollar smile and a welcoming wave. Kind assurances would be offered to the nervous children, warm smiles would be directed toward the long suffering parents. Santa always had a child in his lap and was very good at making sure that child had his absolute attention. He was an expert at making each tyke feel they were the center of his world. And for those precious few moments, they were.

While the child sat on Santa's lap, another elf took a snapshot to capture the moment. The parent had the option of purchasing the photo if they wanted, which they always did. Once the child had told Santa what they wanted, and had gotten their picture taken, a third elf would kindly lead the parent and child away. On the way, they collected the money for the snapshot and made sure the child got a candy cane. Every child who saw Santa was entitled to something sweet to munch on. There were even sugar-free canes so no child was left out. All in all, it ran like a well-oiled machine. Everyone knew their role, and each individual cog excelled at what they did.

Abbey felt completely unnecessary; she was a fifth wheel in every sense of the word. Granted, her primary job was keeping an eye on Santa and blending in with the other elves. However, she had always prided herself on her strong work ethic and was growing frustrated by the fact that she had nothing useful to do. Her assignment was crowd detail, but not the kind that interacted with the parents. More the kind that kept the kids amped up to see Santa. As the lead elf had told her, "Be our cheerleader!"

Not naturally the type, Abbey was trying her best. She had quickly discovered that, for the most part, she had a positive effect on the parents. She was polite, calm, and most of all cheerful. Cheerfulness always helped. However, when it came to interacting with children, Abbey was at a loss. They seemed amped up enough without her. Still, she felt like something was expected of her and she tried to deliver. So, she stuck with "Are you excited to see Santa?"

Most of them would invariably smile, shouting some variation of "Yes!" A few were shy, some painfully so. Abbey could relate. But, every now and then, she discovered how evil children could be. Her first was an unassuming little child with a red striped shirt and close cropped sandy blond hair. He had sparkling brown eyes. They offered no hint as to what he was capable of.

The little boy had a quiet smile that reminded Abbey of Dan. That should have been warning enough. She smiled at the mother, a harried looking middle-aged woman who didn't bother smiling back.

Abbey leaned in. "What are you going to ask Santa for this Christmas?"

With a wet, throaty sound, the kid contorted his features and then spit in Abbey's face. The glob landed smack dab on her forehead. She managed to keep smiling, and most of all not to wring the child's neck. Turning around, she walked across the way and stopped at the corner of Santa's Village. Calmly she reached down, picked up her pink and white purse, and rummaged inside. She had a wipe in there somewhere.

"Abbey, where are you going?" a voice called out. "Are you okay?"

Abbey looked up, pulling out the wipe. As she cleaned the spittle off her forehead, she saw Sandy, the head elf, striding towards her, a big grin on her face. Sandy was the supervisor for Santa's Village and had gone out of her way to make Abbey feel welcome. Sandy's main responsibility was to take the children's photos and Abbey was touched that she was taking the time to check on her.

"Sorry," Abbey said, putting the crumpled wipe in her purse. "I had to get that off."

"Don't be," Sandy said, still smiling. "It happens to all of us. At least he didn't stomp on your foot." Sandy shifted the digital camera in her hand, glancing back at Santa. He was still engrossed, talking to the four year old in his lap. "Look," she continued, smiling at Abbey, "I hate to be the one to tell you this, but you can't have your purse out while you're on the job. It's company policy."

Abbey's eyes went wide, "Oh, I'm sorry." She hid it behind her back as if that would make it disappear.

"It's okay," Sandy waved a hand, still smiling, "Just go put it in the employee locker room. No sense in having Mr. Peters catch you with it."

Abbey nodded, glancing around for him. There was no sign of the boss. In fact, she didn't remember seeing him all day. Not that it would matter with Mr. Peters. She knew he could see everything no matter where he was. She sighed, frustrated with herself. How could she have forgotten about the purse policy? It had been the same policy when she had worked in wrapping; certainly nothing had changed in 24 hours.

Everyone got a locker, and all personal items were kept in said locker. It was an ironclad rule, as all rules were with Mr. Peters. But, at least this rule made some sort of sense. When you were dealing with expensive merchandise it was best for employees not to carry around hiding places. Abbey nodded understanding at Sandy and then glanced at the crowd.

"Oh, don't worry," Sandy checked her watch, "we're going on lunch break in a few minutes anyway. You have time."

"Should I wait until then?" Abbey asked.

"Uh no," Sandy said, a sudden edge to her voice. The smile remained. "How about you go and just take your lunch break now. Be back by 12:30 and we'll all do this again."

Abbey nodded and headed for the exit. Something tickled her senses, she looked behind her. Santa was staring at her with those piercing eyes. He waved, then resumed talking to the little girl on his lap. Abbey waved back, and headed for the locker room.

Dream aside, Santa had been nothing but kind to her. Still, she couldn't shake the weird feeling she felt around him, ever since that awful nightmare. It was strange how much he looked like the Santa from her dream. He was exactly how she'd pictured the evil Santa, minus the ferocity.

She turned the corner, heading into the Employees Only section of the store. The locker room was a small area, fairly spartan by locker room standards. Mr. Peters was a model of efficiency and this space reflected it. Every locker had a label, Abbey's still had her name on it.

She opened her locker, realizing she'd not cleaned it out from yesterday. She smiled at the vertical line of photos. A photo of

Papa and Mama smiling together, Julianne and Gary dressed to the nines, Professor Brown standing by his car, Dan's strange friend Bernie grinning impishly by her Vespa, and of course Dan himself.

Dan's photo was in a set from a photo booth the two of them had gone to in the mall. In the pictures, Abbey was laughing hysterically, Dan had a manic grin. She remembered he had said something, something that had hurt her feelings just before entering the booth.

When he saw her expression, Dan had started tickling her and the camera caught Abbey in mid-laugh. If she remembered correctly, Dan had even apologized to her for what he'd said. Whatever it had been had long since been forgotten.

Shaking her head, she blew out half a breath. He had his moments. Abbey shoved her purse inside the locker, slamming the door shut. Each employee had a locker key, it reminded her of a bus station. Abbey looked around, noting how many lockers there were in the room. Murphy's had lots employees, all of whom needed a locker and key.

She stared at the simple lock, imagining that Dan could break in fairly easily if he really wanted to. She suddenly wondered if he had broken into her locker. Probably, she realized. It would be just like him. He was practically Houdini in that regard, and seemed to take great pleasure in picking locks.

Why, Abbey wondered, did he become a private investigator instead of a locksmith? And more importantly, where was he? How could she miss someone wearing a goofy reindeer sweater with jingly bells on it? She made her way out into the main store and stepped back onto the floor, looking out at Santa's Village. The crowd was dispersing. Sandy was going up to each parent still in line, handing out numbered vouchers. "They're good," she said.

"They sure are," a voice called out behind her.

She turned around. Four men were sitting on a bench. All middle-aged, all with lost expressions on their faces. They had been there for as long as she could remember. Sometimes one nondescript middle aged man would be replaced by another, none stood out. All looked the same, all melded together. She'd never thought about it before, but the one in the middle was vaguely familiar. It didn't click until the man's facial expression reanimated, going from lost and mildly depressed, to a goofy grin.

"Dan?" Abbey called out.

Dan stood up, stretching. The other men didn't even bat an eye, instead continuing their thousand-yard stares.

"Hey Abs," Dan said, then turned back to his compatriots. "Gentlemen." The men glanced up briefly at him in acknowledgement, then continued staring outward. He turned back to Abbey. "Lunch?" He extended an arm.

"How long have you been sitting there?" she asked taking his arm. She was shocked to see the years had melted away. She had never noticed how worn and tired he could look when he wasn't smiling.

"All day," he replied, rolling his head from side to side, stretching the muscles.

"I never saw you."

"That was the idea," he held up the black purse. "I'm a master of disguise."

"Apparently."

He leaned in, dropping his voice low, taking on a husky timbre, "I'm Batman."

Abbey shook her head, hiding how that voice sent a tingle down her spine and turned them toward the break room. Getting closer, she faltered. "I didn't bring a lunch."

"I know, I was there when you didn't pack it. How about I pick something up across the street?" Dan asked.

"You don't mind?" Abbey responded, filling up with gratitude.

They stepped inside the break room, it was deserted.

"No, of course not," He her arm a pat where it lay on his forearm. "What do you want?"

"Oh, just a sandwich. Whatever you get is fine with me."

"How about a Reuben?"

"No!" she shouted with a sudden passion.

Dan jumped back, hands up in surrender.

"Sorry, I had a bad experience once with a Reuben sandwich."

"Fair enough," he stared at her as if she was a bomb about to explode. "I've never seen anyone that afraid of a Reuben."

Shrugging, he headed for the door, but stopped when a thought hit him. "Abs?"

"Yes?"

"Where did Santa go?"

"Aren't you supposed to be watching him?"

"I got distracted watching you."

"Probably headed for the locker room. We're all on lunch break." Abbey looked around.

"Right. Well, keep an eye out for him," Dan frowned, the years returning to his face..

"Yes Sir," Abbey replied, saluting.

Dan laughed and headed for the break room door. As soon as he exited, he made a beeline for the locker room. The bells jingled madly as he ran. He stopped at the door, experience having taught him caution. Opening the door slowly, he looked around, leery of flying fists.

Santa was just stepping out of the bathroom, adjusting his big black belt. He caught sight of Dan, and smiled. "Hello Dan!"

"Santa," Dan smiled back, walking inside. "How's the day so far?"

"Oh most excellent," Santa bobbed his head, "I can't say how much I enjoy doing this. I wish I could do it all year round."

"Have you applied to Santa's Land?" Dan recalled the theme park his parents had taken him to every year, a fond memory from his childhood. The Rudicoaster was a Landis tradition.

Santa stared at him, clearly shocked. "Santa's Land?" he asked. "I've never heard of it."

"Seriously?"

"Mmmm hmmm."

Dan grinned, "Boy are you in for a surprise. Also while you're in the area, go check out Ghost Town in the Sky. They have cowboys and dancing girls."

Santa nodded and Dan remembered his other destination. "Look, I'm heading over to the diner to pick up lunch for Abs and myself. Want something? My treat."

Santa smiled and, once again, Dan had the feeling Santa could read minds. Somehow, his charge seemed to know that this generosity had more to do with the expense account funding it than his magnanimity.

"I don't think so," Santa said. "I appreciate the offer, but I've learned from experience that my stomach can't be too full

while at work. Too much jostling." He punctuated this last
statement with a huge laugh, which forced Dan to join along.

Shaking his head, Dan stared at him. "You're something,"
he said. Santa just smiled in response. "Look," he turned serious
for a moment, "Chris, could you please at least join Abbey in the
employee break room while I'm gone?" He looked pleadingly at
Santa.

"Of course," Santa nodded in agreement.

"Thank you," Dan bowed theatrically. "Thank you so
much. It means a lot to me, and makes Abbey's job a bit easier.
And if Abbey's job is easier, then my job is easier. And I
desperately want my job to be easy. Now if you'll excuse me."
Dan stepped backwards through the door, turning on one heel to
survey the floor behind him.

His eye caught movement, he saw Mr. Peters headed his
way. Dan decided it was time to leave. Hopefully the boss
wouldn't recognize Dan, he really didn't feel like discussing being
out of uniform. Plus, he hadn't submitted his invoice yet.

Invoices, his little voice reminded him, plural.

Two paychecks for the same job, he thought, nice.

So turn in your invoices dummy, his little voice prompted.

Dan ducked out the main door, turning left toward the
diner. The sunshine was bright and clear, the wind was at a

manageable chill. He felt surprisingly good. Except for the fact that people kept staring at him, shooting strange looks his way.

It's the sweater, his little voice pointed out.

Dan didn't bother to respond. He checked both ways before crossing the street. Nothing was coming, and he jaywalked across using the quickest path. The little diner was hopping with a brisk lunchtime crowd, he slipped in behind a lady holding half a dozen shopping bags.

He was shocked when he spotted two familiar faces. One was pretty, smiling, and a bright spot to his day. The other was Billy Kelly, a black hole sucking all the cheer out of his day.

"Katherine," Dan walked up to where she stood, all smiles. He reached out a hand, but she leaned in, kissing both cheeks. He found himself blushing.

"Bon jour," Katherine said, enthusiastic, returning his smile. "What a magnificent sweater, very festive!"

"Thank you," Dan blushed again and glanced down, "it's from my mother."

"Oh how sweet," Katherine tipped her head, trying to catch his eye.

"Nice purse," Billy sneered.

"I found it on the street," he shot back automatically, "I was hoping to locate its owner in here." He looked around, holding up the purse high over their heads. No one paid him any attention.

"You are quite the thoughtful young man," Katherine was beaming at him. A loud and sharp ringing sound erupted from her purse. "Pardon," she deftly removed the offending object and stepped off to one side to answer it.

"So," Dan asked, turning back to Billy. He continued to smile, even as the other man glared. "Finished up your holiday shopping?"

"Bite me Landis," Billy said.

"You have to buy me dinner first," Dan didn't let his tone change.

The young lady at the counter was holding up a bag, waving it at Billy. When Dan pointed, the man looked over, and then stormed over to the counter. Dan followed. "Let me guess, croissants?"

Billy just glared. He opened the bag, closely examined the contents, and then turned his back on Dan, pushing his way back through the crowd.

Dan smiled at the woman eyeing Billy's retreating back curiously.

"Can I help you?" she blinked back to him.

"Two meals," Dan said, holding up two fingers. "Reuben and a tuna on rye please, fries with both."

"You betcha," the lady said, "Sweet tea?"

"Yes, please," Dan replied. "Thank you very much." He went overboard on the kindness to counter Billy's negativity on the poor woman.

The clerk smiled her appreciation and rang up the order. She looked up at Dan, "Fourteen-fifty."

Dan handed her a twenty and waited for his change. The light scent of roses brought his head around. It had been a long time since he had smelled roses and perfume. The past was a performance of *Puttin' on the Ritz* danced in a minefield.

"So sorry Dan," Katherine breathed seductively. It probably wasn't intentional. She just had allure coming out of her eyeballs. "I must go, there has been a new development. Billy, could you join me?"

Bill Kelly had come back, shadowing the exotic beauty. Now he nodded at her then turned to Dan, "Be seeing you Landis." Dan nodded at Billy, then gave his most winning smile to Katherine.

"Au revoir, parting is such sweet sorrow." He took her hand, kissing it gallantly. Katherine laughed. Even her laughter was sexy.

Billy glared and finally turned away. He jerked the door open. Katherine followed. The crowd was staring at them as they left. Most likely they were really staring at Katherine, who wouldn't? Dan turned around, taking his change and his order. He didn't see Katherine and Bill Kelly head across the street. Instead, he debated on whether to eat his sandwich in the diner and enjoy the friendly atmosphere, or return to the break room. Realizing Abbey was waiting for food and probably only had a half hour lunch, Dan's choice was easy.

He sniffed the bag, enjoying the sweet scent of a hot fresh Reuben. Traffic was heavy, he had to wait before jaywalking back to Murphy's. The early lunch crowd was all heading downtown to go shopping, all trying to beat the mad rush.

Dan made a beeline for the main door. When he got there, he felt a pang on his conscience, wondering if he should go around to the employee entrance. No sense inviting trouble.

Who are you kidding? His little voice asked.

Dan opened the main door, the noise of the crowds hitting him like a hammer. He headed for the 'Employees Only' section, and the relative safety of the break room. It was surprisingly deserted, though he figured it was a little early for most employees to go to lunch. Only Santa's posse took their breaks together.

Dan placed the bag on the table, looking around for either Santa or Abbey. They should have been together. He also trusted in the crowd of the store at this hour to dissuade an attacker from taking a crack at Santa. Figuring someone would show up for food eventually, he rooted around in search of condiments. He was having some difficulty deciding what he wanted on his sandwich and perused the options outside his bag.

Someone had a bottle of hot sauce stashed behind the microwave, it was still half full. Dan also knew there was some relish in the refrigerator. When he opened the fridge's door, he discovered a new bottle of mustard.

"I love you guys," Dan said to the room at large. He pulled out the found items and set them beside the hot sauce on the table. He rifled through the bag, pulled out the Reuben and his fries and set them to one side. Then he pulled out Abbey's tuna and fries, setting them on the opposite side of the table. He carefully pulled the two sweet teas from their carrier and rifled through the bag in search of straws. Finding them, he was disappointed that they weren't bendy. With a shrug he put the straws in the teas, then sat for a minute, staring expectantly at the door.

When Abbey still didn't appear he unwrapped his Reuben, deciding it wasn't rude not to wait. First he slathered on relish, then added hot sauce, and finally dabbed just a hint of mustard. He smashed his sandwich down before bringing it to his mouth. He glanced at the door, hoping she'd catch him in this perfect Dan position. Nothing.

Where is she? Dan wondered. He bit into his sandwich, savoring the flavor explosion. As he chewed, he tried not to worry. Abbey had probably gotten distracted by something. Or someone.

Maybe Santa had been accosted by some eager kid or overzealous parent. Distracted, right. She could be a bit flighty, with the attention span of a puppy.

Glass houses, his little voice chided.

Yeah, he told it, but I'm ADD, mine's medical.

She's smarter than you too, the little voice chided him.

He nodded in agreement, chewing thoughtfully. With Maggie just a voice in his head, it was good to have someone physical to talk to. He took another bite. With a dry swallow, he put the sandwich down and reached for his tea, bringing the non-bendy straw to his lips. He took a drink.

"She's not this flighty," he frowned, getting angry for himself. Standing up, tea still in hand, he walked over to the bathroom and pounded on the door. There was no response.

"Abs?" he called out, a lump rising in his throat. He took another sip from his tea. A blinking light caught his eye and he looked up. Security camera. Duh, Dan rolled his eyes at himself. If you were going to find someone, the Batcave was probably the best place. He took another sip of his tea. He spun on one heel, taking in the spread. After another sip he walked back to the table.

Dan set his cup down, and then started packing everything up. No sense letting someone steal their food. Stealing food was his job. He put the drinks back into the tray and headed out, bags and carrier in hand. Time to go visit security.

Normally, when Dan went up to the fourth floor where the security office was located, he would have bounded up the stairwell. But, after the concoction he'd eaten, there was no point in tempting fate. Dan opted for the elevator. It was a really cheap elevator, meant to be used only to transport heavy loads upstairs. And for disabled customers. At least, that was what Mr. Peters had said when he'd caught Dan riding it on his first day. He probably wouldn't have said anything, had Dan not been riding up and down all day, killing time and enjoying himself. Fun was forbidden at Murphy's. Nothing eventful happened on the lift this time. Dan wasn't sure if he was glad or disappointed, maybe a little of both.

Dan stepped out at the fourth floor, turning right toward Security. The door was closed. He paused, knocking on the doorframe with his foot. The heavy door, cheaply hung on thin sheetrock, wobbled on its frame before closing.

"Hello?" Dan yelled knowing anyone inside could hear him, "Karl you in there?" He leaned in to press an ear against the wood, listening to the gentle hum of electronics. No answer.

He stared at the floor. It wasn't the kind of place he wanted to put his sandwich bag down. It had a "Not been cleaned since the Jurassic Age" kind of look. The Security door had wobbled open, he realized with a pleased grin. This kind of door, heavy as it was, would shut itself. Karl had stepped out, but not locked the door behind him. It was so out of character, Dan just couldn't believe it.

He started to get a bad feeling in his gut. It had nothing to do with the hot sauce. With one foot he nudged the door open ever so gently. It swung open and then slowly shut itself behind him. When it stopped at the lock, it didn't click shut.

Bending at the knees, Dan gently nudged the door ajar, leaning in to examine the lock. There was tape over it. Someone had taped over the lock to keep it unlocked. That's so not good, he shot straight back up.

With his foot, he pushed on the door again, putting his weight against the door to keep it open. Dan peered in, waiting for someone to jump out at him. No one did.

A big figure was sitting in Karl's chair, back to the door, turned towards the monitor. He was wearing a red Santa hat. And is apparently deaf, Dan hoped.

"Hello," he said loudly, "someone order lunch?"

Santa didn't move. Dan glanced around, ready to run. There was an open space next to Karl's candy dish. He set the bag and drink tray down. His now free hand automatically reached for his gun, before he realized it was at his office. This is bad.

Yes it is, Danny Boy, his little voice agreed.

"Look," Dan said loudly, "I don't know what you're doing here, but if Karl catches you in here, he'll kill you." Please be alive to let Karl kill you, he didn't add.

He reached out, touching the shoulder. It was limp and cold. Pulling on the shoulder, he rotated the chair around to face the occupant. He tried not to scream. Karl was sitting in the chair, his round head topped by the cheerful red hat, a fake white beard hanging askew covered only part of his slack jaw. The drooping features were an unhealthy shade of green. Dan backed away, fighting to keep down his lunch. Now wasn't the time to lose it.

You know, Dan thought, some people go their whole lives without ever finding a dead body. Me, I find three in 24 hours. It was amazing what came to your mind at moments like this. He pulled out his phone, still staring at Karl's former body. His cell rang before he could think to dial.

"Oh thank you," Dan said as he checked the I.D. He answered it, "Gary?"

"Dan!" Gary said, his voice tense, close to yelling.

"I was just going to call you," he continued to take shallow breaths, desperate not to vomit.

Dan didn't dare contaminate the crime scene.

"You heard?" Gary asked, his anxiety boiling over. Something clicked in Dan's brain. Gary couldn't possibly know about Karl.

"Heard what?" Dan said, his nausea instantly forgotten. He knew that tone of voice. Gary was near panic. That was definitely not good.

"About Abbey," Gary said, "they've just arrested her."

Chapter 17

"You want to repeat that?" Dan asked, looking down at Karl's dead body. He backed out of the security office, trying to get away from the stench death brings with it. He doubted Karl's face would ever be forgotten.

"I just found out myself," Gary went on, his voice shaking with barely contained anger. "They're bringing her down to the station. I just got the call. Abbey!" He was mumbling about "of all people" and other partial rants.

"Who's bringing her down?" Dan asked, trying to remain calm at the thought of his Abbey in cuffs. Without fuzz on them, "Wait, never mind. I have a sneaking suspicion who might be behind this." He suddenly had the urge to knock the smug grin off Billy Kelly's face. "What's the charge?"

"I don't know the exact charge, but it's got something to do with the jewelry store robbery," Gary said, then as if reading Dan's mind, "Listen, Billy called me as a courtesy, because he knows she's a friend. I won't, I can't be involved in the case."

"Why not?" Dan shot back, angry at the lack of solidarity. This was about family. "You know Abbey had nothing to do with the stupid robbery."

"I know," Gary was starting to calm down some. Dan suspected the man's initial panic might have been from fear that Dan would overreact and do something stupid. In any other situation, he would have been right.

"Trust me, Katherine's a good cop," Gary continued. "Hopefully, it's all just some kind of big misunderstanding."

"Misunderstanding," Dan said flatly, "Right. Well you need to get up to the security office at Murphy's."

"Why?" Tension of a different kind crept into his voice.

"Because I found another damn body!" Dan screamed into the phone. There was silence. Dan looked at his phone, checking to make sure they were still connected.

"Daniel," Gary said slowly. Dan was taken aback. Gary had never called him Daniel. Only Doc and Mama Landis did that. "I want to make sure I heard you correctly."

"Gary," Dan began again, his voice tight as a wire. He felt like he was getting emotional whiplash and he was getting frazzled. "I'm in the Security office, and I've found…its Karl. He's dead, and someone put a beard and little red hat on him."

"I'll be there in five minutes, don't touch anything!"

The slam of the phone rang in Dan's ear. He slipped his cell phone back into his pocket. Looking at Karl's body, Dan sighed. He looked from the body, to the door with tape over the lock, and back to the body. There were no obvious signs of a struggle, just Karl's body.

Yet, something felt out of place. Something was wrong. Dan couldn't put his finger on what was wrong, what was missing. Missing. He looked around, forcing his mind to relax, to superimpose what he saw every day with what he was seeing now. Nothing. He just couldn't think in this room.

He grabbed his lunch bag and backed out into the hall. With another shaky sigh, he plopped down on the floor against the opposite wall and pulled out his Reuben. The door obediently swung shut behind him. He was grateful. No sense staring at what was formerly Karl. The Karl he'd known wasn't in there. The door closed, and then bounced open a crack.

Dan snorted, close to hysterics. "It's a curse," he grumbled, biting into his sandwich. He continued to talk to no one in particular while chewing on his corned beef and sauerkraut. "I'm cursed. I'm just going to keep finding holiday themed bodies for the rest of my life."

Dan envisioned finding dead cherubs on Valentine's, bunnies on Easter, maybe a bunch of Ents on Arbor Day. That earned a half-smile. Hot salty tears ran down his cheeks. He thumped his head against the wall. The shock of pain felt good. He did it again, and again. It might have been five minutes; it felt timeless to Dan. No one so much as passed by or made a sound while he waited. The store felt like a ghost town.

Gary arrived after what seemed like forever. Dan was still methodically thumping his head against the wall. When Dan heard the heavy footsteps, he didn't bother to stop thumping or even to look and see who it was. Those footfalls were distinct. Instead, he just continued thumping his head against the wall in synch with his sandwich chews: thump-chew-thump-chew.

Gary halted in front of him, his back to the Security office. He stood there for a long moment, not saying anything. Dan stopped thumping his head, and finally turned his bloodshot blue eyes up at his brother-in-law. Gary didn't say a word. His face was like stone, but his brown eyes were soft. Turning around slowly, he pivoted to face the Security office. Pulling a handkerchief out of his pocket, he cautiously opened the door. Stepping inside, he closed the door behind him.

Dan waited.

The door opened again and Gary went to close it. He paused and bent down to stare at the lock. Nodding to himself, he stood back up, his knees and joints cracking as he taxed them. Carefully, Gary closed the door, watching it swing back open a crack.

"Emergency exit had the exact same thing," Dan pointed out.

"I noticed," Gary agreed, putting away his handkerchief.

Of course Gary knew that, but he probably didn't know that Dan knew that. Or maybe he did; Gary knew everything.

Dan watched as Gary pulled out his cell phone, punching in a number. "This is Sgt. Jones, I'm at Murphy's," he said, "I got a 10-54 here in the store Security office. I'm calling a Code 2; we got another Double-K DB. 10-55 and 10-95. Right." Hanging up, Gary walked over to the wall and leaned against it. He slid down beside Dan. His long legs almost covered the width of the hall.

"Double K?" Dan asked.

"Kringle Killer," Gary advised him, hesitating.

"Kringle Killer. Catchy. It rhymes." Dan noted how much lankier his brother-in-law's legs were lately. They used to be solid muscle, larger than life. Now he was almost, human. The thought was frightening to the young man who considered him to be more than a mere human.

"Not the name I would have chosen," Gary's frustration leaked through. "It was something the Coroner came up with. It got the Captain's attention and this whole thing has become a Red Ball case."

"Magic words," Dan said knowingly. Red Ball meant high priority, which meant all department resources were available to this case, other crimes be damned.

"Pretty much," Gary agreed. He turned to Dan, "I'm sorry." There was nothing but sincerity behind his words.

"Chips?" Dan offered him Abbey's fries.

"No," Gary held up a hand, "thank you."

"Did you know Karl?" Dan asked him.

"Only by reputation. Heard he's good. Got blue in his veins. Former P.I."

"I didn't know that. Karl never mentioned it."

"Yeah. I think he worked in Chicago maybe? Got injured on the beat, came here. Karl was sending us some stuff over. I guess CSI will find it."

"What was he sending?"

"No idea," Gary shrugged, "probably the store footage we asked for. Karl sent an email, said he'd give us hard copies of everything, and hoped we could find something. Probably figured the Kringle Killer had ducked through the Emergency exit. Apparently it was at a blind spot. Karl was hoping we might recognize some faces."

"Yeah," Dan agreed, "it would have been nice to have had that." He'd finally realized what was missing. "Crap, the tapes."

"Noticed that, huh?" Gary asked, staring at the door. "All the copies are gone. Whoever our culprit is, they are thorough."

Dan sighed, "Karl could have been spring cleaning, boxing up all the extras. Could be that we're dealing with an incompetent serial killer who didn't get to Karl before he sent out the tapes." He ran the back of a hand across a wet cheek. "Dollars to doughnuts, we'll never find those missing security tapes."

Gary nodded, staring at the door.

"We'll find him Dan," Gary said quietly. Then, without turning his head, he put an arm around his wife's brother. Dan leaned his head against the big shoulder. After a minute of quiet tears, Dan wiped his eyes and straightened back up.

"Thanks," Dan cleared his throat. "I'm okay."

"No judgment," Gary said, looking at the closed door.

Dan started on Abbey's fries and then offered them again to Gary. The big man reached out. "Just one," Gary gave him a closed lip smile.

"Yeah, right. No one can stop at one."

"Yep. Every cop's nightmare." He chewed thoughtfully on the fry.

"Gary. You got to get on this robbery case. I'll bet my black book that these two are connected."

"No chance. No chance at all. I'll be lucky to keep the Kringle case."

"Why's that?"

Gary stared darkly at Dan.

"You think they're going to suspect me?"

"You got an alibi?"

"Probably. Give me a time of death and you bet I will. Even better, I got the best defense attorney on the planet in my corner."

Gary took a breath, hissing air between his teeth.

"What?" Dan asked, cold fear clutching his stomach.

"I tried calling her," Gary said, "about Abbey, I rang her the whole way over here. She didn't answer. I hope she answers Abbey's call."

Dan's hand was a blur, whipping out his cell. He hit Julianne's number, not even bothering with speed dial. It went straight to voice mail. Hitting end, he tried the office.

"J. Jones' office," a matronly voice said.

"Marsha?" Dan asked, picturing Julianne's grandmotherly secretary. She always smelled like cookies.

"Yes?" Marsha's tone didn't change, "Who may I ask is calling?"

"Marsha," he said in a rush, "this is Dan Landis, Julianne's brother."

"Oh hello Dan," Marsha replied, sedate. Her smile radiated through the phone.

"Is Julianne in today?"

"Oh, I'm afraid not dear," Marsha replied, "She's going to be in court all day."

Court, he thought, great.

234 | T h e   F i v e   S a n t a s

"Which case is she at?" he asked.

"I'm afraid it's a closed session, dear," Marsha said, her firm voice dripping in honey. Of course.

"If you'd like," Marsha said, "I can have her call you, just as soon as she checks in."

"Okay," Dan tried not to sound desperate, "Please do. Tell her it's an emergency."

"All right dear," Marsha remained calm, "You have a good day."

He hung up. Crazy old bat, he thought. She wouldn't get rattled in an all-out bombing campaign. But, she was the perfect legal secretary. Sweet as honey, stubborn as a mule. Do not disturb meant under any circumstances.

"Court?" Gary asked, knowing the response.

"Yep," Dan answered.

"That's what I figured. She's busy lately."

Dan wondered if he should bother asking what was going on with the two of them. He wondered if Gary would try lying if Dan brought up the subject. Best to save it for later. He could only handle so many crises at a time.

"Nice sweater," Gary flicked a bell, smiling for the first time.

"Thanks," Dan twitched his lips back, "Camouflage. I needed to blend in, keep an eye on Santa."

"Good idea. Very effective." Gary nodded in approval, flicking a bell again.

"Speaking of keeping an eye on people, what happened with Abbey?" Dan asked, savagely biting into a French fry.

"No idea. Kelly just said he was bringing her in. They got a tip."

"Well, my dead body beats their tip."

"Dan," Gary warned.

"No," Dan argued, "Come on Gary, you don't think this whole thing stinks like yesterday's…"

Footsteps cut him off. Dan and Gary looked over. A man in a blue jacket, with "POLICE" emblazoned on it was walking towards them. The man was accompanied by a security monkey and a couple of uniformed patrol officers. He recognized the Assistant Coroner, and appreciated the thoughtfulness of whomever had sent him specifically. The Assistant was especially considerate of his charges and their loved ones. When you dealt with the dead, you worked extra hard to be good to the living.

"Waldorf isn't it," Dan said to the kid in the crimson coat.

"Yes Mr. Landis," Waldorf didn't bother giving his last name. Or maybe Waldorf was his last name. In which case, what was his first name? Dan didn't really care at this point.

"Would you please show this gentleman," Dan pointed to the man in the blue jacket, "how to get from the elevator to the loading dock?" He turned to Gary, "Would circumspect and unobtrusive be alright with you?"

"That's fine with me," Gary shrugged, unaffected.

"I don't understand, why are so many officers here for a theft?" Waldorf asked, frowning his confusion.

Dan stepped close, "They're very thorough. Please, show the gentleman to the loading dock."

Waldorf and the Assistant Coroner left together.

Gary motioned for one of the officers to step forward. "Take Mr. Landis down to the station, do the report," Gary ordered. "I'll take charge of the crime scene."

The young man in uniform nodded.

"You're not going to take me downtown?" Dan asked, worried he would run into problems getting to Abbey without Gary.

"Reggie's great," Gary nodded to the officer drawing up beside Dan. "And I'm already involved in this case up to my neck. I can't get away."

"Which is saying something," Dan said, making a show of looking him up and down. When Gary turned to stare at him, he rolled his shoulders, "Considering how far off the ground your neck is." The officer named Reggie snickered. Dan turned to him. "You and I will get along great."

He took a good look at Reggie. The guy looked like a younger, leaner, slightly shorter version of Gary. They even had the same ebony skin tone. Even the kid was taller than Dan. Not fair, he thought to himself. By the dark shadow becoming visible under his nose, Dan could see that Reggie was starting to grow a mustache. Dan recognized hero-worship when he saw it. He extended a hand, "Dan Landis."

"Reggie Wilson," the kid said, shaking Dan's hand. "I know who you are Mr. Landis, Gary's talked a lot about you."

"Only half of its true," he said with a wink.

"Alright," Gary broke in, "clear out you two. Reggie, call me when you get to the station." He leaned in, stage whispering, "And don't let him out of your sight."

"I'm standing right here," Dan whispered loudly back.

"Go," Gary straightened up and nodded at the end of the hall.

Dan led Reggie toward the nearest elevator. The door opened to reveal Mr. Peters standing there.

"Mr. Landis," Mr. Peters started, "Are those police officers I see?"

"Yes Sir," Dan said, not interested in explanations.

"My goodness," his even tone didn't match the scene, nor the anger the boss would have felt at the presence of so many law enforcement officials. "When I called the police this morning, I never expected so many people to be involved in the investigation," Mr. Peters blinked at Gary's tall form down the hall.

Reggie stepped into the elevator, Dan was frozen in place.

"What are you talking about?" he asked. His voice had dropped a few octaves, taking on a harsher tone. If Gary had been within earshot, he would have put Dan in cuffs. He was one of the few people alive that knew what Dan Landis' killing voice sounded like.

"I simply meant that I received a report of some ostentatious jewelry in the employee locker room," Mr. Peters said matter of factly. If Mr. Peters sensed what kind of danger he was in, he didn't show it. "I called the police, as is my duty."

"Was it lying around?" Dan pressed.

"Well," Mr. Peters continued, staring nervously from Dan to Reggie, he was beginning to get an idea not everyone was pleased with his report. "It was in a purse, inside an employee's locker. I don't know where the jewelry came from," Mr. Peters sniffed with visible disdain, "Since it's obviously not the kind of low quality we carry here at Murphy's. And, well, what with the robbery and all, I thought it best to let the police handle this matter."

"Mr. Landis," Reggie said, his voice soft and calm, "We should probably get going."

Dan turned to Reggie, catching his friendly brown eyes that were so similar to Gary's before they got tired. When had they gotten so tired? The young cop nodded and pointed behind them, Dan mechanically stepped into the elevator. He could feel the fight going out of him, too much was happening. It was beyond his capacity.

"Thank you for doing your civic duty, sir," Reggie said, as the doors closed in front of them.

"You didn't tell him." Dan pictured Karl's dead eyes in the blank expanse of the faux wood elevator doors.

"He'll find out in a minute," Reggie said calmly.

"Does that jewelry thing sound like a setup to you?"

"He doesn't seem the type…"

That earned a less convinced look, and Reggie smiled toothily. Dan realized he hadn't breathed since seeing Mr. Peters. He exhaled, some of his anger going with it; he inhaled hungrily. Looking down, he noticed his knuckles were white. Dan relaxed his fists.

"You did good back there," Reggie commended him, keeping his eyes forward.

"Not really. If you hadn't been there I'd have beaten him senseless."

"Yeah," Reggie nodded, "if the dude had gotten my woman arrested, it wouldn't have mattered who was around me."

Dan smiled at that, "Abbey's not my woman."

"Uh huh," Reggie gave him a sideways look.

Dan sighed, leaning his head against the elevator wall. He hoped Abbey was okay. Well, he thought darkly, what's safer than the police station?

Chapter 18

It was a quiet drive. Dan had talked Reggie into letting him drive, and somehow Reggie didn't laugh at the car's terrible condition. Though the lackluster stereo did elicit a snort from the young cop.

"Is that a tape deck?" Reggie pointed out, helpfully. "I thought the last of these was in the Smithsonian."

"Yeah," Dan said, "I got an adaptor for it so I can play mixed tapes."

"Hey Dan," Reggie said, buckling up, "The Flintstones called, they said its time for an upgrade." Dan laughed. Having Reggie in the car was a much needed distraction. Of course it also meant he couldn't swing by his office. Dan desperately needed to collect his thoughts. And get his gun. He had a burning desire to be armed right now. It was amazing what problems the sight of a gun solved. Even if it only had blanks.

"Turn right up here," Reggie instructed needlessly.

Dan dutifully turned. He didn't have the heart to tell the kid, "Yes, I've been to the police station before." Instead, Dan went over the facts of the case in his mind, automatically following Reggie's directions.

Of course, Reggie couldn't pass up the chance to talk about his hero. "So," he asked, "How long have you known Gary."

"Me?" Dan set his thoughts to one side, "Oh, going on five years. Our anniversary is coming up; I should probably pick something out. Do you think Gary would prefer slippers or a robe?" Reggie laughed. The kid had a rich, earnest laugh that reminded Dan of a younger, happier Gary.

"Is it true he's married to Boom-Boom Jones?"

"Nah, that's just a rumor I started. Boom-Boom actually plays for the other team. The only time she likes to see men is in court."

"Man," Reggie said, staring out the window, "She got a hold of me one time for a public intoxication case I handled. I thought she was going to eat me. I mean, who goes to bat for a drunk?"

That's my sister, Dan thought. It was some half-crazed homeless guy who first gave Julianne the nickname of Boom-Boom, because as he said, "She shows up, and Boom-Boom-Boom you gone!" It stuck, and it was accurate. Julianne was a sucker for the dregs of society.

Dan checked his mirror and caught a glimpse of his own reflection. His haunted eyes had the same expression as Gary of late. Not as bad as Jules had last night, but still. He glanced over at Reggie, hating to lie to the kid. But, Gary fought hard to keep his professional and personal lives separate. It didn't pay to advertise the fact that one of the city's most respected cops was married to the city's most successful criminal defense attorney. True, all the senior cops knew, but you still didn't offer it up as general knowledge.

"Turn here," Reggie ordered again. He studied Dan's face. "You know, you look a little like Boom-Boom." Dan pulled into the visitor's lot, threw the car in park, and turned to Reggie.

"Fine," he said straight faced, "You caught me. I'm a brilliant legal mind by day, and play private investigator by night. Also, I'm a cross-dresser. Size 8 if you were wondering. Please don't tell anyone." Reggie threw his head back and laughed again, fumbling to open the door while wiping his eyes.

You really can't help but like the guy, Dan thought. The kid even held the station door for him. The check-in process was fairly routine. Just as he'd done a million times before, Dan had to sign in as a visitor and get his visitor's badge. Then Reggie had to sign in, making it official that he would take responsibility for Dan. Poor guy, that was a lot to ask of anyone. The duty clerk was Yolanda. Dan loved Yolanda. She was a bright ray of sunshine at this station.

"Yolanda," Dan smiled at her, "You make coming here worthwhile." She smiled, handing him his I.D. Today her dreadlocked hair was dyed gold, her chocolate skin glittered with

244 | T h e   F i v e   S a n t a s

sparkles. With a smile that beautiful, Dan had no idea how she was still single. He realized she wasn't looking at him. Checking over his shoulder, he caught Reggie staring cow eyed at her. Dan rolled his eyes at the two of them and cleared his throat.

Allowing herself to be distracted from her object of adoration, Yolanda reached beneath her desk and buzzed them in. Reggie waved as they went back and Dan saw her wave perfectly coifed nails toward the kid. Young love, he thought with a smile, those were the days.

The station wasn't especially noisy. This close to Christmas most cops were either out on the street or hiding out, trying to stay out of sight from the brass. Everyone in the station moved quietly, trying to stay under the radar. No one wanted to be caught doing nothing at the busiest time of the year and get assigned extra work.

Dan walked past Reggie and led the way to Gary's desk. He flopped down across from it, sitting at Billy Kelly's desk. He gestured for Reggie to sit down in Gary's chair.

"Take a load off," he said putting his feet up on Billy's desk. He glanced at the paperwork, noting Billy's bank statements lay on top. When would people learn not to use the ATM in the strip club? He mused seeing the familiar name of a particularly seedy locale on the East side.

"Right," Reggie said with a shake of his head and walked away.

Seriously? Dan thought. He couldn't believe the guy had left him alone. The kid really was a rookie. Reggie came back before Dan could get into too much trouble though, carrying a yellow legal pad and a cheap pen.

"So," Reggie started, still standing, "What happened?"

Dan gestured toward Gary's seat. "Please sit," he said using his friendliest client voice, "You make me nervous." He watched as Reggie reluctantly sat down. The kid didn't have Gary's ability to intimidate. Even sitting, the big guy was terrifying. Dan leaned in. Reggie mimicked his move. "All right, I'd just come back from picking up lunch at the diner across the street from Murphy's where I bumped into Billy Kelly and Katherine from Robbery. Any idea what Katherine's last name is?"

Reggie shook his head, continuing to make notes.

"After that I went to the break room to wait on my friend Abbey. Turns out she was indisposed, so I went up to the security office, looking for Karl. I found him."

"That's it?" Reggie asked, sitting back.

"Well no," Dan said, wondering how much this kid knew, "I called Gary as soon as I stumbled across Karl. Then I went into the hall to wait on him." Dan took a deep breath, "You might need to know I also discovered the first Santa." What did it matter, the kid would find out soon enough anyway?

"Any idea who found the second?" He didn't look up, Reggie's pen was flying.

"You don't know?" Dan rubbed his temples. There was something about those kind brown eyes that made him sorry to bring the look he knew was coming. "I found all three." There was a long pause. Reggie's pen hesitated. "Blame Gary for you not knowing. I've gone to him with each and every one. The second, I think he put down as a concerned citizen. He probably wanted to protect me from suspicion."

Reggie nodded, his pen starting again.

"I do have an alibi," Dan added, "A good one."

"Uh huh," Reggie said. Dan began to worry about his tone. It wasn't as friendly as before. The laughter was gone from his eyes, they'd flicked up at him twice in the last two sentences. Kindness had been replaced by the brusque professionalism Gary used when he was on a case. Dan was starting to have flashbacks to the first time Gary had arrested and interrogated him. This kid could be good yet.

"Look, it's important that you know Karl was a friend. A really dear friend."

"You really found all three?"

"Yes. I thought I saw a shoplifter running out the emergency exit and gave chase. I went to the alley, but didn't find anyone, and when I was looking around, I found the first Santa stuffed behind the dumpster. I called Gary." Dan began ticking them off on his fingers, "The second one was behind a diner, the same diner I later met Bill Kelly and Katherine at, just before they arrested the wrong woman. I only found that one because he smelled really bad. You know, now that I think about it, the first one smelled kind of bad too, and so did Karl."

"You've obviously never been around a lot of murder victims," Reggie said, his eyes betraying a bit of world weariness. "Bowel evacuation. Death isn't pretty or clean."

"I see," Dan swallowed the acid creeping up his throat, nodding with a forced look of calm. "Anyway, Gary was down the street from Santa #2 talking to Katherine at the jewelry store, so I ran to get him. And Karl, I found him when I was looking for my friend Abbey. And you know where she is."

Reggie's careful note taking was grating on Dan.

"Look Reg," Dan began, not sure what to say. The young man looked up, "Yes, I found all three victims, purely by accident. I have unbelievably freakishly bad luck."

Dan moved papers around Bill Kelly's desk with his finger. Reggie went back to writing everything down. Dan wondered if he should stop talking. He had never been good at keeping his mouth shut. He froze, a thought forming. He had never been good at keeping his mouth shut. It kept getting him into trouble. Especially on the job. He slammed his hand on the desk, the sound making Reggie jump.

"I am a BLOODY idiot!" Dan yelled. Reggie stared at him. "Does the name Mortimer Hasselberg ring any bells with you?"

"Is he a friend?" Reggie asked. He looked ready to Taser Dan.

The thought of 50,000 volts coursing through his nerves calmed Dan down some. In a more conversational tone he clarified, "No, he's a stick-up man, a touch on the crazy side. Serial killing isn't normally his style, although I wouldn't put it past him. My point is, he would definitely not be opposed to robbing a jewelry store. And, it just hit me; he's got a pretty big grudge against Murphy's." Karl and I specifically, he decided not to add.

"You think this Mortimer..." Reggie began, searching for the name.

"Hasselberg," Dan supplied.

"Right, is a person of interest?" Reggie continued writing.

"No, I think he's a multiple offender with a penchant for larceny and armed robbery who got arrested when I spotted him casing the store." Dan thought for a second, "Except he went quietly with minimum fuss. No one got shot."

"What do you mean?" Reggie asked.

"Huh?" Dan snapped out of his thoughts, "Oh just thinking out loud. Mortimer carries these twin six-shooters..."

"Wait," Reggie raised his voice excitedly, "are you talking about Tex?"

"Exactly." Reggie looked down at his notepad and Dan suddenly got a bad feeling in the pit of his stomach. "Reg," his tone similar to a parent to a naughty child. Or, almost every time Gary talked to him. "What happened?"

"He sort of disappeared."

"Disappeared like David Copperfield, or like Chuck Cunningham?"

"Who?" The young cop was unable to mask his confusion.

"Not a fan of Season 1 of *Happy Days*? Never mind," Dan gave a dismissive wave of his hand. "Tex disappeared?"

"He sort of vanished during processing. It's been all over the station. We were busy and apparently no one was keeping an eye on him. We still have his guns in impound." Reggie responded.

Dan buried his head in his hands. He wondered if he should tell Gary. Somehow, "Gee Gary, I think the psychopath you guys lost has a grudge against the store and finally snapped. I think he might have robbed the jewelry store and gone on a killing spree," just didn't have much Christmas spirit. And it didn't explain the Santa fixation either. Why would Tex have gone after the Santas if his targets were Karl and Dan? He leaned back in the chair and a smiling face he spotted out of the corner of his eye, caught his attention.

Katherine was talking to the only other woman in the office. Dan stood up and Reggie shadowed him. He smiled at Katherine who smiled back, making a beeline in his direction. Dan shot a glance at Reggie, but the guy made no motion to stop him. Extending his hand, Dan smiled at her. "Bon jour Katherine."

"Bon jour Dan," Katherine took his hand and grasped it warmly in both hands, "What on earth are you doing here?"

"He's helping out on the Kringle case," Reggie offered.

Bless you, Dan thought.

Katherine glanced from Reggie to Dan. "That's fantastic," she said, "Have you found out anything?"

"A couple of things." He looked Katherine in the eye, "I have to be honest, I'm more worried about my friend Abbey right now."

"Who?" Katherine said.

"Blonde, wearing an elf costume?"

"Oh," her eyes went wide. "I had no idea she was a friend. Billy's handling the interview." Dan's heart stopped for two beats and then he took off running.

"Dan!" he heard Reggie yell behind him. It didn't slow him down. He knew Billy too well. The light above the door on interrogation room 3 was the only one lit. He burst in.

Billy was sitting on one side of the gray table, Abbey on the other. She was drinking coffee from a Styrofoam cup, he was doing a Sudoku puzzle with a pencil.

"Wondered when you'd get here Landis," Bill Kelly said calmly, not looking up from his puzzle. Dan didn't trust a calm Billy K.

"Just checking on my employee," Dan forced himself to take slow measured breaths. He ran a hand through his hair, fighting to regain his composure. He glanced at Abbey who was blushing. "You okay, Abs?"

"Why wouldn't she be?" Bill Kelly cut in.

"I'm fine," Abbey answered, keeping a wary eye on Billy Boy. She doesn't trust him either, he noted. Good for her.

"We're waiting on my lawyer," Abbey continued, "Isn't that right Officer Kelly?"

"Absolutely," Bill said nonchalant, working on his puzzle, "I've advised Ms. Smith of her rights, and she's asked for an attorney to be present."

"Oh, of course," Dan could guess who that might be and was proud of how quickly Abbey had protected herself. "Well, when Boom-Boom gets here, I'll send her your way." Billy's head shot up so fast, it was a wonder it didn't pop off his neck.

"Jones is coming here?" Bill Kelly asked.

"That's right," Dan smiled, "She owes me a favor." He looked at Abbey, "So Abbey, is there anything I can get you while we wait?"

"I'm good," Abbey held up her coffee.

"Okay, I'll just tell Boomer you're in here." He feigned a long look at his watch. "And that you've been here for a while."

"No need Landis," Billy said. He picked up a sheet hidden beneath his puzzle. "We ran her fingerprints against the stolen items found in her locker, as well from the crime scene, neither of which were a match. I would have told Ms. Smith this before," Kelly said, his voice dripping with smugness, "But I'm not technically allowed to speak to her without an attorney present."

"So you don't need her for anything else?" Dan asked, trying to keep his voice casual. Finding it hard to keep his hands away from Bill Kelly's throat.

"No," Bill said, and then turned to Abbey, "But, I would advise you to stay in town."

"That shouldn't be a problem," Abbey stood, smoothing her festive mini skirt. "If you need to reach me, Mr. Landis knows where to find me."

Dan nodded, smiling at Billy. The guy had nothing behind him when it came to playing power games. He was all bluff. Dan extended his arm and Abbey took it. A shock ran up his arm at her touch. He fought to keep his expression neutral. Katherine and

Reggie were standing, waiting at the door. He smiled at them and then gestured toward Abbey.

"Katherine, I believe you already know each other. Reggie," Dan waved a hand, "Let me introduce you to my associate, Abbey Smith. Abbey, this is Officer Reggie Wilson."

"The dancer?" Abbey asked with a wink.

Reggie flashed a smile that would make any girl swoon. "Most people guess the football player," he said, "but no to both. Though, I can do a mean two-step."

"Nice," Dan admired watching a natural lady's man in action. He had to work to be that good. "Do you need anything more from me?"

"No," Reggie shook his head, hesitating at the thought of letting the two of the walk out the door. "Just let me type up the report, and I'll have you sign it. Like Officer Kelly told Ms. Smith, I'd stay in town. Both of you."

"Don't worry Reggie," Dan assured the nervous young officer, "Gary knows where to find me." He glanced into the interrogation room. "And Billy, I promise I'll know where to find Abbey. And Katherine…" She looked at him, a hint of a smile curving her lips. He had to fight back the overt French accent. "You know where to find me. We've certainly seen enough of each other lately to know the other one's routine." Dan told her with a sly wink.

Abbey rolled her eyes and tugged at his arm, "Please."

Katherine gave him a knowing look. Dan shifted his weight, leaning towards her. "Could you do me a favor?"

"If it is at all possible," Katherine assured him, enjoying the attention.

"Could you check the crime scene prints against a guy named Mortimer Hasselberg."

"Tex?" Billy asked with a laugh, "We aren't as stupid as you think Landis. We already checked all the prints from the safe against knowns. The creep wore gloves."

"Sure," Dan failed to hide his disdain, "But what about the jewelry displays?"

Dead silence. Dan was tempted to drop a pin. "I mean, it's obvious whoever broke in cased the place," he said. "Probably saw the manager enter the safe combination, maybe even the alarm code. He wouldn't have worn gloves during the day, it would be suspicious. Of course, that's just me speculating." He faked an epiphany, "Wait, isn't that what you brought Tex in for, planning a jewelry robbery?"

Billy pulled out his phone, hitting speed dial.

"Gary?" Billy spat, "Yeah its Kelly. Listen, when you get done with the lab boys can you have them do a print check on what we pulled from the jeweler's cases from the robbery? Yeah we think there might be a connection to the Kringle case. Mortimer Hasselberg. Yeah, Tex.”

Billy took a breath and then glared at Dan. “Yeah, Landis is here, he had one of his harebrained theories. I know how much you love those. We’re going to release the bird into his custody. Alright, fine.” Dan watched him hang up the phone, slow to release it into its cradle and return to his conversation with Dan. “He’ll do it,” Billy said, “And, thanks to you, Murphy’s is in an uproar. He’s got the manager buzzing around his ear every step of the way.”

Dan sighed. He could imagine how much fun it must be to have Mr. Peters hovering around, asking a million questions. He heard Abbey suck in a breath. He glanced her way and they shared a wince on Gary’s behalf. They both had the same thought: I hope we get paid. If Gary and Mr. Peters both got mad at them, or each other, paychecks might not come. Abbey didn’t need to worry though, Dan would make sure she got her money.

“Okay,” he said, gesturing for Reggie to lead the way, “Let me sign whatever, and then I’m going to get this young lady back to work. The show must go on.” This last part was directed toward Abbey, who nodded in understanding. He glanced at Billy, studying his Sudoku puzzle with exaggerated intensity. Dan stuck out a hand to Katherine who laughed and wrapped him in a hug.

“Monsieur, I hope we see each other soon,” she said, her slight frame belying a steel grip. “I am new here and am trying to learn the ways of my new American peers. I think that you too have some things to teach me." She winked. Katherine kissed Dan on both cheeks, and he felt himself blush. And, unless he was mistaken, she had slipped something into his pocket.

Releasing him, Katherine took a step back and, noticed everyone staring at her. She grinned and pivoted on her heel, exiting stage right.

Abbey squeezed Dan's arm.

"Right," Dan took the hint, "We should probably go. I'm sure Billy has important cases to solve."

Reggie led the way out. Dan could feel Billy's glare on the back of his neck. Reggie gestured for Dan to sit in Gary's chair, seeing the rookie's rapidly fraying nerves, he did. No sense rocking the boat, he thought. Abbey sat down opposite them at Billy's desk. Reggie grabbed his pad and paper and took a step back.

"I'll be right back," Reggie told Dan, "Try not find any bodies while I'm gone."

Dan nodded, watching him leave. Abbey leaned in.

"Who's Tex?"

Dan leaned toward her, "Jewel thief."

She raised an eyebrow, asking for more.

"He's a certifiable psychopath, not afraid to kill. Also jaywalks. Other than that, a

nic++++++++++++++++++++++++++++++++++++

e guy. What'd Billy ask you?"

"Nothing," she shrugged, "He read me my rights, and I asked for my lawyer. I know how the system works."

He smiled at her and patted her hand resting on his forearm. He liked that she hadn't tried to remove it after they'd sat down. "You did great."

"Thanks," she said with a short laugh, temporarily giddy from the close brush.

"So, what's this about a body?" Abbey came back to herself.

He took a breath.

"Karl."

Her mouth dropped open, tears springing to her eyes. He reached out, stroking her hand. She took a breath, pushing her emotions to one side.

"Tell me what happened."

He filled her in being as considerate to their friend's privacy and Abbey's sensitivity as possible.

"Someone was after the security tapes?"

"Probably. They're definitely missing."

"And you think this was Tex too?"

"It makes sense."

"Did you know I was his secret Santa? I spent days trying to weed out what he might want."

"What did you get him?" Dan asked, admiring her ability to master her emotions under stress.

"I got him a gift card to the theatre. He seems to like movies from what I could tell."

"That's a good idea. Better than mine, I got him a brick because he's really into masonry."

Abbey looked like she'd smelled something foul, "You can't get someone a brick for Christmas. That'd be like getting someone a lump of coal."

"Right," Dan agreed with a nod, thinking to himself, "How do you return a chunk of the Berlin Wall?"

Dan hated that he'd had no idea Karl liked movies. He had probably been chattier with a beautiful girl than a sarcastic kid who thought he was all that because he got paid to follow people and take pictures. Before Dan could ask what kind of movies Karl had liked, Reggie came back with a handful of forms.

"Sign here," Reggie instructed them in a neutral voice, handing him a form, "Also, Gary told me to give you this." He handed Dan a second sheet. Looking at it, he was shocked to discover it was an invoice. Good old Gary, he thought. He quickly signed the first form, before filling out the invoice. He decided to play it straight on his rates.

"Thanks man," Dan gave a winning smile.

"Hey," Reggie shrugged, "thank Gary. He's the one that thinks you're innocent."

"Right," Dan tipped a finger to his brow in a mock salute. It crossed his mind that Reggie might not. Which hurt, surprisingly. "If he calls, could you tell G-Money I'm on my way back to Murphy's."

Reggie nodded and then looked at Abbey.

"Sorry about the hassle, ma'am," he apologized, with obvious sincerity. Abbey stuck out her hand. He took it, favoring her with a warm smile.

"Maybe you can show me some of those dance moves sometime," Abbey teased.

Dan cleared his throat. They both glanced over. "Come on Abbey let's get you back to work." *After we make one detour,* he added to himself. *It's time I got my gun.*

Chapter 19

"Taking me back to work, huh?" Abbey asked, as they pulled up in front of the old two-story brownstone. Dan's office was on the second floor. He didn't reply, instead he jammed the car in park.

"This is a detour," he told her sharply.

"Uh huh."

"Try not to slam my door."

In a complete shock, she didn't. As they walked toward the building, Abbey stopped to look inside the downstairs bakery. The giant glass window displayed a wide variety of cakes and cookies. She sniffed the air. It smelled good, like cinnamon and chocolate, with a hint of peanut butter. "Aren't you worried about Gary calling?"

Dan figured they had ten minutes, fifteen on the outside, before Gary would start hunting them down. "Nope. I just need to pick up his Christmas present for tomorrow." He headed for the stairwell door. It was to the right of the bakery's entrance, only a few feet. Then there were twenty-eight steps leading to his office door.

"We wouldn't have time for a muffin or something, would we?" Abbey asked with a pleading look, she hadn't eaten since her sticky bun this morning. Dan handed her a twenty.

"Go for it. Grab me a bear claw." Mario, the owner, made the best pastries. Thanks to its location in a practically deserted part of town, it didn't do much walk up business. They baked for local coffee shops and grocers. Dan headed up the stairs to his office entrance, pulling out his keys.

"Yeah right," she told his back, crumpling the money in her fist, "I'm not letting you out of my sight." She followed, bounding up the stairs two at a time.

As Dan opened his door, he ran through his mental checklist. Change clothes, grab gun, catch bad guy, and get change back from Abbey. When he breathed out fog in the cluttered space, it occurred to him that he had left the heater off again.

"Good grief!" Abbey stepped up beside him, wrapping her arms around her middle for warmth. "You can hang meat in here!"

"Where's that coat I loaned you?"

"At work," Abbey said, her teeth chattering. "And I'm pretty sure it was Julianne's coat. I don't think you own a whole lot of women's clothing."

"You'd be surprised," Dan said with a faint grin. Walking over to his office closet he rummaged through its contents, finally pulling out a woman's jacket. It was amber with purple flowers running down the sleeves and on the back. He handed it to her.

"Let me guess, undercover work?"

"I've got a skirt to match. Although, you'll have to supply your own heels."

She threw the coat over her shoulders. She continued jumping up and down, rubbing her legs. Dan considered the entertaining sight for a moment, noticing her shapely pale legs were turning dusky blue. With a snap of his fingers, he walked over to a chest of drawers on the far wall. Opening the bottom drawer, he pulled out jogging pants. JHS was emblazoned in dark blue letters, a roaring cat stenciled above them. He tossed them over to Abbey.

"Tigers?" she asked as she pulled them up beneath her uniform's skirt.

"Wildcats. I was a wildcat in high school." Dan gave a wink.

"I bet you were. How do I look?" Abbey held her arms out. Green and white elf costume, amber jacket, and gray sweats.

"You look beautiful. Just perfect." He grabbed one of his black shirts off its hanger and checked what kind of pants he was wearing. The jeans he had on should work with it. He was tired of the ludicrous sweater, plus it was hard to hide a gun under it. He headed for the bathroom to change. Taking off his shirt in front of Abbey would probably send the wrong message.

"Can I wear the sweater?"

He stuck his head out of the bathroom. She smiled at him. He threw her the jingling abomination. Abbey took off the jacket and slipped Dan's sweater over her head. The bells jingled. As she put it on, static made her blond hair stick up in all directions.

"It's you Abs," he teased, buttoning his shirt as he walked back out, feeling a lot lighter. The cold air cutting through the cool silk of his shirt was a welcome sensation.

"Thanks," Abbey blushed, catching a glimpse of his bare middle when the shirt flared. She hung onto the coat, intending to rehang it. The sweater should be enough and she didn't want to have to carry two coats home from the store later. She reached into the closet and pulled down a metal hanger, and paused. She could see several pieces of women's clothing.

All about the same size too, she thought. One of the green dresses looked vaguely familiar. She turned away, trying to remember where she'd seen it before. Glancing in Dan's direction, Abbey noted he was rifling through his collection of shoes. Apparently, he didn't want to wear his dress shoes anymore.

Still holding the jacket under her arm, Abbey walked across the egg shell painted office, stopping at the room's only window. It looked down on the street. A silver framed photo rested on the windowsill. The light of the streetlamp shining on a beautiful woman with fiery red hair, smiled for the camera. She was in her mid-forties with a grin that begged for trouble and sparkling blue eyes.

Same shade of blue as Dan's, she noticed. More importantly, she was wearing the same green dress as the one in Dan's closet. Abbey traced a finger along the frame.

"You caught me," he broke into her thoughts.

She turned around. He was sitting at his desk pulling on a pair of boots.

"What?"

"I'm a pack rat."

She looked around the room at the dozens of items that congested it. A healthy variety of gadgets, memorabilia, bric-a-brac, and just plain old junk all around the room. There were four or five sets of shelves all filled with stuff. Against the far wall was a door with a beaded curtain partition she knew hid Dan's small living area from the general public.

In addition to the cot, mini-fridge, and sink behind the curtain, it was also crammed with books, movies, and more electronic gadgets. And one small blue teddy bear. It's true, Abbey thought, you are a pack rat. She looked down. There was a newspaper, The West Falls Gazette.

"Where's West Falls?"

"Somewhere in South Carolina." Dan felt a stinging pain in his chest. They were now tap-dancing on the minefield, and he'd forgotten how to step-ball-chain.

"Dan," Abbey was clearly aiming for delicacy, "those clothes in your closet, did they belong to your old partner?"

He took a shaky breath. After five years it was still tough, and the events of the past few days didn't help his emotional balance. "Eh," he confessed, "it's just some junk that I never got around to tossing out."

The specter of Dan's former partner, Margaret "Maggie" O'Bryon, hung between them like an asparagus fart.

"Can I ask you a question?" she picked up the photo frame.

"You just did."

"When did she die?" She was sitting on the windowsill. She was holding that silver framed photo, which Dan had bought Maggie for their one-year anniversary, and she was sitting in the spot. Maggie's thinking spot. He felt an unsettling sense of déjà vu. They both sat the exact same way. Though admittedly, there were only so many ways you could sit on a windowsill. His vision of Maggie shifted into that of a redhead in a green sweater, one with the same emerald eyes as Abbey. For a moment, a glimmer danced across Dan's consciousness. "Uh…February-ish," he said, with a noncommittal shrug.

Abbey glared at him, with a look that said, "You're not fooling me for a second Mister." Same look Maggie gave too. He was powerless against that look.

"February 26th. And before you ask, it's been five years, 9 months, 29 days."

She stood up, placing the frame back in its original spot. "I just thought she might have died…" she said, shrugging, "Around Christmas time."

"No, my hatred of Christmas is entirely home grown."

"Fair enough."

He sighed. "Alright, after we solve this case, how about we go look at the Christmas lights. There may even be some caroling involved. Would that work for you?"

You old pushover, his little voice added.

Yes, I'm aware I'm going soft, he thought back, that's very helpful of you to notice.

The little voice, Maggie's voice, didn't respond; but, Dan could see her smiling at him, just like in the photo. Abbey's face lit up. She loved Christmas, she'd told him so and he'd been less than enthusiastic about sharing in the joys of the season.

"Do you mean it?" she asked, her voice a fight between playing coy and jumping for joy.

"Absolutely," he promised, and strangely enough, he meant it. He had a warm feeling spreading outward from the pit of his stomach. Probably that Reuben, he thought cynically. Walking over to his hat rack, Dan pulled down his shoulder-holster. He put it on, walking over to his desk drawer.

He removed the gun from the top drawer, double-checking that it was clean, and then inserted the full magazine of blanks. Double-checking the safety, he holstered it. Now for something to cover the holster. Reading his mind, Abbey walked over to the closet, pulling out his leather bomber jacket, coffee brown and fresh from the cleaner's. She handed him the jacket.

"You're the best," he slipped his arm into the jacket.

"Really?" she asked, wincing at the hopefulness in her voice.

Dan gave her an unflinching gaze, blue meeting green, "Yes."

She blanched and ducked her eyes. He adjusted his coat, checking the mirror for any sort of telltale bulge in his silhouette. He patted his hidden gun and went back to the rack to fetch his favorite hat.

"I feel a lot better knowing that those are only blanks," Abbey stepped forward, adjusting his collar for him.

"That's what she said," he joked. Little did she know, he'd been shooting blanks for years. She rolled her eyes and kept her sights on the costume adjustment. The jacket completely covered the gun like he knew it would. He smiled at her, "I will have you know, I'm a fantastic shot."

"It's what you're aiming at that worries me." He laughed. She walked over, pulling down his brown fedora. "Perfect."

His cell phone rang. It was Gary. "I'm on my way," he said in answer.

"Where are you?" Gary yelled.

"I left the police station a few minutes ago and I'm heading right for you…" He had never heard Gary yell like this. Gary simply wasn't a screamer. It was anger, that was normal, but behind it Dan could hear fear. That wasn't a Gary emotion.

"Where are you right now Daniel?" Gary asked.

"I'm at my office. We needed to pick up a few things."

"Is Abbey with you now?" Gary shouted.

Dan's heart was starting to skip around, butterflies pounding into the sides of his stomach making him queasy.

"Yes. What's wrong?"

Abbey stared at him, her brow scrunched and mouth open in question.

"Dan," Gary said, slowly, "Can you verify exactly where you are?"

"I've got a surveillance camera with a time stamp over my front door. And you can call the office phone if you want."

"No. Just hang tight."

"Gary, what happened?"

"Shots have been fired over by the bus station."

Dan sighed. "Let me guess, another Santa?"

"Bingo. Kelly's breathing down my neck about that Tex theory of yours. Which is fine, since I also got my Lieutenant, Captain, and now the Commissioner on me as well. But, you're okay?"

"Right as rain," Dan lied. Lead settled in his stomach, crushing the butterflies. "If I remember my city layout, isn't the bus station right by the interstate?"

"Congratulations, you're absolutely right. You've now figured out what every one of the higher ups has yet to figure out. They want to lock down the city, throw up road-blocks, and generally make life fun for everyone. On Christmas eve."

Dan sat down at his desk, approaching this like a client interview. Gary sounded like he could use a calm voice of reason. "They're idiots," he offered.

"Yes, they are," Gary admitted, "You never heard that from me."

"Never ever," Dan agreed, "there aren't any chances of a few witnesses are there?"

Gary started to sound a little calmer. "Aye, therein lies the rub. It was dark, and Santa was coming out of a convenience store. Another street corner Santa. Just picking up a bottle of something to keep him warm. The clerk says he didn't see a single vehicle in the parking lot, and could see to the road."

"That's not good," Dan looked out the window. He hadn't even paid attention to how dark it had gotten. Darkness fell a lot faster this time of year, when the winds of winter started calling.

"You're telling me." Gary snorted. "Everyone else is thinking a drive-by. I mean, no one saw a vehicle, but that's not stopping the brass from wasting resources locking down the city looking for a phantom car we know nothing about. The Commissioner has the wonderful theory that this is all some kind of gang-related initiation."

"Oh," Dan kept his voice even, trying not to laugh, "I bet that went over well."

"Yeah," Gary said, with a dark laugh, "It's all I can do to keep him from going to the press with that story. You know they'd love to get a hold of this thing and make a mess of it."

"Want me to call him for you?"

"No!" Gary yelled.

Dan yanked the phone from his ear to save his hearing.

"Sorry." Gary huffed. "No, not one word to the Commissioner, the media, or anyone. Not even to your Mother, who is at your Auntie Ruth's now. You sit tight in your office and stay out of trouble."

"I can do that," Dan said agreeably.

There was a long pause. Dan wondered if Gary had hung up.

"How well do you know Tex?"

Dan let out half a breath, "A little." Something was wrong; something didn't sit right in the deepes part of his brain. This killing didn't make sense. More importantly, he didn't trust Gary when the man was trying to feign casual. "He's no one I would want to hit the town with."

"After all this," Gary told him, "Maybe we should track him down."

"Or I could do it right now. Before things get worse."

"No," Gary said, his voice cold and distant. The hot rage was gone, replaced with a tone that wouldn't have looked out of place on Frosty, "You stay put. Don't leave that office under any circumstances. Do you understand?"

"Absolutely."

"You're going to leave aren't you." It wasn't a question.

"Would I do that to you?"

There was a frustrated groan as Gary hung up.

Dan pocketed his phone. Abbey was watching him closely. "Come on," he moved toward the door, "Let's get back to Murphy's."

"What was that all about?"

"I'll tell you in the car," held the door open. When she was out, Dan turned off the light. Handing her his car keys, he slipped back across the room. He probably wasn't coming back here anytime soon. He stopped at the photo.

"Merry Christmas Maggie May," his voice cracked. Putting two fingers against his lips, he kissed them and touched the frame.

Merry Christmas Danny-boy, his little voice whispered back.

He double-checked the locks on the back and front doors, and headed down to meet Abbey at the car. She wasn't there. He looked around, in a sudden panic, until he spotted her inside the bakery. Dan followed her inside remembering how to breathe.

"What are you doing?"

"Buying you a bear claw."

"I don't want one."

"Yes you do. You need it. And I need a cookie." She turned back to the counter.

Mario, the owner, was nowhere to be seen. His wife, Marcy, smiled at Dan when she saw him enter and made the connection that Abbey was with him.

"Dan!" Marcy yelled, "What are you doing here?"

"I finally convinced her to come in, to try something," he yelled back, nodding toward Abbey. "She doesn't believe this is the best bakery in town!"

"Heh," Marcy frowned and gave Abbey a speculative look, lowering her voice while still remaining far too loud for someone only three feet away, "What can I get you?"

"Uh," Abbey said, "a bear claw and a cookie?"

"A what?" Marcy yelled.

Dan leaned in to whisper in Abbey's ear, "She's a little deaf, speak up."

"A bear claw and a cookie!" Abbey blushed.

"Sure thing," Marcy smiled, "What kind?"

"Peanut butter and chocolate. And…" she turned to whisper to Dan, "Do you want your bear claw warmed up or anything?"

"She knows how I like it," he whispered.

Abbey rolled her eyes.

"Same thing, right?" Marcy yelled to Dan, who nodded his answer instead of screaming. The co-owner gave Abbey a confident smile. "Okay girl, we're going to show you who's got the best cookies in town."

Abbey smiled tentatively at Marcy.

Poor kid, Dan thought, you really need to live a little.

Marcy turned around, yelling their order at a young man in the back. He looked like a younger version of Mario. Dan wondered if his name was Mario Jr. Or maybe Luigi Mario.

Abbey stepped up to the display case and watched as they scurried toward the oven for fresh pastries. Seeing it would take t a few minutes to grab what they needed, she turned away and pulled on Dan's arm, leading him away from the counter. Junior might have better hearing than his mother.

"What's going on?" Her emerald eyes were tight at the edges. Say what you wanted about her, Abbey didn't miss a trick.

"Another Santa. Someone sniped him outside a convenience store."

Dan paused, the full implications hitting him.

"Oh no," Abbey covered her mouth, her eyes growing wet, "who would do something like that?"

Someone with a good scope. But who would want to kill Santa? That was a good question. "Chris, our store Santa?"

"What? Why?"

"I don't know…because there can be only one?" he quipped, frustration making him sarcastic. He needed time to think. Suddenly he wanted nothing more than to be alone. She stared at him like he was going nuts. Maybe he was, calling Father Christmas a murder suspect. "Highlander? It's a movie? Christopher Lambert and Sean Connery? Queen did the music?" She continued to stare unblinking at him. "Bernie would have laughed at that," he muttered. A thought sparked.

"This is no time for jokes Dan."

"I know. That's the best time to for jokes."

Abbey sighed. She did that a lot around him.

"Honestly, the store Santa kind of gives me the creeps. There's something about him that's too good to be true."

"I think so too. But, creepy doesn't equal killer."

"I think," Dan paused, rubbing his eyes and throwing out a hand before whispering, "He believes he's the real Santa."

"So?" Abbey whispered, shrugging.

"So…You do know Santa isn't real right?"

"Yes, I'm not an idiot. But what's wrong with someone believing they're the embodiment of all that's good in the world? It would most definitely not make them a killer." He shouldn't have been surprised. Abbey probably was the embodiment of all that is good in the world. She liked to think the best of people. Her features softened, "He scares me a little too."

He grinned and nudged her with his shoulder. She smiled back. "Thanks. Okay, giving people the creeps aside, he's probably not a bad guy. But, he's the only Santa in a ten mile radius who someone hasn't tried to kill."

She raised an eyebrow, "So far."

"So far. Maybe it's because we were watching him." Dan roughed up his hair. "Someone has a grudge against that store, probably someone who works there, maybe someone fired for having shoes unpolished, and my Spidey-senses are telling me there's more to our Santa than he's saying."

"You two want your food?" Marcy yelled.

Dan and Abbey both jumped. Abbey stepped up, handing Marcy the money. The cash register sang out, and Marcy handed back the change. Abbey pocketed it.

Little sneak, he thought, that's my money.

She turned around, bag in hand and a slight smile on her face. She was daring him. "Let's roll Chief," she tried to sound tough. With the jingling sweater. It was adorable.

"Don't call me Chief." When they got in his car he cranked up the heater, but didn't shift into drive. She wrestled the bear claw out of the brown bag. She handed it to him.

"Alright," she prompted as he took a bite out of his aromatic pastry, "the store closes in three hours." He stared at her while he chewed. "So," she suggested nibbling on a cookie, "We keep an eye on Santa for today, tomorrow's Christmas, and this whole thing will be over then, right? Did Gary say anything about us going back to Murphy's."

Dan nodded. Gary had definitely said something. No was something.

"Did he say we should?" Abbey had been around Dan long enough to know how evasive he could be. He shook his head. "So you want us to disobey Gary, the senior officer who may be the only one keeping us both out of jail, mind you. You want us to go against his direct orders?"

He nodded, pretending he wasn't done chewing.

"Let's roll out," Abbey said, a smile on her face. Dan guffawed and inhaled a crumb which kicked off a coughing fit. "You alright?"

He nodded, finally able to breathe. "Sorry, you sounded like Optimus Prime for a minute there."

"Who?"

"Never mind." He leaned back against his seat.

"Or we can sit here. I'm cool with that too." She leaned back against the cold headrest.

He gave her a once-over.

"What?" she asked, self-consciously checking her mouth for cookie crumbs with the back of a hand.

"You're something," Dan said, counting his blessings.

"And don't you forget it," Abbey gave a wink and a smile.

"Can I ask a favor?"

"Sure."

"I need you to keep an eye on Santa for me. A discreet, far off eye. Stay out of sight, and call me if there's any trouble."

"How will I know there's trouble?"

"Well, if a big blond guy who answers to Tex walks in," he frowned, "You'll know something went wrong. Also, look for someone sporting a sniper rifle. Possibly in a gunny suit.

Dan grinned at Abbey's odd expression and patted her arm where it lay on the center console. "Just, you know, keep a general eye on things. And watch out for Mr. Peters. And Tex. And camouflaged men carrying sniper rifles."

"And, while I'm keeping an eye on everyone," she put a hand over his, trying to ground him, "where will you be?"

"I need to talk to some people."

She raised an eyebrow.

"Okay, Bernie. I need to talk to Bernie."

Abbey started to ask why, then stopped. She closed her mouth. The car became the slightest bit frosty. He turned up the heater and the charm. "Trust me, I know what I'm doing. Right now, Bernie is the best chance for answers."

"Why?"

"I have no idea. I've got a bunch of pieces to this puzzle, and I'm just looking for the corners. And my highly trained detective skills say Bernie might be able to help."

"Plus she's a doctor, so obviously she likes puzzles."

"Who Bernie? No, she hate's 'em. She's kinda lazy for a woman who passed medical school."

"And flirty," she mumbled.

"What was that?" he asked, shifting the car into gear.

"Nothing. And I do."

"What?"

"Trust you. Always."

Dan was at a loss for words. He was a cynical, conniving cheat and swindler. And one of the smartest, most honest people he knew trusted him. Without reservation.

Well, said the little voice in Dan's head, it's important for partners to trust one another.

Dan's mouth twitched as he pulled onto the open road. Hey, he justified to the ghost in his head, she's just going to babysit Santa Claus in a department store. What could possibly go wrong?

On later reflection, Dan realized, that was a stupid thing to say.

Chapter 20

Dan was kind enough to drop Abbey off at the front entrance. It was just dark enough she could convince herself it was any other morning at Murphy's. Abbey liked routine, it was comforting, and it made her feel safe. She'd grown up with routine. She could see herself walking into the wrapping department, excited about setting out the various papers. Freshly unfurled wrapping paper had a unique smell. It was the part of her job she'd enjoyed. She could almost smell that special odor. Almost.

Abbey glanced back over her shoulder to see Dan at the end of the block already, turning at the light and heading off to see Bernie. Perfect, wonderful Bernie. A proper doctor, beloved by everyone, saving lives and healing the sick. Abbey wished she could hate the woman, it would make life so much easier. But, what Abbey hated the most was how gregarious and charismatic Bernie could be. Full of life and vitality, no wonder Dan was rushing off to pull her into this case.

Part of her wanted to run after him and beg him to take her along. Except, Dan needed her here. This strange turn of events was pushing everyone to their limits, and Dan Landis simply couldn't be in two places at once. So, Abbey the Babysitter was riding to the rescue.

She opened the main door, noting the main floor was packed with people of all shapes and sizes. She looked around, remembering how well Dan had blended in amongst the sea of humanity. It had been nothing for him. The row of interchangeable men were still there. Sitting in a line against the wall, waiting on their wives. They never really moved, just sat there in a trance until they were summoned. Just a bench full of guys, waiting on a woman.

She kicked herself for ignoring the mundane, not paying attention to little details. It was completely natural to tune out the ordinary. If you didn't, if you observed every little detail all the time, you would go insane. Yet, it was possible that any one of these tiny little details could tip her off to the identity of the killer. Maybe, just like Dan had done, she should camouflage herself. To hide. To blend in as it were and observe these bits of everyday searching for clues.

Abbey hadn't told Dan how much she hated this place. Oh, they'd joked about the rotten conditions and oppressive management, but she'd never revealed the depths of her feelings. He'd gotten her the job and she hadn't wanted to seem ungrateful. That and she needed the money, her student loans were coming due and she was scraping the bottom of the barrel at this point.

282 | T h e   F i v e   S a n t a s

Now, here she was in a place she hated, dressed like a color blind monkey had given her fashion advice. But, Papa had always told her to make the best of a bad situation. She examined her outfit, seeing for the first time, some possibilities. It could work with if she played it right. The skirt was not immediately recognizable as an elf costume. It was just a green skirt that, to her hopeful eyes, looked like something a cheerleader might wear. Add to that she was wearing a pair of sweatpants with the logo of a local high school. Someone might think she'd come straight from practice. That she was a cheerleader.

It was perfect. She could blend in, be someone else. Someone that no one would pick on, no one would bother. Well great, Abbey thought, this is easy! This is just acting. Channeling all those preppy girls she'd known, the ones who'd always ostracized her well into adulthood. Abbey strolled through the mall, head held high. She began to craft a story, her story.

Abbey wasn't trying to look for a Christmas gift, she was doing something she wanted to do. She was going to go shopping for herself.

Keeping an eye on Chris, situated over at Santa Village, she stayed on the lookout for this Tex fellow. This was going to be easier than she thought. She just had to keep her head high, maintaining a haughty gaze to cut down on interference from sales staff.

Santa's Village was fairly central to the first floor, all departments flowed out from it like spokes on a wheel. Abbey decided to head for the shoe department first. Not only would a girl of her status want to buy shoes, but it would be a perfectly natural opportunity to sit in one spot for an extended period of time. It would be a piece of cake to keep an eye on Santa from the shoe department.

Plus, Dan had given her his credit card. Well, he had given her a credit card. With Dan you could never guarantee whose it actually was.

"Buy something for yourself," he had said handing it to her. "Consider it an early Christmas present."

An early Christmas present he had said. Ha! "Because I don't know what to get you and I know you're expecting something from me," was what he really meant. Abbey had spent every dime she had on his gift, she'd picked it out months ago. She wondered what he'd gotten Bernie. She stopped, and forced the scowl from her face along with the negative thoughts.

Bernie the happy go lucky doctor with the jolly British accent and carefree attitude. Bernie never had to worry about being sadled with a name like Bernice Agnes. Being called "Baa" all the time. Wonderful Bernie. Perfect Bernie. Beautiful Bernie.

"Bunny," Abbey said, amazed at what could pop into your head at the strangest times. That was going to be her character's name. Bunny was self-confident and could take on any problem. The boys all flocked to Bunny and girls fought tooth and nail to be her friend. She walked proudly toward the shoe department.

Bunny was on everyone's radar, she decided, strolling casually across the store. She may not have had enough money to buy real, designer shoes as Abbey, but Bunny never worried about money. Poverty was something that happened to other people.

Maybe a nice pair of work shoes, Abbey thought. Something comfortable that I can wear for a long time on my feet. And of course it had to be something expensive. Expensive was the only way Bunny shopped.

As she continued walking, she passed the entrance to the Employees Only hallway. Someone, a cashier if she remembered correctly, was coming out. She shuddered at the public humiliation she had endured in the locker room.

Abbey didn't dare tell Dan how scared she had been. He would have laughed. Public humiliation didn't bother him. He didn't care what people thought, not like poor little mortified Abbey. No one intimidated Bunny, Abbey added another detail to her character.

The P.A. system had called all employees not working at a register, roughly thirty of them, to the employees' locker room. They had shuffled in, all of them barely fitting into the confined space. A shiver of nervousness ran through the crowd; no one believed they had been called for something good. Murphy's wasn't big on team building exercises.

Mr. Peters was there, along with the two people Abbey would later learn were Lieutenant Katherine Picard and Detective Bill Kelly.

Abbey had never met either one of them before, but the man was holding up a purse. Abbey's bright pink purse, the one she'd stuffed into her locker that morning. He was asking the crowd if they knew who it belonged to. She could still see all the lockers hanging open. She had stepped forward, claiming it as hers. It had all gone downhill from there.

"You're under arrest," the male officer had even pointed his finger at her like a school girl. And she'd blushed like one. "For possession of stolen property."

She had been shocked, even more so when she looked around, into the eyes of all the people she'd worked with for nearly a month. Everyone Abbey had taken shifts for, traded lunch breaks with, tried so hard to make friends with. No one had stood up for her; no one had stood up and shouted that it was impossible. That she would never dream of stealing anything. They had just left. Sandy, the head elf, had started the exodus. Soon the room had cleared, leaving only Abbey, Katherine, Bill, and Mr. Peters.

"I trust we can keep this quiet," Mr. Peters had said to the officers before he too had abandoned her.

Her boss, the man who had trusted her enough to hire her, to handle money, and close registers, had left. He never even looked Abbey in the eye. She had tried so hard not to cry. Instead, she locked away all of her emotions, keeping quiet and polite. They had left out the back door, through the far end of the employee break room. Through the stock room and to the exit. That one locked, unlike the smoker's exit. The one whoever had killed Santa had used.

Of course, it had all worked out in the end. Dan had ridden in at the last second, saving her from a long wait for his sister. He did have a knack for dramatic entrances. Well, she thought, at least I won't have to worry about working here again after this job is over. After tomorrow, I can go back to the school. I can have a normal life again. Probably, a Dan free life after the mystery trip over New Year's. Dan wanted someone more exciting. Like Bernie. He would be gone as soon as he saw that Abbey was nowhere near Bernie's level.

Bunny reached out, touching a fantastic black pair of pumps.

And, she added to herself, I'll have the best footwear on campus. The clothes Julianne had given her would probably even match these. If not, well she had Dan's credit card and plenty of time to shop. She looked around for a place to sit so she could try her wonderful shoes on. Just then, movement caught her eye.

287 | T h e   F i v e   S a n t a s

Looking up, she was startled to see Mr. Peters had drifted through her line of sight. He was walking slowly, arms held to his sides as always. His posture was stiff, though his head was in constant motion, a slow, rhythmic rotation. As she watched, Mr. Peters never moved his eyes. Instead he glanced back and forth by moving his head, like an owl.

What is he doing? Abbey wondered until she realized what should have been obvious. He's looking for shoplifters, or Dan. The head of security was dead, two Santas were killed outside his store, and Dan was MIA. She almost felt sorry for the poor man. Almost. He'd left her hanging, left her alone with the police.

She watched for a few minutes longer, trying to figure out the best plan of action. Mr. Peters was now a few feet away, walking in what he probably thought was a circumspect manner. He was definitely coming her way.

I'd better not push my luck, she decided, slowly edging away from him. She knew better than to run, that would obviously attract attention. If there was one thing she'd learned over the years, it was how not to attract attention. A thought froze her mid-stride.

Sure, Abbey had always been good at not attracting attention, but Bunny ran from no one. Bunny wouldn't sneak away, she decided. Bunny relished attention. Turning around, and with her head held up high, she began walking boldly forward, straight at Mr. Peters.

She refused to acknowledge him, instead continuing to evaluate the various items in her line of sight, like the shopping connoisseur she was. Bunny only wanted the very best and she could afford it. Not finding anything to pique her interest, she headed for the make-up counter. She walked at a leisurely pace, keeping an eye out for Mr. Peters.

The girl behind the counter obviously didn't recognize Abbey, as she smiled brightly, delighted to have a customer. Abbey, or rather Bunny, decided she needed to try a little bit of everything. The girl, who Abbey recognized as Mandy, was happy to oblige.

"How about," Mandy asked, "We start with some blush? You have lovely cheekbones."

"Thank you," Bunny replied carelessly. Abbey decided that Bunny should at least be civil to the hired help. Especially if they were paying her compliments. Abbey had dark memories of Mandy. She'd called her Flabby Abbey because Abbey had worn a pair of dated, over pleated trousers weeks ago. It was amazing how similar to high school this place was. Bunny had a velvety Southern accent; Abbey had always been good with accents. Mandy smiled brightly. All in all, it was a good start.

As they tried different colors of blush, looking for what might match Bunny's skin tone, she glanced in one of the mirrors. Mr. Peters was still making his circuit around the store. Best of all, he hadn't glanced Abbey's way.

"How about that?" Mandy asked.

Bunny adjusted the mirror, and noted how nice the coloration was. "Absolutely lovely," Bunny smiled warmly. Mandy offered up some eye shadow and Bunny agreed. Abbey had never bothered with makeup, but there was nothing wrong with a little indulgence now and again. Besides, she thought, glancing at her cell phone's clock, I've got time to kill.

Bunny kept an eye out for Mr. Peters as he made his rounds. For now he was taking an ambling path toward electronics.

"Oh this would be so great on you," Mandy showed off a light shade of pale bluish gray that accentuated her green eyes perfectly. Mandy even put some sheer eye shadow beneath her eyes, to make them look more defined. By the time Mandy had rung her up, she felt like a new woman.

It really was Bunny staring at her back in the mirror. No one would ever call Bunny names. She decided to head back toward the shoe section. On her way, she spotted a private little corner that would allow her to try on shoes while keeping an eye on the entire store.

She started untying her cheap sneakers, wondering what Dan would say when he saw the bill. Oh well, she thought, he said buy yourself a Christmas present. She glanced toward Santa who was talking to a child. The well-oiled machine of Santa's Village was running at peak efficiency.

Mr. Peters was nowhere to be seen, but even if he did wander by, he wouldn't recognize Abbey anymore. After all, she thought with a grin, Abbey was downright unmemorable. Bunny, on the other hand, was going to be unforgettable.

Bunny settled in to the vinyl chair trying to get comfortable. A quick look at her phone confirmed the time. Still over two hours before closing. Well, she giggled to herself, at least I have something to keep me busy. She grabbed the pair of black pumps, sliding them slowly onto her feet one at a time. They felt wonderful.

Chapter 21

Dan turned left, driving as fast as he dared down the slick streets. He was in a race against time, only he wasn't sure if he was running away or toward something. But, some unexplainable feeling told him Bernie could help, that answers were out there. Just waiting to be discovered. Now he just needed to know the right question.

A flashing OPEN sign caught his eye, just below GOLDEN TRAVEL. A bolt of inspiration hit him. He slammed on the brakes and jerked the wheel hard, the car screeching into a U-turn. He could feel the car beginning to fishtail and he took his foot off the gas, slowly and gently moving the steering wheel in sync with his rear bumper. The car regained traction and he floored it back to the neon sign. He turned right into the strip mall's parking lot. It's a long shot, he thought, a complete long shot.

When did that stop you? His little voice asked.

He pulled into an empty space and shifted the gear into park. He paused, taking a breath. No sense getting overexcited, best to just calm down. Dan glanced in the mirror, checking his reflection. His friendliest smile grinned back at him. Time to work that old Landis charm. As an afterthought, he reached into his backseat. He had a box full of things he kept for emergencies: back-up lock pick kit, first aid kit, his passport. He rifled through the box and found a hardcover book. Stuffing it beneath his arm, he walked into the shop.

There was one person inside, a woman who looked up expectantly when the door chimed open. "Can I help you?" she asked an edge of sleepiness to her words and eyes that came from disuse.

"I hope so," he said, smiling back. It was worth a try, he told himself. She smiled back. The kind of smile that only the experienced salesperson gets, when they see a fat commission walk in. Her name was Eileen and she smelled like peaches.

Not only was she able to help, but it only took twenty minutes, and a signed copy of Doc Brown's book. It was amazing how helpful people could be if you knew what buttons to press. Of course, when you had a picture of Dan Landis and Doc Brown in one of the bestselling travelogues of all time, all sorts of doors opened. Especially when you were in a travel agency. And all he had to do was promise to book Doc's next vacation with her.

Hopping into his car, Dan took a slow, measured breath. He now had leverage in his pocket and still enough time to get everything done. Speaking of pockets, he fished out what Katherine had slipped him. It was a business card with a second number scribbled on the back. Still got it, he thought. And now, it was time to visit Bernie. Fortunately, he knew where she was: off doing rounds like she did every religious holiday.

Merry Christmas to my favorite atheist, Dan thought with a dark chuckle. He glanced at the clock. Still enough time if the traffic would just play along. He just needed to make one phone call. And check that no one had called him while he'd been working his magic on Eileen.

If Abbey ran into any trouble whatsoever, she was supposed to call Dan at once. Nothing yet. He double-checked that the ringer was on, and turned to high.

"Be careful Abs," Dan prayed, "watch out for the bad men and the crazies."

He kept his eye out for pedestrians, especially the drunk ones. There were quite a few out and about. Christmas was a great time for doing something stupid, and people in this city always liked to start things early. Dan had no time for accidents.

As he floored it toward the hospital, his eyes scanned the dark streets. His brain went over the facts of this bizarre case. Someone had killed four people, specifically four people dressed as Santa. Granted, they had dressed Karl up as Santa after the fact. Someone broke into and robbed a jewelry store less than a block away from the store. They had emptied the store's safe but not the glass case of merchandise. Both were within a one block radius of where the bodies had been found. Three bodies, he corrected himself. Someone had also stolen Mr. Peters absurdly valuable coin collection from that jewelry store. Mr. Peters who was store manager at Murphy's, the most hated man in the store.

Someone knew which door was unlocked from the outside. Someone knew where Security was, and had killed Karl, probably to get the tapes. And someone had set Abbey up to take the fall for the theft, knowing there was no way she could be a believable murder suspect. Was it the same someone? A team? Too many questions, and not enough answers.

"Who benefits?" Maggie always asked. For her, all crimes had to have a motive, and if you could figure out the motive, you could solve any crime. Of course, Dan knew differently. Sometimes people just did things because they were human. Evil, depraved, soulless human beings.

Driving on autopilot, he turned left at the light, then right at the hospital entrance. He parked in an open Clergy spot, and laughed darkly.

"Who knows what evil lurks in the hearts of men?" he asked no one in particular. "Me! That's who!" Unbuckling, he turned off the car, making sure to lock his door. He headed straight for the doors to the hospital's reception area. Keeping up his frantic pace on foot, he ran as fast as he could. The sidewalk was icy, but he could handle ice. He had on his steel toed boots with great grips. He was done playing around.

The thrill of danger gave him a tingling sensation that lit his nerve endings on fire. He glanced up at the imposing hospital. He hated hospitals. They did good work and he certainly appreciated having them around. But he had never forgotten that not everyone walks out of a hospital. And here he was, coming to see Bernie again.

Dan kept his dislike under wraps. Right now, he needed to see a doctor and he knew just how to reach her. It was amazing what you could get away with if you knew what you were doing, and issued orders authoritatively. Dan strolled right in, kept his eyes forward, and went into the first open exam room. Everyone ignored him because he looked like he knew where he was going.

Every exam room had a phone, and he used the one in #2 to have Bernie paged. The first three exam rooms were empty, and he had picked #2 because it made him chuckle to say number two. Everyone in the area was too busy to ask questions. Besides, he didn't have the time or patience to make up any answers. The exam room was quiet.

"Paging Dr. Wilkins," a nasal voice rang out over the P.A. system, "Dr. Wilkins to Clinic Exam Room #2 please."

Dan sat on the paper sheet, waiting. He stared at the walls, hating how uniform the paint was, hating the smell. Within moments, the door opened and she walked in.

"Good evening, I'm Dr. Wilkins…" she started, scanning the bed for a chart, and then saw who was sitting there, smiling. She stared for a minute, mouth agape before snapping it shut with a click. "What's happened this time?"

"Hi Bernie," Dan gave her a little wave. Bernie looked beautiful despite the fact that her long dark hair was up in a bun, which for some reason always made her look a lot like a librarian. Of course, no librarian he knew would wear a turquoise business suit to work, or have a white lab coat on over it. Nor would they look that good doing it.

"You don't look injured," she said with an appraising glare. The "yet" was unspoken. Even angry, her eyes held a hint of her ready laughter.

"Before you say anything," he pulled the envelope out of his jacket pocket, "check this out first." She took the envelope reticently. Watching her open it, he forced himself to relax. If you were going to have leverage, you had better make sure it was good. And he had some great leverage. Thank goodness for last minute inspiration.

She looked up, shocked. "When? How?"

"Twenty minutes ago. Because I'm good like that."

"This is real?"

"Would I be here if it wasn't?"

Bernie's chocolate eyes softened and her lips curved upward. "How the devil did you get a first class ticket to London on Christmas Eve at this late date?" Her thick accent poured out at the thought of home. When she was talking to patients it was with a charming, light British lilt. When addressing Dan, her accent was pure North Country.

"Merry Christmas," he smiled, throwing his arms out wide.

"So says you. And since it is you, what's the catch?"

He sighed and cast his eyes at the ceiling, "I can't do something nice?" She glared and crossed her arms. "I need a favor."

"Obviously," she said, staring at the ticket in her hands. She sighed and handed it back to him, her shoulders slumping.

"They'll never let me out of work. Not in a million years. However, I appreciate the gesture."

"Hey," he said with calm assuredness, "trust me."

"I've heard that one before and it came back to bite me." She tapped the ticket now in his hands. "Is this even the real deal? Or are you just teasing?"

"You're the tease, I always deliver on my promises. Besides, if it wasn't the real deal would it be a one-way flight?"

"That's true. You wouldn't bother taking the piss out of me with something this cheap." Bernie gave him an approaising look. The problem with medical professionals was, they never turned off the professionalism. It was the same problem hair dressers and dog groomers wrestled with. The struggle was real.

"You think that's cheap? I'll have you know that's a good chunk of my meager life savings right there." Dan protested, a bit too hard.

She stared at him, giving him the usual thoughtful expression that read, "I don't believe you for a minute." He would have been hurt by her distrust, if not for the fact that she knew him all too well.

"All right, I cashed in my frequent flyer miles." He held up a finger, "But I was saving those."

"For what?"

"Scotland. I want to visit the Highlands."

"If this is real, I'll take you there next summer."

"Excellent."

"So how am I getting out of rounds?"

"Pardon me madam. I need to contact my daughter, Bernadette Wilkins."

Bernie rolled her eyes.

"I'm afraid," Dan continued smugly, "There's been a motoring incident, and her dear mum has been injured. Not sure she's going to make it through, so if you could be a dear and let her know, we would be eternally grateful."

299 | The Five Santas

"They're never going to fall for that. No one would believe an accent that terrible." Her phone buzzed. He waggled his eyebrows at her. She flipped him off and answered it.

"Dr. Wilkins," she paused, listening and turned her back to Dan. "Oh no, when did this…are you sure? We're swamped, are you sure? Oh thank you," Bernie's voice choked. "I'll grab my things and head for the airport. Thank you, I will tell them that. No, thank you. I'm really sorry for the timing…Oh, thank you!" Wiping away her crocodile tears, she hung up the phone and whirled around to face the manufacturer of this farce.

"You're insufferable when you're right, did you know that."

"Yes, I do. Before you go, I need a favor."

"Please tell me this favor doesn't involve pharmaceuticals."

Dan held up his palms defensively. "All I need is for you to take a look at something."

"Thanks, I've seen it," Bernie replied, reading over the tickets.

"No, I need you to help me break into the morgue and look at some bodies."

Bernie glanced from Dan, to the ticket, and then at the phone.

"Well?"

"I'm thinking about it."

"I'm kind of on a deadline."

She sighed, staring at the ticket, "Whose body do you need to look at?"

"Santa's," he said, "Well, several Santa's actually."

For the first time since they'd met, she was speechless.

Chapter 22

"Is there anything I can help you with dear?" the clerk asked Bunny. Abbey smiled up at the lady, shifting her weight against the plastic seat. The shoe department wasn't known for its comfortable seating or friendly staff. However, this clerk did look surprisingly cheerful. It was a welcome break to find someone like that this close to Christmas. In Abbey's experience, the closer to Christmas it got, the testier the sales staff.

She had a carefully stacked assortment of shoe boxes, still unsure what exactly she wanted. "I was looking for something comfortable for work," she waved a hand, "And price is no object." The clerk sighed, the kind of relief only a person behind on their quota can have. Especially when they see dollar signs in their future. She sat down in the chair next to Abbey/Bunny.

"Can I tell you something?"

Abbey smiled kindly at her, "Yes."

"I was just praying for another customer, and here you are!"

"You were?" Abbey smiled tentatively, more her than her alter ego.

"I was," the clerk grinned back.

"I'm glad to help." She waved at the stack of boxes. "Would you happen to have any suggestions?"

The clerk winked at Abbey, "Do I ever."

Abbey had never thought of shopping as fun. It was something that you only did when absolutely necessary. Shopping was only enjoyable for other people. People with money. Bunny was one of those people. The clerk, Catherine Cahill, mother of three and originally from California, was an expert in her field. She also tended to talk while she worked, quickly sorting out the shoe boxes Abbey had already tried, and scouting for new options.

"I love the soles on these," Cathy handed over one box. She reached for another, "These have a higher heel, but you have the figure for it. I could never wear heels, I'd look like a wobbly little clown with these ankles and hips."

Bunny laughed confessing, "I hate heels. I feel like I'm on stilts."

"Oh but you would look so good, I bet all the guys will love you. Although you probably don't have to worry about that." Catherine chose six different options. When Bunny decided to take all of them, the poor woman cried.

Mr. Peters, Catherine confessed, was breathing down everyone's neck to make their quotas this month. As the Season drew to a close, Mr. Peters was getting increasingly anxious to maximize profits. Poor performance during this time of the year could lead to pink slips. Catherine had two kids she was supporting and couldn't afford to lose this job.

Abbey understood completely and silently made a decision. Bunny was going to get some toys for Catherine's kids. She wanted to give them anonymously though and wasn't sure how to do that. Maybe, she thought, I can put them in her locker. She would be sure to see them when she picked up her things after work. It was worth trying at least.

Bags in hand, Bunny strolled over to the toy section, searching for toys appropriate for a four-year old girl and a two-year old boy. A board game? Stuffed animal? Abbey tried to remember what she liked as a kid. A book, she thought worrying it wouldn't be enough, I loved books. What would Bunny buy?

"Are you Santa's elf?" a small voice asked. Startled, she looked around. A little redheaded girl was standing there, looking up at her. The child's auburn locks fell across her ears. The girl looked no older than four and was staring with wide green eyes at Bunny. She smiled, revealing two missing front teeth. Abbey smiled back, looking around for the child's mother. The little one continued to stare at her, her head tilted to one side, a thoughtful expression on her face. Abbey realized she was waiting on an answer.

"Yes, I am," she lied.

"Why are you looking for toys here?"

"I'm picking out something for Santa," she invented wildly. Dan made it look so easy.

"Oh," the little girl nodded, stepping closer. Her delicate features ignited with the draw of forbidden knowledge as she whispered, "Why are you looking for something in the little kid's section?"

"Well," Abbey made a show of scanning for eavesdroppers before whispering back, "Santa still loves toys." She could feel her cheeks starting to burn.

The little girl nodded wisely. "I like the kitty," she said, pointing.

Abbey followed the direction of her finger to an adorable stuffed gray kitten. "Thank you," she said, glancing back down. The girl was gone. Abbey stood up and glanced around, but the kid had vanished into thin air. She breathed out heavily, relieved. She hated lying. Still, she worried about where the girl had gone. Probably back to her Mom, there were a number of likely candidates not far away none of whom appeared concerned that they were missing someone.

Abbey aka Bunny grabbed the kitten for Catherine's daughter. That little red headed girl was about the right age to have steered her correctly. She found a big red fire truck for the boy; all boys loved fire trucks, and according to the box this toy was age appropriate. She glanced at Santa's Village. Chris was winding down. She checked the time on her cell phone. Closing time was fast approaching. She decided there was still enough time to pay for her purchases.

Making her way toward the cash register, Abbey struggled to stay in character. She didn't imagine Bunny would be one to carry a fluffy kitten and a fire truck. But surely everyone, even Bunny, had a kid in their lives thus making it acceptable. She noticed Mr. Peters was making another pass, continuing his sweep of the store.

The bells on her sweater were jingling, drawing unwanted attention with every step and sway. She bit her lip when she got to the registers. There were too many lines, each one impossibly long. She was terrified of not having enough time to get back to Chris. Picking one at random, she stepped into line and breathed a prayer. Fiddling with her packages, she tried to juggle watching Santa, keeping an eye out for Mr. Peters, and following the person in front of her through the check-out line. The woman ahead of her moved, and Bunny nonchalantly strolled forward. Outwardly, she was nothing but cool and collected.

She glanced around. The crowd was thinning, heading for the registers. A cough made her turn around. The middle aged woman behind her was glaring. Abbey looked to see that the line had moved another inch closer. Another step forward and she was one person away from check-out. That was when her phone rang. She quickly adjusted the items to one hand, struggling to get to it.

"Hello?" Abbey muttered, trying to keep her voice low while glancing around. She felt her stomach seize up. She hated the idea of being on the phone checking out; it was one of her pet peeves. Bunny or no Bunny, she didn't want to be that lady.

"You alright?" Dan asked. He sounded nervous.

"Fine," she replied hurriedly.

"Okay," the tension she'd heard initially eased, "where are you?"

"About to check out. I'll call you if there's trouble." She hung up and jammed the phone back in its place. Abbey took a breath, trying to calm down. The person in front of her finished checking out so she stepped forward, spreading out her items on the counter. The cashier smiled, although it was obviously forced.

Though, to be fair, the poor woman had worked all day, and was probably fresh out of kindness. Abbey offered a sincere smile of encouragement. The cashier volleyed with a withering stare. Can't win them all.

Handing the cashier Dan's credit card, Abbey continued smiling. She didn't know what else to do, it was hard to not speak or smile at someone facing her for that long. The cashier swiped the card. She was holding her breath, praying it would go through. It did. She exhaled, relieved. With Dan you could never be 100%

sure. The cashier handed her a receipt to sign. Abbey signed
Bunny's name, trying to make her handwriting illegible. "Thank
you," she beamed falsely, intentionally making it extra bright.

"Next," the cashier looked past her. Abbey stepped aside,
getting out of the way of those behind her.

Quite an efficient process, she thought. Murphy's ran like a
well-oiled machine everywhere. Glancing up at Santa's Village,
she realized Santa had one last child waiting in line. There was still
time to play Good Samaritan and fulfill her duties. If she hurried,
she could sneak into the locker room and put the toys in
Catherine's locker. And to kill two birds with one stone, she could
grab the black coat Dan had loaned her, or rather stolen from
Julianne. Consolidating the toys into one bag, Abbey decided to
head for the locker room.

Cahill, Abbey repeated to herself, Catherine Cahill. The
nice shoe clerk is named Catherine Cahill, and thinks my name is
Bunny. She glanced around the store one last time, although she
couldn't see Mr. Peters anymore. She hoped he'd gone back to his
office. Trying to look nonchalant, she strolled over to the door
marked Employees Only.

Opening the door, Abbey noted at once that the locker
room was completely empty. Not a soul in sight. Most of the
locker doors were still hanging open, unlocked. Only a few,
probably those who had gone on break since the "confrontation,"

had been closed. Abbey was grateful Catherine wasn't one of them.

It took her longer than she expected to find C. Cahill's locker. Surprisingly, Mr. Peters had not arranged the employees alphabetically. Catherine's locker was toward the center, two rows from Abbey's. As she walked by, she noted that almost none of them had been searched. It was just her luck that she had been singled out. But, why would anyone put jewelry in her locker? Was it a prank? She didn't go out of her way to anger people, but somehow she always ended up a target for pranks. Some of them horrible, mean spirited pranks. People could be so cruel, she thought sadly.

At least with Dan and Professor Brown, even Bernie, she was accepted. That was worth a few odd television references she didn't get or a minor case of jealousy. Even the heartache she was sure to suffer when Dan started bringing a girl around as he would inevitably do.

Reminding herself why she was there, Abbey looked into Catherine's locker, noticing the children's photos first. They were unbelievably cute. It was probably Dan's influence, but when she was talking to Catherine, a part of her thought the story about the children was an act. Something to make Bunny sympathetic, more willing to buy from the poor hapless worker bee. It was reassuring to know some people were truthful. Abbey always tried hard to see the best in people. It felt good to be proven right once in a while.

The two girls in the picture looked just like Catherine, right down to the dark curly hair and hazel eyes. The boy, well into his teens, with dark skin and soulful eyes, looked, presumably, like his father. Both had adorable grins, smiling happily at the camera.

Abbey hung the presents on the locker's coat hook in plain view. She thought about leaving a note, then decided to remain anonymous. She slipped the gift receipt in the bag. No employee could leave the store with merchandise without a receipt. Abbey certainly wanted to avoid causing Catherine any trouble.

As she was closing the locker, Abbey felt something on her periphery. Without knowing why, she suddenly had the impression she wasn't alone. Whirling around, she looked for anyone else. There was nothing behind her but more lockers. Taking a deep breath, she walked quickly around the corner. A swish of clothing caught her eye; a hint of red flashed at the far door, in the opposite direction of the entrance.

Santa? Abbey wondered, her pulse taking off. Could he already be done with the children? If so, why was he going through that door? Why would he go out the far side when he knew he was supposed to stay here and wait for them?

I should call Dan, she thought. This smells like trouble.

Standing up straight, pushing back her shoulders, Abbey took a deep breath. It might be something Bernice Agnes Anastasia Smith is too scared to do alone, but Bunny? Bunny is another story.

Abbey couldn't think of a witty middle name for Bunny to have, but her last name was definitely going to be Hayes. The first day Abbey had formally met Dan, after he'd climbed out of the dumpster, he'd named her Mattie Hayes. Bunny Hayes was afraid of nothing. She also wasn't stupid, and it was with reasonable caution that she approached the door, then paused. The urge to call Dan flared up again.

"Call me if you run into trouble," he had told her. He had been very specific about that. Maybe I can just stick my head around the corner, Bunny told herself, see if there's any trouble. She hated to cry wolf if it was nothing.

Convinced she was doing the smart thing, she walked quietly as she closed the short distance remaining between her and the red painted door. It was labeled in black stencil Warehouse Storage. The two cops had taken her this way, when they arrested her. Opening the door, she saw the room was pitch black. A single shaft of light was all that illuminated the inky darkness. It had been much brighter when she was arrested.

She stuck her head in, looking around. Nothing. She thought about calling out, and realized that would be stupid. With trepidation, Abbey started to pull her head back. A sharp crack sent stars into her eyes. She felt herself go limp, crumpling to the ground. Someone caught her, strong hands. She felt fur against her skin.

The last thing Abbey remembered before she blacked out, was red clothed arms and white fur on the cuffs. "Santa?" She breathed, as she slipped into unconsciousness.

Chapter 23

"You're out of your bloody flipping mind," Bernie yelled as they drove.

"Maybe," he shifted in the car seat.

"Let me make sure I understand this," she said, leaning against the window, "You want to sneak into the city morgue to examine a bunch of dead Father Christmases?" She shook her head and closed her eyes, "Why?"

Dan blinked. "You haven't heard?"

Bernie frowned at him, then glanced down at the ticket back in her hands. She pulled out her phone to check the time, "Look, this flight leaves in three hours, and I've spent the last two days locked in this hospital. Can we just skip to the end so that I can have a hope to at least pack clean pants before I go?"

"Right," he drummed his fingers against the steering wheel. "Short version: someone is killing street corner Santas."

"How many?"

"Four. So far." Dan didn't want to split hairs about Karl's inclusion in that group.

"Why do you want to look at the bodies?" Bernie asked.

"I have a crazy theory." He ignored the snort from his passenger. "I need your medical opinion, and your badge."

Bernie scratched her nose. "Fine, but you should know we have no chance of seeing those bodies. This ticket isn't worth that kind of trouble."

He sighed, "So what is it worth?"

"Well," she met his curious gaze with a devilish grin, taking flirty to a whole other plane. "I can't show you the body, but I can give you a very, detailed, description."

"Can you now?" He grinned. She returned the expression.

"How about the autopsy reports? I have a friend working in the Coroner's office. Also," she pushed his face back toward the road, "Stop picturing me naked." A hint of a smile played on her lips. This was a familiar game, a dating version of chicken. They had tried making a real relationship work, but Bernie was a free spirit, and Dan needed someone to come home to.

Dan's mouth twitched, "You look good."

"I look fantastic, but that's not helping." Bernie fired back.

"Helps me."

She hit him with the ticket.

"Right, autopsies. Excellent! Is this friend working tonight?"

"It's still Christmas Eve right?" He nodded. "Then yes."

Traffic was starting to pick up as they wove their way across town, the car bobbing and weaving. Dan had only been to the Coroner's Office once, but thankfully Bernie knew every shortcut. In between mutterings about the amateur driving skills of all Americans, she directed him toward a nondescript concrete building. He parked in the handicapped spot. She turned to him, giving a dirty look.

"Limp when you get out," he told her with a wry grin. She gave him a two-fingered salute. He jogged ahead, keeping an eye out for ice. The front door was locked, the lights on. He pulled out his lock-pick kit and Bernie, quickly catching up, slapped his hand. She knocked on the glass and a pimply faced young man emerged from a corner room and over to the door.

His face lit up when he saw Bernie, and he rushed to unlock the door. Opening it without question, he allowed them both to step into the anteroom. The place was warm, something that struck Dan as odd. He had always assumed a morgue would be a cooler temperature throughout for the sake of their silent residents.

The place was not brightly lit, not completely dark, just generally mild and pleasant. It was far more pleasant and comfortable than any morgue had a right to be. Dan kept staring at the kid's thick-rimmed glasses. It was like he had two glass bottles strapped to his face. There was even a piece of tape over the bridge of the glasses. The kid looked like the poster child for *Revenge of the Nerds: Electric Boogaloo*. Dan decided not to make a joke. There wasn't time, and it would probably just go over the kid's head anyway.

"Rupert!" Bernie called too loudly at the man staring at her. She was jacked up. Rupert was breathing slowly through his mouth. Bernie wrapped both arms around Rupert's neck, giving him a ferocious hug. He blushed, his pasty white skin going scarlet. Dan felt bad for the poor kid. Rupert had no idea how out of his league she really was.

Bernie let go, waving a hand in Dan's direction. "Rupert, this is my friend Dan."

"Hi," he gestured to himself, "I'm Rupert." Dan smiled at the kid, feeling a pang of guilt for getting him in trouble. He looked and sounded all of fourteen.

"Hi," Dan offered him his hand, "Pleased to meet you."

Rupert gave a wet noodle of a handshake and Dan tried to be discreet about wiping off his hand. Rupert had cold sweaty palms.

"I need a favor," Bernie said, "a really big favor." She ruffled Rupert's greasy hair.

She really wants to go home, Dan thought to himself.

"Umm sure…" Rupert stammered.

"Good," Bernie's words dripped honey. "Is it true someone has killed Father Christmas?"

"What?" Rupert blinked out of his stare.

"Santa," Dan offered helpfully.

"Oh," Rupert shot Dan a nervous glance, "I'm not allowed to talk about that."

"I'm not a reporter," Dan pulled out one of his cards, handing it over. "I'm a private investigator, just trying to find some answers."

"And I merely want to look at the medical files," Bernie purred.

"Why?" Rupert's eyes were trained on Bernie. Dan put his card back in his wallet; he could have been holding a gold bar and Rupert wouldn't have cared. Bernie was still stroking his hair. Dan had to admire the kid's resolve. As well as Bernie's.

"Because I said...please," Bernie spoke into Rupert's ear, her voice dropping into a husky whisper. Dan was surprised the kid didn't melt.

"Oookaaayy," Rupert was trembling. He pointed behind him, "Only, I have to get the files."

"You do that sweetie," Bernie released him.

Rupert backed away, keeping both eyes on Bernie as he led the way into a small reception area just past the front room. Dan watched the kid back out, afraid to take his eyes off Bernie for even a second. He bumped into the door. Dan didn't dare laugh. He understood the kid's puppy love completely. He watched as Rupert rounded the corner, and spotted him through one of the back windows rifling through some filing cabinets. While they waited, Dan grabbed a seat, checking out what magazines were in the Coroner's office reception area.

Lots of *Highlights Magazine*, apparently. Bernie leaned against a wall pulling out the plane ticket.

"Laying it on a bit thick?" Dan asked, over Goofus and Galiant. He'd always identified with Goofus.

"I'm in a hurry," Bernie replied in a harsh whisper.

"Right."

"What are you hoping to learn from this?" she asked, watching Rupert pulling out several files. He glanced up and she waved. Blushing, he waved back before resuming his work.

"I don't know," Dan admitted in a normal voice, he doubted Rupert could hear them. She gave him an appraising stare and he rolled his shoulders. "Something's been bugging me about the first two murders, except I'm not sure what. There's something there, I just can't put my finger on it. What I really need is a second set of eyes, preferably with medical training."

"And," Bernie started, "you don't think the authorities have noticed whatever's tweaking your interest?"

"No," Dan shook his head, "because they're trying to find a serial killer."

That remark earned a thoughtful stare. She sat down. The plastic seat made a squeak. "So let me make sure I have a handle on this, if you will," Bernie studied him. "Four Santa's turn up dead, each murdered, and you don't think that it's a serial killer?"

"No," Dan put down the magazine. "And I know how crazy that sounds. I just can't shake the feeling that…Yes, I think the same person has killed these Santa's, but I think there's an explanation other than psycho killer or someone on a spree. It's just, for the life of me I can't think why anyone would kill a Santa."

"Who do you think did it?"

"Well," he fidgeted with the corner of the magazine resting on his lap. He was going to say he didn't have a suspect. Only Bernie knew him too well. "All right, I've got two candidates."

"Oh?" she leaned back in her chair. "Do tell Mr. Holmes. I never fancied myself for a Watson. Go on."

"Bear with me," he held out a hand to stay any objections, "The first suspect is a six foot, two hundred pound bad, bad, bad man named Mortimer Hasselberg. He goes by the name Tex. The problem with that is if it is Tex, they're never going to catch him." Dan tugged on one ear.

"Why not?" Bernie's eyes stared into his soul.

"Because the man's a ghost. The only time you'll ever see
him is when he's on a job. And then you don't want to see him. I
spotted him my first day at work, purely a fluke. I called, the cops
arrested him, and he vanished from custody. Except," he
interrupted himself, "here's the thing: Tex sticks to robbery with a
little B&E. I could see him killing a clerk that gets in the way. But,
there'd have to be a good reason. He has loaded guns, but he's not
known for firing them. Anyway, the cops are after him already.
Why come back?"

"You said two," she reminded him.

"Did I?" he asked, trying not to look her in the eye.

"Yes," she said.

"The other is Santa…"

"The dead one?" she asked, "Because Dan, I know you
love *Shaun of the Dead*…"

"No, not Zombie Santa," he huffed, "the department store
Santa."

"Really?" Bernie asked, there was a touch of laughter in
her voice. "So, why is the department store Santa killing his fellow
Santai?"

"Because there can be only one?" Dan threw it out again,
desperate for distraction from his uncertainty and growing fear.
She tossed her head back and laughed. "Thank you. I told Abbey
that joke and she didn't laugh."

"That's because it's a terrible joke," she said. He laughed at that. Rupert came back out carrying a fat bundle of files. "Don't feel bad," Bernie said to Dan, "it was a great, bad joke." Turning to Rupert she gave him bedroom eyes and a sultry "Thank you so much," drawing out the "o's" for a mile.

"If you want," the kid helpfully offered, "you can use our conference room. It's more comfortable, the chairs are anyway. The table's a little stiff. I nap on it sometimes. Not that I think you need to nap or anything." He tripped over himself in his nervousness.

"That would be delightful Rupert," she wrapped an arm around his shoulders, "thank you again!" Rupert smiled and Dan could tell the kid's Christmas wish had been made. He led them down a narrow white hallway, lit by heavy fluorescents and decorated with bad art meant to be comforting, and only coming off as gauche.

They headed towards a small room and Rupert hurried to turn on the light. The whole place was painted a dull white, almost gray. It was also possible the paint had faded. Either way, Dan could feel the life being leeched out of him much like the paint's color. The conference room had an oblong faux mahogany table surrounded by crimson upholstered chairs that looked very uncomfortable. The whole room was standard Government Issue bad.

Bernie sat down at the head of the table with Rupert placing the files reverently in front of her. Then he sat next to her in what Dan considered an uncomfortably close proximity. If she minded, Bernie didn't say anything, instead devouring the files, flipping through each one at a rapid pace. Dan remained standing, leaving the files to be handled by the expert. Still, he remained close by her shoulder opposite her admirer and new slave for life.

"What are we looking for?" Bernie asked, still reading.

"Cause of death," Dan said simply.

"Well I could have told you that," Rupert said quickly, then seemed to regret his outburst. "I mean, I typed up the reports. I'm sorry, I didn't mean to be rude."

"No," Dan said, sitting down across from Rupert. He waited for him to continue. "No, that's good. Can you go through each of them? Let's start with David Barr."

"Umm," Rupert touched his temple as he thought, "I'm not sure of his name."

"The first Santa who died," Dan waved him off, "what was the official cause of death."

"Asphyxia," Rupert said, "bruising around the neck and shoulders suggests manual strangulation. Spacing of bruises suggests hands, though irritation of the skin would most likely indicate that the attacker was wearing gloves. Slight abrasions suggest fabric or leather."

"Wait," Dan tugged on one earlobe, "I thought someone hit David on the head."

"Maybe he hit his head after being strangled?" Bernie asked.

"I'm sorry to interrupt," Rupert said after Bernie had finished speaking. "Did you say David Barr?"

"Right," David said.

"Oh, I'm sorry, I thought you meant the first Santa Claus killed. David was the first found." Rupert looked down crest.

"Yeah, I found him. My bad, Rupert. What was the name of the first Santa?" He caught Rupert's expression and clarified, "The first one who died, not the one who was found."

"Cody Rodney Brown."

"I have no idea who that is," Dan admitted.

"Neither do I," Rupert said.

"I only know him in the Biblical sense," Bernie fired back. The two stared at her. She grinned devilishly. "You'll never know."

"Santa Cody, Santa #1, was strangled?"

"Correct," Rupert nodded.

And, Dan noted to himself, you knew all this without ever looking at a file. Guy had an amazing memory. "Santa #2, David Barr, first Santa found."

"Whack to the head," Bernie stated before Rupert could interject. She looked up from the files she was holding, saw the kid's hangdog expression at her stealing his thunder and patted his head. "Sorry sweetie, we're in a hurry."

"Okay," Dan kept things moving, "Karl, Santa #3…?

"Poison…" Rupert said simply.

"What?" Dan's jaw dropped. He hadn't expected that.

"Overdose of toxic substances, specifically arsenic. Blood tests reveal high sugar levels, which coupled with the residual candies found inside his stomach…"

"Someone poisoned his candies?" Dan guessed the source, going pale. "I…I ate those candies." His whole life began flashing before his eyes. Too much of it had been lacking, in his opinion.

Bernie looked at the papers and shot him a knowing smile. "Relax pickle," she said, "if you had eaten one of those poison candies, you would already be dead."

"Really?" he asked, not quite ready to believe her. "It was that random?"

"Yep. If this dosage had been lead instead of arsenic, you could have written your name with one of those candies."

"Wow," Rupert exhaled slowly, "this is just like TV."

Dan inhaled, relieved at the bullet he'd dodged. He stood up and began pacing back and forth, scratching his head.

"What are you thinking?" Bernie's eyes followed him.

"That this doesn't make any sense whatsoever," Dan admitted, "fourth Santa."

"Still haven't gotten the report," Rupert said, "they're retrieving the body as we speak."

"Oh that's not good," Dan said, suddenly realizing his predicament. He couldn't be there when the officers brought the body in. "Rupert," Bernie said, leaning in, "we weren't here."

"No," Rupert agreed without argument.

"Okay, time crunch," Dan banged the heel of his hand on his forehead, "Think, think, think. What do we know? Gary told me Santa #4 was shot."

"Poison, strangulation, shooting, and blunt force trauma," Bernie ticked them off on her fingers, "this is like *Clue*. All we need are Tim Curry, Madeline Khan and a candlestick."

"What?" Rupert asked. He was too young.

"Never mind," Bernie patted his hand, "four different methods, yet given the similarity and proximity of the victims, possibly the same perpetrator?"

"Possibly," Dan admitted, "and if not, then it's one of the strangest coincidences ever. Hang on, what you said isn't right. That's not the order."

"What?" Bernie asked, her face scrunching up in confusion.

"The order of methodology...first strangulation, then blunt force trauma, then poison, then a gun," Dan said, ticking them off.

"So?" Bernie asked.

"So," he said, walking over, "When you strangle someone…" He reached out. Bernie glared at him, stopping his attempted reenactment in its tracks. He looked over at Rupert and then decided against it as well. He wrapped his hands around his own neck. "Alright, when you strangle someone, it's up close and personal. How much you want to bet they were looking Santa in the eye when they strangled him. Rupert?" Dan pointed at the kid.

"It's true," Rupert agreed, "judging by the finger indentations, whoever killed Santa was facing him."

"Really?" Bernie asked, looking from Dan to Rupert. "That's some serious psychic work. Did you read the report?"

"No, it was actually a wild guess," Dan glanced away, slightly embarrassed. "I did discover the body. The way Santa was in the alley, buried under some garbage bags, it felt like a spur of the moment thing."

Bernie rifled through the papers. " So, we're dealing with a Santa Strangler?" Alliteration had never sounded so sexy. "Huh, according to this, he'd been dead long enough for rigor to set in and then dissipate."

"So, a while," Dan paraphrased.

"Actually, Dr. Kepler believes the weather may have affected lividity," Rupert offered helpfully.

"Right," Dan added, trying desperately to keep the medical nerds from derailing the conversation, "Then the method changed. The second one was blunt force trauma, and that is what's confusing. If they'd died in the order I found them, then it would make sense. The killings would be escalating. Except they didn't. First, he strangles one guy and hides him behind a restaurant. Then he whacks the second guy in the back of the head and hides him behind a dumpster. I could maybe believe the guy likes killing…"

Bernie lifted a finger, her mouth open to interject.

"But," Dan said cutting her off, "here's the part that's got me confused. Even if he killed those two Santa's, strangling is personal but a whack to the back of the head isn't."

Dan stopped, as Rupert and Bernie were staring at him.

"What?"

"When did you start channeling Mr. Poirot all of a sudden?" Bernie was smiling, shaking her head mildly.

"You pick up a few things along the way," Dan said offhand. Bernie raised an eyebrow. "Okay, mostly from watching lots of TV. But…am I right?" He looked from the Emergency Room doctor to the Coroner's Office Assistant. Wrong crowd, he realized. Where's an amateur psychologist when you needed one?

"Makes sense so far," Bernie agreed.

"I agree," Rupert hurried to side with Bernie.

"Thank you," Dan bowed with a tight smile. "That's why the poison makes even less sense. Poison is a crime of passion, of rage. It can also be anonymous, an expression of powerlessness. It was very clean, unlike strangulation and blunt force trauma. I'm thinking this was personal; you have to know something about your victim's habits to put arsenic in a candy dish."

He rapped his knuckles against the wall, "A whack to the head isn't personal, yet it requires proximity and rage. There is definitely passion behind it. The same thing with strangulation, if you want to get down to it."

"So," Bernie said, "What you're saying is, all of these killings are personal?"

"Maybe the serial killer's got something against Santa?"

"No," Dan said, slamming his hand down. The two others jumped. "Sorry. See, that's the problem. Personal doesn't explain the shooting. Gary said witnesses didn't see anything, which says distance, a shot from something like a rifle. That kind of distance dehumanizes your target, meaning it wasn't personal or passionate. Which takes us back to anonymous. Everything in my gut says this death, the shooting, is a distraction."

"Distraction from what?" Bernie pursed her lips, she did that sometimes when she was thinking.

"Exactly," Dan said. "If I could figure that out we'd be handing this guy over to the police, and we'd all be heroes.

"A jewelry store gets knocked over; a Santa gets killed right down the street. Then a second Santa gets killed nearby," Dan was glaring at the window as if his answer was out there somewhere, waiting for him.

"What was stolen?" Bernie asked.

"Some cheap jewelry and a coin collection…" He stared into space.

"Well," Bernie said tracing her finger against the table, "this is me thinking out loud, but, what if our thief accidentally gave some coins away. Complete happenstance."

"Ooh," Rupert sat up and twisted his neck to watch them both in his excitement, "Just completely by accident?"

"Exactly."

"Then why'd he kill two Santas?"

"What if he forgot which Santa he gave the coins to? Maybe they switched corners on him and when he went back, the Santa he wanted had moved?" Bernie asked.

"They all look the same to me," Dan said, as he continued to stare into space.

Bernie watched him, knowing he was working something out. "What?"

"They found the jewelry," Dan's voice was distant, "someone planted the jewelry on Abbey…" His eyes widened. He looked askance of Bernie.

"Go…"

"Are you sure?"

She patted Rupert's hand, indicating Dan's taxi services had been replaced.

"Are you…"

"Go!" Bernie shouted.

Dan spun around, slamming into the door in his haste. He bounced off and backed up. Wrenching open the door, he barreled through, pausing as he exited. "Rupert you've been a huge help," Dan touched two fingers to his brow in salute. "Thank you!"

"You're welcome," Rupert called to Dan's retreating back. He turned to Bernie. "Did I miss something?"

"He's figured it out, I pity whoever did this. When Dan finds them, they're in for a world of hurt." Bernie frowned. "I just hope Abbey's all right.

"Who's Abbey?"

"I'll explain it on the way to the airport," Bernie said with a smile.

Chapter 24

Dan bolted down the front steps of the Coroner's office, skidding on the ice. He grabbed onto the handicapped sign and swore a blue streak working frantically to keep his legs under him. The Coroner's van was stopped in the road about to turn into the office. He was going to be lucky to get out of there unseen. He wrenched opened his car door, falling into his seat. The fabric was cold, his breath fogged up the windshield.

She's probably just hanging out some place, he hoped. Some place nice and public. He fired up the ignition. The Coroner's van passed by and as soon as it was out of the way he threw it into reverse, whipping the nose around. He popped the gear into drive and got ready to hit the gas. He glanced in his rearview mirror out of habit to see Bernie waving frantically at him. With a hiss he hit the brakes and waited. Bernie wrenched the back passenger door open, pulling out her bag. Rupert was running toward her.

"Lover boy's going to sneak out to the airport," Bernie told him. Dan was staring at her. "What are you waiting for? Go!" She slammed the door. Dan floored it, almost skidding on the ice. He struggled to pull out his cell phone, hitting Abbey's speed-dial.

"Hello?" she answered.

"You alright?" he tried to keep his voice calm.

"Fine," she replied. He could hear the noise of the store on her end.

Witnesses, that was good. He forced his lungs to work. "Where are you?"

"About to checkout," she was tense about something, "I'll call you if there's trouble." She hung up.

Dan let loose a long and creative stream of obscenities, and was about to call her back when the car in front of him slammed on brakes. He swerved to avoid it, and saw that traffic had come to a standstill. He jerked the wheel, the car hopping up onto the sidewalk. He followed it to a cross-street, and pulled a hard right. Scanning the street ahead of him, he cursed all inexperienced winter drivers while filing through his mental map of the city. He desperately needed to find a detour.

Turning left, Dan took a deep breath. It was going to be a long drive. He had to keep reminding himself to breathe as he went through one shortcut after another. The entire town was dark. A power line must have gone down. Of course, the people in this city had no idea how to deal with a power outage and snow. They didn't seem to realize that if a stoplight was out, that meant you stopped. Not raced through it all at the same time.

The snow wasn't helping either, but Dan could deal with the snow. He was worried about panicky people who might do stupid things that would further delay him and put Abbey at risk.

"It's all my fault," he kicked himself. "I put her there, I got her into this. If something happens, I'll never forgive myself."

You forgave yourself for me, his little voice said.

"I have a shrine in my window," he shot back angrily, "You think that's me forgiving and forgetting?"

His little voice chuckled, mocking him. He looked over. His phone lay on the seat beside him. He didn't dare stop to retrieve it, and he couldn't risk calling while driving on this road. An accident would just slow him down further.

"Case in point," he muttered, swerving to avoid a pickup. Dan kept one eye on the drivers, and the other eye on the inky darkness, scanning for street signs that might offer escape. His headlights were due to be replaced, he could barely see ten feet in front of him. He almost missed his turn, and had to make such a sharp left that spun the car around. He didn't panic. He didn't have time.

This little side street had no traffic. All the crazies were on the main thoroughfare. Without traffic, with just his car spinning like a top, it was kind of fun. At least it would have been fun if he didn't have a cold feeling in his stomach.

"Maybe it was dumb luck they picked her," he said out loud, his voice was too loud in the quiet car. It was a bit like whistling in the dark.

Yeah right, his little voice said. She gets framed right after you hire her? Just when you start sticking your nose into the store's business?

He could always count on Maggie, or the ghost in his head, to be the pessimist. Even if she was just voicing Dan's own thoughts.

A beacon of light illuminated the horizon. Apparently the power hadn't gone out at the store. He breathed a sigh of relief. Darkness would only make people panic. Right now he needed a calm and collected crowd.

The last thing Dan needed was a mob scene or Abbey getting lost in the chaos. He touched his gun with his arm, reminding himself to be cool. "Just blanks," he reminded himself. No one needed to get hurt tonight.

He parked in the fire lane, turning off his car and jumping out all in one smooth motion. He slammed the door, eyes scanning the crowds coming out. Pausing, he went back, opening the passenger back door. He rifled through his emergency box, looking for something to even the odds. He pulled out a set of gloves, special gloves for special occasions. Slamming the door, he let his eyes pass over the exiting shoppers.

"Abbey," he called out, still scanning, before realizing she wouldn't have left. Not without calling him first. He slipped on his gloves, the lead powder woven into the lining gave them a heavier than normal feel. They made pulling out his gun more of a challenge, but they also gave him an edge if it came down to a fight. With Abbey at stake, Dan wanted every advantage he could get.

Stepping around, he opened his front passenger door, grabbing his phone. He dialed Abbey. It rang four times and went to voicemail. He tried it again. Same. The cold in his stomach spread. He headed for the store's main entrance, still looking from face to smiling face. No one looked familiar, and every time he didn't see Abbey, his heart got a little heavier. When he finally got inside, it was like walking into an oven. Feliz Navidad played over the P.A. system. He felt like he was going to be sick. He dialed Abbey again. Nothing.

He scanned the registers, looking from one dour face to the next. Every one of them was checking out the last of their customers. He felt an inherent pressure, a drawing down of the day. It was the close of business, the end of the Season. He walked over to the nearest cashier.

"Excuse me," he asked the tired woman, "Did an elf just check out?"

The cashier, already exhausted looked at him blankly, and then turned away.

"Hello?" he prodded, following her along the counter. "Elf? Blonde, sort of short, great legs?"

"Abbey went that way," another female voice answered.

Dan glanced over to the other woman working in the department, straightening up. He recognized the voice as belonging to one of the girls from the break room only 48 hours before. The blonde, the one with the pretty eyes and snide remarks about his Abbey. The owner of the voice was pointing toward the employee locker room.

"Are you sure?" he didn't care what kind of person she was or whether he liked her, she had seen Abbey.

"Yeah," she nodded at him, "I remember, because I thought it was weird that she was back. Wasn't she fired or something?"

"Or something," he said over his shoulder, already heading that way. He paused, turning around to smile at her, "Thanks."

She smiled back, "Sure, Merry Christmas."

Feeling a hint of forgiveness creep in, he gave a wave and a nod, and then headed into the locker room. It was empty, though the lockers seemed to all be unlocked, a few were hanging open. Dan scanned the room carefully, it was completely deserted. One open locker in particular caught his eye. Walking over for a closer look, he saw there was a bag of toys hanging on the coat hook. A gift receipt poked out of the bag. Glancing inside, he noted it was toys and moved on.

Dan looked around, trying to spot Abbey. A splash of white caught his eye. Down by the far door, at the end of the room, was another bag. Several bags, he realized, bending down to look at the scattered pile. Makeup, lots of shoes…someone went on a shopping spree. This receipt had his name on it, though not his signature. Abbey.

He looked up at the door, noting the sign. Warehouse storage. His first day, Mr. Peters had given him a tour of the facilities. Dan knew that on the other side was a big room with lots of places to hide oneself, or to hide someone else. Of course, if memory served, there was also an exit to the outside. Standing up, he carefully pulled out his gun. It took a moment to adjust his grip with the gloves on, though he finally found a comfortable arrangement.

Stepping forward, he kept his finger off the trigger and the muzzle pointed at the ceiling. He eased the door open a crack with his free hand, barely enough to see the room. A dim light shone against the concrete floor. Someone had recently turned the massive overhead lights on. They were still humming to life, slowly clicking on one by one.

Within his tiny sliver of vision, Dan couldn't see anyone. He edged his toe against the door frame, getting down on one knee. Placing his free right hand against the door, he shoved it open. Rolling into the room he came up on one knee, trying to make the smallest target possible. He whipped around, trying to find his target. He spotted someone in his periphery, immediately pointing his gun in their direction.

"Hold it," Dan shouted.

What he saw made his heart stop. He stood up automatically, all thought to his own safety gone.

Abbey was lying on the floor with blood marring her forehead. Looming above her was Santa. And pointing a rifle at Dan was Mr. Peters.

Chapter 25

Mr. Peters and Dan stared at one another. One pointing a rifle, the other a pistol. Pivoting on one foot, Mr. Peters turned the rifle on Santa. "Mr. Landis," Mr. Peters' voice was hoarse and shaky. He cleared his throat and tried again. "Mr. Landis, I would like to report that I have caught our killer."

Dan glanced at Santa, who continued to loom over the prone form, his face expressionless except for the eyes. The twinkling green eyes showed only the barest signs of awareness behind the bushy beard. Abbey lay at Santa's feet, her forehead bleeding. Dan couldn't tell how severe the injury was from this distance. He noted the shoulder stock of the rifle glistened with wet blood. He looked back at Mr. Peters, shivering, making the gun's barrel quiver. Shaky hands did not make for safe guns.

Dan's throat tightened. "Excellent work Sir," he kept his voice calm, "Why don't you give me the gun."

"I can't do that Mr. Landis," the man barked out, visibly struggling to remain in control of himself. Shock, terror, and confusion played across his face. "I assure you it was some work getting this gun away in the first place. I regret I was not in time to prevent the young lady from being harmed."

Dan extended his arm, now pointing his gun fully in the direction of Santa. "Its fine, Sir," Dan assured him, stretching out his free hand toward Mr. Peters, palm open. "I've got them covered, Sir. See?"

Mr. Peters focused on Dan. His eyes were haunted, and in the flickering overhead light they looked hollow. His face was pale, worn, and showing signs of the strain he'd been under the last few days. What little hair the man had was sticking out wildly; sweat glistening on his sallow complexion. He was obviously close to cracking.

"You believe me?" he asked, surprised.

"Of course," Dan kept his voice level, "Of course I do. In fact, I've figured the whole thing out. I know exactly what happened."

"You do?" Mr. Peters eyes bugged out, relief flooding his voice. Behind the thick glasses, he blinked rapidly.

"Yes sir," Dan nodded, continuing to reach out for the rifle. Carefully, he shuffled forward a step. His pistol remained pointed at Santa. "It all started with your coin collection, when our big red friend here found out about it, about how much it was worth. He," Dan nodded toward Santa, "broke into the jewelry store, emptied the safe, and made it look like a run of the mill robbery. No one had any reason to suspect what he was really after."

"Really?" Mr. Peters said. "No one knew he was after my coins?"

"No, Sir," Dan's voice soothed. "That is, until he made a mistake."

"What?" Mr. Peters croaked and hastily swallowed. "What mistake was that, Mr. Landis?"

"He was feeling generous and put some change into Santa's bucket," Dan shrugged, "Maybe even more than one Santa's bucket. See, I don't think our robber had ever stolen anything in his entire life. The guilt was overwhelming. What he didn't realize, however, was that he'd accidentally put some of your coin collection into one of the buckets."

"But how could he make that kind of mistake?" Mr. Peters asked, clearly troubled. "Isn't that foolish?"

"I wouldn't say foolish, it's just one of those things that can happen," Dan nodded his head to one side in sympathy. "It happens. He probably had the coins and jewelry in his pockets. Did you know Santa had pockets? I just found that out recently. He probably put maybe one or two in the wrong pocket, with his normal change. Happens to me all the time." Dan glanced down at Abbey, and when he turned back, Mr. Peters was staring at him, his mouth agape. "It isn't unheard of for things to go off plan," Dan assured him. "We hear about those sorts of things all the time."

341 | T h e   F i v e   S a n t a s

"Then, you don't think that means the thief was," his voice shook, "incompetent?"

That *would* be of utmost importance to Mr. Peters. Dan divorced himself from the tightly wound man's concerns. The thought crossed his mind that this man had checked out, he had broken from reality entirely. Dan pressed on regardless, his voice calm and soothing, a leisurely passenger on a tranquil sea. "So, Santa had to track down your coins."

Mr. Peters nodded again, and must have realized his mouth was open again. He closed it with a sharp snap.

"He went to the Santa down the block from the jewelry store first, the one that stands over by that diner across the street," Dan explained, "probably thinking that's where he put his change. Except, something happened along the way."

"What?" Mr. Peters was captivated, "What happened?"

"I'm not sure," Dan admitted, "maybe Santa wouldn't cooperate and there was an argument. Or, our man was just impatient. The point is," he sneezed into his elbow, "pardon me. Something happened that threw a wrench in his plans and he grabbed Santa. Choking him was an accident."

"An accident?" Mr. Peters asked.

"Purely accidental," Dan reiterated with a dismissive wave of his free hand. His gun remained steadfastly pointed in Santa's direction. "Unfortunately, the same thing happened with the next

Santa. The one nearest Murphy's. He probably just wanted to conk Santa on the head, grab the coins, and leave. Except, the human head is a very fragile thing. Presumably between Santa #1 and Santa #2 he found all the coins."

Movement caught Dan's attention. For the briefest of moments, it looked like Abbey was stirring. He didn't dare call out to her, she was safest if no one knew she was awake.

"How do you know?" Mr. Peters asked with watery, pleading eyes.

"Because there wasn't a Santa #3," Dan assured him. "Or there shouldn't have been. Only Karl, Mr. Anderson, saw something."

"Saw something?"

"Maybe our killer didn't know about the missing video camera out back, maybe Karl said the wrong thing at the wrong time."

"Or tried to blackmail him," Mr. Peters added, nodding his head fervently.

"Quite possibly," Dan said with a swallow. He closed his eyes for a second, took a breath and continued. "Whatever he did, whatever he said to Santa, Karl ended up being next on Santa's list. He knew enough about Karl, about his habits, to take him out. That gave Santa the opportunity to poison the candies," Dan said, casting an eye from frozen Santa and back to his disheveled boss.

"Poison's pretty easy to come by. Arsenic makes a great industrial rat poison. There's probably some in this very warehouse. Though of course by this point, the cops were onto the scent. I mean, three bodies is kind of a hard thing to keep quiet. So, Santa had to distract the police, he used the jewelry."

Mr. Peters' eyes trailed down to his hands, startled by what they held. His mouth opened and closed repeatedly, a fish suffocating out of water. "I got this rifle from him," Mr. Peters gasped, staring wide eyed. "I think he was trying to hide it in here. He was going to hurt the girl…get rid of all the witnesses."

"Exactly," Dan said, reaching out again with his free hand. He closed the distance with another sliding step. "And we have him now. We have all the evidence we need to put this guy away for a long, long time. We have means, motive, and opportunity. Please give me the gun, Sir, and we can call the police. We can end this."

"The police?" In his voice was, for the briefest moment, a touch of the old Mr. Peters.

"They'll be discreet," Dan assured him, "I promise." He took a few more small steps towards the man, coming shoulder to shoulder. Close enough to see the rifle, he glanced down and swallowed hard. The hammer was back, cocked and ready to fire.

Then, as Dan shifted his weight, the view changed as he saw down the gun sight to where it was actually aimed. His heart froze in mid-beat. The rifle wasn't aimed at Santa. It was aimed at Abbey.

Mr. Peters stopped breathing when the barrel of Dan's pistol came to rest firmly against his head.

"Give me the gun," Dan said his voice cold and barely above a whisper.

"What, what are you doing?" Mr. Peters whispered back, his voice trembling.

"I'm asking you very politely to give me the gun," he hissed.

"But, Santa, he…" Mr. Peters'began to beg.

"Santa didn't kill those people, you did. You know you did, and I know you did. And that's all well and good. I would have gladly talked you around. I was willing to do things nice and discreet. But, right now, you are pointing a gun at my friend."

"How sweet," Abbey mumbled, coming around, "You really care."

"You okay Abs?" Dan didn't break his gaze from Mr. Peters. The rifle hadn't moved.

"Head hurts," Abbey said, her words slurred.

"I…" Mr. Peters tried again, "It was Santa. He did this."

"No," Dan barked, his voice bounced across the dark warehouse. When the echo stopped, no one dared move. Dan leaned forward, cheek to cheek with Mr. Peters. He whispered in the older man's ear. "Santa didn't. You did. Santa just stumbled into this whole mess, didn't you Chris?"

Santa continued to stare ahead, silent and possibly catatonic.

"See," Dan continued, his nose almost touching Mr. Peters' fragile shoulder. "You made a few mistakes. Want me to point them out?" He took a step back, his gun remaining pressed to the back of Mr. Peters' head, at the base of the neck, while his free hand held up a finger so that his boss could see it. "First, you disarmed the burglar alarm at the jewelry store and opened the safe. That was, can I just say, amazing. That's Mensa level memory. You saw and memorized those combinations, probably after seeing them once, when they locked your collection up for you. Beautiful work. That would have been fine with me. What does it matter to me if you steal your own collection? But," he held up a second finger. "You went and killed two sweet old men; two old farts who volunteered to stand out in the cold and the wet, for hours at a time for a good cause. And you killed them. That is not something I can let slide." He took a breath, exhaling slowly. His free hand trembled in his fury. His gun didn't move. "Then you fired Abbey. Of course you did, she ran into you; she's clumsy. That's why we call her Grace."

"Ha ha," Abbey grumbled from the floor, her voice edged with pain.

"And you probably couldn't stand the thought of someone knocking you down," Dan continued, his anger building momentum, "even accidentally. That was where your perfect plan ran into a hitch. Somehow, you dropped something that ended up being picked up by Abbey, something incriminating. Something coin related."

Abbey shifted, ever so slightly.

"I bet it was routine," Dan whispered. "You putting money in those buckets. Every day you did it. You had to, it was expected of you. And then, after killing two Santa's to get your coins back, they were picked up by the most honest and efficient employee you had. She'd have gladly returned it to you, if you'd asked. Doesn't that just fry you?"

Mr. Peters didn't respond. The rifle's nose dipped just a hair.

"So you had to get it back," Dan told the room at large, feeling off balance from the rapid turn of events. "You couldn't let it all fall apart after all you'd done. But, you had already fired her, so why would she come back to the store?"

"I knew it," Abbey twisted her head to catch Dan's eye, a smile playing across her lips. "No one in their right mind would hire you on purpose."

"Thanks Abs," Dan grinned at her, his eyes wide and reckless. He fought to maintain control. "You made me Santa's bodyguard to get Abbey back into the store, to get your coins. You knew I'd bring her in, I couldn't be everywhere at once."

"Which," Dan nodded respectfully, "I have to admit is a downright Xanatos-level gambit."

Mr. Peters blinked rapidly his body shivering, "I don't know what you're talking about. I wanted to protect Santa. The Season."

"Right," Dan narrowed his eyes and a chill returned to his voice. "The Season. Couldn't have anything obstruct The Season. What'd they find in your purse Abs?"

"Jewels," Abbey said, gingerly feeling her forehead. Blood stained her fingertips.

"Jewelry," Dan repeated, "the same jewelry they found in the store. Stupid, cheap jewelry that no one, especially a man of your experience in sales would hang onto. Two birds with one stone. All because Abs can't bother to clean out her purse."

Abbey rolled her eyes and groaned for her efforts.

"For want of a nail, the shoe was lost," Mr. Peters said a faraway expression on his face. Dan took a step back, extending his arm. The gun was still pressed against Mr. Peters head. He put one gloved hand underneath the magazine, adopting the two-handed Weaver stance favored by the FBI.

"All for the want of a horseshoe nail," Dan said. "Give me the gun, Mr. Peters," he ordered. His voice was subzero. "Or so help me, I won't think twice about pulling this trigger."

"Why don't you give him the gun Andrew?" Santa said, his voice calm and gentle; he had come back to life. His face was kind, no hint of shock or worry lined his features.

At the sound of Santa's voice, a strange thing happened. The room seemed to get warmer, the lights brighter. Mr. Peters seemed to melt, his shoulders drooping. His whole body appeared to deflate, and slowly, he relaxed his arms, holding the rifle out.

With his right hand, Dan grabbed the rifle and held it pointed safely at the ceiling. With his other hand he holstered his pistol. Turning his attention back to the rifle, he flipped the safety back on, and slid the bolt slowly to the eject position. Pulling out the cartridge, he laid it carefully on a nearby shelf. Finally, releasing the rifle's trap door, he removed the magazine, closed the trap and set the magazine on the shelf next to the cartridge.

Completely unloaded, Dan propped the stripped weapon in the corner, wedging it firmly against the metal shelving, barrel pointed at the floor. It was only when he let go of the rifle that he felt his shoulders lose some of their pinch. "Thanks Santa," Dan glanced over to see that all was well with the red clad man. He showed no signs of distress.

"No problem Daniel," Santa replied easily.

Dan leveled his gaze at his soon to be former boss, "Now Mr. Peters."

Mr. Peters met Dan's gaze, tears in his eyes. Dan lashed out with a hard left, his fist connected with Mr. Peters chin and the man crumpled, landing in a limp heap. "My name is Dan, Andrew!" he shouted, shaking out his hand. The one problem with these gloves, it always ended up hurting both sides. Although, admittedly it was usually more painful for the other guy. He looked down at Mr. Peters' unmoving form, "That was a long time coming."

Abbey cleared her throat and Dan looked around, feeling somewhat sheepish about his uncharacteristic display of emotions. He took a breath, released half of it, and looked up at Santa. "I owe you an apology."

"I can't think why."

"Can I trust you?"

"I should hope so Dan."

He handed Santa his phone.

"Should I call 911?" Santa inquired casually, as if they were talking about the weather.

Dan felt his temper cooling considerably, making thinking easier. "No, call police dispatch. It's in the contact list."

"An ambulance as well?" Santa suggested.

"No," Dan exhaled, "I'm going to take Abbey to the hospital myself."

Santa nodded toward Mr. Peters.

"Then I shall remain with your former employer until the authorities arrive."

Dan glanced over to make sure the rifle was safely out of reach, and began searching the room for something to bind their captive.

"Good," Dan was careful not to disturb anything. "Tell them to search this place for poison. Should be a vat around here somewhere, maintenance probably uses it to kill rats. It'll probably match what killed Karl."

He found a length of jump rope, and used it to tie Mr. Peters' hands and feet together. It was a fairly good knot, Maggie the former sailor, had taught him all the good ones. He was generous enough in his ties, it wasn't going to cut off his circulation. Abbey was out of danger, Dan was no longer interested in hurting Mr. Peters. Finished, he knelt down beside her.

"Hey you," she blinked drowsily.

"Hey you," Dan responded softly. He glanced at her head. It was bleeding lightly with a nasty bruise, but it looked otherwise superficial. "Abs, can you wiggle your fingers?" He watched as she did. Then she thumped her leg against his and giggled when he yelped like a little girl. "Thanks Abs," Dan laughed. It was loud and overreactive, and completely cathartic.

"Anytime," she laughed along with him.

He looked up at Santa who was pulling off one glove, all the better to scroll through contacts. The big man's hand was old and wrinkled, his fingers slightly curled with arthritis. He didn't join in their laughter.

"Santa," Dan instructed, "when you call, tell dispatch to patch you in directly to Sergeant Gary Jones, priority call. Give Sergeant Jones this message exactly: Gertie wanted me to call you; he's found the Double-K. Then, you can explain everything else, but make absolutely sure you begin with that phrase exactly."

Santa nodded, then repeated back the instructions exactly. Dan watched him find the contact and press CALL. He could hear the phone buzz as it rang.

"Sergeant Gary Jones please." Santa having handled the police, Dan gently scooped Abbey into his arms.

She wrapped both arms around her neck. "My hero," she mumbled into his neck.

"Come on Abs," he said gently, "Let's get you out of here." He paused at the door.

Santa shot a look at Dan. "I'm on hold." A grin played across his bearded face.

"Figures. Let Gary know the whole thing was recorded."
He gestured at the security camera just above his head. Santa
nodded. "And," Dan added, "Thanks."

"For what?"

"For not being offended when I accused you of murder."

Santa laughed that rich hearty laugh. In this dark room it
bounced all around, the echo sounding like the laughter of a
thousand Santas.

"My dear boy," Santa's deep baritone rang out. "It was a
first for me, and trust me, it's been a long time since I've
experienced a first. Though, admittedly, I don't wish to experience
this one again."

Dan's eyes ran from Santa, down to Abbey's face.

"Me either," he said with certainty, then kicked the door
open.

No one asked any questions when he carried Abbey out.
All the employees just silently cleared a path. One of the crimson
sport coat wearing personnel, who Dan recognized as Waldorf,
approached him. Nodding toward the locker room, Dan spoke
clearly and with utmost authority.

"Santa's in there," he said, "and is calling the police. Mr.
Peters has been caught stealing company funds. Mr. Claus and I
have been part of a sting to catch Mr. Peters," Dan invented wildly

on the spot. "Listen to Santa, do what he says, and if anyone needs me, I'll be at the hospital."

Waldorf nodded emphatically.

"Move!" Dan shouted. The kid jumped to one side, and Dan headed for the door, kicking that one open as well.

The cool evening breeze was welcome and gave Dan a much needed splash of reality. For a minute there, things had gone all topsy-turvy. Somehow he managed to open the passenger door, put Abbey in, and shut the door without incident. He slid into the driver's seat and slammed the door.

Abbey winced. "Not so loud," she grumbled.

"Stay awake," he cranked the ignition. "You may have a concussion."

"Yeah yeah," Abbey said, "I was the one who got him. Hit by him. Him dim." She reached up, putting her hands over her eyes. "Oh, I'm so getting hazard pay for this!"

Dan shifted the gear into reverse, and gently pressed the gas. This was no time for reckless driving. He stopped, and then carefully shifted to drive, ambling as slow as he dared down the street. Though he bobbed and weaved down the side streets, Dan kept his speeds low. Meanwhile, he kept pestering Abbey to keep her talking, to keep her awake.

"Did you buy something?"

"Yeah," Abbey replied with a heavy sigh, "for one of the employees. She was really sweet to me."

"That's nice," he offered, watching the road ahead. "What'd you buy?"

"A kitty for her daughter and a fire truck for her son. Also some shoes. The shoes are mine though. We'll have to go get them later."

"What kind of shoes did you get?"

This went on for the whole trip, all fifteen agonizing minutes. He pulled right heading for the parking lot, coming to a stop in a reserved space. They could have the car for all he cared.

Turning off the ignition, he opened the door and leapt out, his feet carefully planted. He stopped to take a breath. Slow down and take your time, he reminded himself. Calmly, he walked around to Abbey's side, mindful of where he put his feet. She opened her own door, though she needed his help to get out. Leaning against him, they walked toward the ER.

"What time is it?"

"About nine-thirty."

"Then this is early," she mumbled.

"What is?" He asked confused and worried.

She leaned over, giving him a peck on the cheek.

"Merry Christmas," she whispered into his ear. His cheeks flushed. She leaned her head on his shoulder.

"Merry Christmas to you too," Dan seconded, holding Abbey close. As he helped her into the ER, he decided that hers was one of the nicer Christmas presents anyone had ever given him.

Chapter 26

Waylon and Johnny used to sing that there ain't no good chain gang. Well, Dan wanted to add that there ain't no good waiting room. He hated hospital waiting rooms. It was as if someone had taken a normal room, removed all hope, took away comfort, and designed it to be infinitely soul crushing. Also, the chairs were uncomfortable. And the contrived feng shui of the room was starting to annoy him. To top it off, the magazines were out of date; apparently Jaws was the hit movie of the summer.

Dan suspected whoever had built this particular waiting room was actually engaging in a psychological experiment. They wanted to see how long it took for people to crack. He hated waiting rooms, and airport terminals. He suspected there was a dark conspiracy behind both. It was doubly unnerving that the room was empty. Part of him, the dark sarcastic part, felt an ER waiting room on Christmas Eve should be more crowded. Maybe it wasn't until Christmas Day that all the people showed up.

Dan leaned back in the hard metal chair barely covered in equally firm plastic, wondering if he should turn off the TV. It was broadcasting one of those weird live concerts that people loved doing around the holidays. Who has a live event on Christmas Eve? Besides Bill Murray in *Scrooged*. That elicited a thin smile.

The harsh overhead lights bounced off the pastel walls, creating a bizarre ethereal sensation. Not quite day, not quite night, it was just all around uncomfortable. He glanced out the window, hoping for a sight of blessed night, some sense of normalcy. Instead he got a full blast of artificial illumination from the outside floodlights. He turned away, rubbing his eyes. He kept seeing spots.

The smell of coffee tantalized Dan's nostrils.

"You look like you could use this," a voice right next to him offered.

Dan looked up, blinking rapidly. Santa, still wearing his bright red suit, giving him an appraising look. He was holding a cup of coffee out, a gentle smile on his face. Dan took the coffee with a grateful nod. He took a sip, it was strong and sweet. Sweeter than he normally liked his coffee, but appropriate given the person who had handed it over.

"Hi Chris," Dan said, "shouldn't you be heading home? You've had a day." He took another sip before adding, "Thank you, I needed this." Santa was still standing, and Dan gestured for him to take a seat. Dan took another sip of the coffee, the sugary goodness starting to grow on him.

"Actually," Santa said, as he sat down, "I thought I'd check on the two of you first."

"Well," Dan replied, "Abbey's getting checked out now. I'm just waiting."

"How are you Daniel?" Santa asked, watching him closely. The man's green eyes were warm and sympathetic.

"A bit tired. But, I'm glad this whole thing is over." He sipped the coffee before asking, "What did Gary say?"

Santa pulled out a small leather bound notebook from his coat pocket. There was even a gold plated ballpoint pen to accompany the wintergreen notebook. It was so quaint and old fashioned; it fit with the overall image.

Of course you take notes, Dan mused, because after all, the list has to come from somewhere, right?

"Sgt. Jones informed me that when they looked in Mr. Peters office, they found the stolen coins, in addition to the missing security tapes. The recording of the incident in the warehouse including what happened before you arrived has also been collected by now."

"The jar of arsenic was near the entrance to the storage room," Santa continued. "Mr. Peters was looked over by an EMT but seems to be fine. He has given a complete confession. The good Sergeant hopes that you will stop in at the police station tomorrow, for a complete statement." He paused, giving Dan a kindly look and a sincere smile, "However, you can wait until after Christmas Dinner. Family first. Also, he sends his best for Abbey, and hopes you are both well."

"That," Dan said, smiling into his coffee, "Sounds nothing like Gary."

"Well," Santa chuckled, "It may have gotten embellished in the translation. But, the spirit of what was said is there."

"I don't doubt it," Dan sighed, shifting around in the seat. He adjusted the sweater in his lap. Abbey had asked not to take it back into the ER with her, and Dan couldn't bring himself to take it to his car. That would mean leaving. Bad things happened when he left.

"Are you curious why?" Santa asked.

"That's the great question," Dan nodded, exhaustion making him feel philosophical.

"I meant in reference to motivations," Santa clarified. "Specifically, why Mr. Peters turned to a life of crime."

"Insurance fraud," Dan told his coffee cup with an unconcerned shrug.

"You peeked," Santa said with a chuckle, his eyes sparkling with laughter.

Dan gave him a wry look. Santa had a weird sense of humor. "No, but I know people. It's a gift."

"A valuable gift," Santa replied, a hint of respect in his voice. "But, I'm curious as to why he would do such a thing?"

"Why do we do anything," Dan asked, resting his head against the wall. He turned to Santa, "All right, you want to hear me make a wild guess?"

Santa nodded.

"Money. When in doubt, it all comes down to sex or money. And knowing the little I do from observing Mr. Peters, I'm going to pick money." Dan didn't want to think about what sex with Mr. Peters would mean. Peanut butter and a gimp suit sprung to mind. Somethings simply shouldn't be discussed with Santa Claus.

"Go on," Santa said, giving Dan a look that, once again, made him think the big man in red could read minds.

"My theory, and this is just a theory mind you. I think Mr. Peters was having money troubles and saw his coin collection as his only way out."

"So, he had his collection appraised by the closest expert?"

"Exactly," Dan took a deep pull of the sweet coffee. "But, a guy like that, he couldn't let that coin collection go. It represented his life's work. And, more than likely, he was getting screwed out of the deal. That jewelry store owner didn't look like the most upstanding merchant. Mr. Peters probably snapped. Plus, with the theft, he could have gotten the insurance money for their full value and kept the coins for himself. When I first heard about the robbery, when I found out only the safe was emptied, I thought either someone had a grudge against Mr. Peters, or it was insurance fraud. I just couldn't picture Mr. Peters as a fraudster. I guess he was just too easy a guy to underestimate."

"Fascinating," Santa rubbed his brow, "And circumstances led to murder?"

"Yeah," Dan nodded, "And if it wasn't for those meddling kids, he would have gotten away with it too." Santa chuckled. Dan appreciated the laugh at the bad joke. Maybe Santa was just being polite, and didn't get Scooby-Doo at the North Pole. "Some people have a hard time letting go of things," he said, absentmindedly stroking the sweater.

"But not you?"

"Me? No never. In fact, do you think the Missus would like this sweater?"

Santa looked at it, examining it closely. "I thought it belonged to Abbey."

"No. This is just an old thing I had for today, belongs to my sister. Actually, I have a bunch of stuff I need to get rid of. I have a really nice women's jacket, too big for Abbey."

"Well, I appreciate the offer. But, I don't think Mrs. Clause needs another jacket."

"That's okay. There are always charities."

"It's not just any jacket, is it."

"No." Dan closed his eyes.

"I thought as much." Santa's voice was gentle and kind. "What was your partner's name?" Santa pressed gently.

"Maggie. Doc Brown introduced us. She was the one that got me started in the P.I. business. She put me on the right path."

"I see."

"You're scarily easy to talk to."

"It sort of comes with the job," Santa winked.

Dan took a breath, "When Maggie got shot...I came here, to this hospital. Doc was about to leave for Machu Pichu. He left me here. Took a while for me to forgive him for that. Never occurred to me, we all grieve in different ways." Dan pointed to the door leading to the interior rooms, "A young doctor stepped out through those doors. She had too sad an expression on a face that beautiful. I knew the answer before she even opened her mouth."

"I'm sorry," Santa's eyes showed he meant it.

"I wasn't there when Maggie got shot. The cops said it was a random street mugging. Afterwards, I tracked down the guy. It took me a week."

"I see," Santa said solemnly.

"And I was too late." Dan admitted. "For a lot of things. The guy bit it the night before I found him. The news was all over the street, apparently the guy was a real sleaze bag. Ding dong the witch is dead. I found out from a friend who worked in a halfway house. You know who that friend was?"

"No idea," Santa took a sip from his coffee.

"David Barr. He was very kind to me. Weirdly enough, it was at the halfway house that things went south. Some tall drink of water was coming down the street toward me. All flashy badge and bad attitude. Except this was the wrong neighborhood for that kind of rookie braggadocio. Some young punk took exception, and took pot shots at the poor guy." Dan pointed at his chest, "Got him right here. Being a smart copper, he had on his bulletproof vest. But, what they don't tell you is how much it's going to hurt to get shot. He still broke a few ribs, couldn't move because of the pain. I shot the punk, saved the big goober's life." Dan snorted, "Gary's regretted it ever since."

"Then it would seem you were not too late after all," Santa commented, "you were, it appears, right on time."

"Don't let Gary hear you say that," Dan gave him a wry smile. "I owe you an apology."

"You've already apologized for accusing me of being a murderer. Have you done something worse?" There was a twinkle in Santa's eye.

"I pointed a gun at you. I'm sorry I had to do that."

"Nonsense," Santa waved him off, "you resolved the situation without anyone being harmed. Not permanently, at least."

"I just…" Dan began, and then swallowed hard. No sense holding back now. "For a while there, I thought you were the killer. It wasn't just for Mr. Peters that I said those things. For a while I'd believed them."

Santa turned to him, and raised an eyebrow.

"I'm sorry, I really am. There's this indefinable vibe, something odd about you."

"Ah," Santa glanced out the window with a bemused expression.

"However, you should know I never would have shot you."

Santa gave Dan an unflinching gaze, green eyes meeting blue, "I know."

"I mean literally," Dan said with a dark laugh, "my gun only has blanks in it." He paused, running his fingers through his hair and shot a look toward the emergency room door. "Uh…keep that to yourself. I don't, I mean that's not public knowledge. After that punk Gary and I made a deal…"

"Your secret's safe with me," Santa assured him.

"To be honest, I really don't have the stomach for death anymore," Dan swirled the last dregs of his coffee. "Not since that stupid kid. But, you know, even blanks can kill at close range."

"Indeed?"

"That's why I take gun safety very seriously." Santa didn't respond. Dan looked into his kind, sympathetic eyes, "I would have done it. I really would have. When I saw him threatening Abbey, I got so angry. I would have pulled that trigger."

"You wouldn't have killed him," Santa said.

"I wanted to," Dan retorted. "and at that range he would have been just as dead if I had bullets. I was ready."

"I believe you," Santa eyed him steadily and nodded. "Except, you're forgetting one important detail."

"What's that?" Dan took a sip of coffee.

"You never took the safety off." Santa winked.

Dan blinked. He reviewed the events in his mind. "I didn't, did I?"

"Not while you held a gun to Mr. Peters head. Never while you pointed it at me. And, do you know what's more?"

"What?"

"I don't think you ever would have. You don't strike me as the killer type. And believe you me; I'm an excellent judge of character."

"Look Santa, before you lay it on too thick here, you should know…I'm no angel."

Santa laughed heartily, his belly shaking like a bowl fuel of jelly, "Oh, you are a naughty little one, Daniel Landis!"

Dan threw his head back and laughed. It felt good. "You've no idea. I'm so getting a lump of coal!"

Santa's expression turned serious when he finally stopped laughing, his sparkling eyes gone piercing, "You're no murderer."

Dan drew a deep breath, looking around. The ER was deserted, apart from the two of them. The nurse who had checked Abbey in must have gotten bored and left. "I promised her Christmas lights."

"Abbey?" Santa asked.

"Yeah. I told her when this was all over, I'd take her to see some Christmas lights." He looked down at the sweater, lying mangled by tense hands in his lap. He played with one of the bells. "You know, I'm surprised my sister still has this. I'm the packrat of the family."

"I know the feeling," Santa rested a gloved hand on his wide black belt. "Do you know, I have never thrown away a pair of shoes."

"Really?"

"Absolutely. I still have the first pair I ever bought. Somehow I feel that if I can keep hold of them, then I will never forget where I've walked in them."

"I understand that."

Santa pulled out an ancient silver pocket watch. He opened it, and Dan heard a tinkling sound. It took a minute for him to recognize *Santa Claus Is Coming To Town*. "I do believe it's getting late."

"You got rounds to make?" Dan teased, smiling.

"I do indeed," Santa said, his eyes back to merry. He handed Dan his cup, "Would you mind?" He pointed toward the trashcan nearby.

Dan stood, holding both cups. He glanced back; making sure Santa hadn't wandered off. Santa, who always seemed to know his mind, smiled up at him.

"Remember," Santa touched the side of his nose, "even though I haven't thrown away the old ones, it doesn't mean I'm opposed to new ones. And Daniel…"

"Yes, Sir?"

"I've got my eye on you," Santa said with a wink.

Dan smiled, and then pivoted. He did a free throw shot, both cups landed in the trashcan. "Nothing but net. Chris, I have to tell you, you've got the act down…" He turned around. Santa was gone.

Dan whipped his head around. There wasn't a soul in sight, the sliding doors were closed firmly. He heard a rustling sound and glanced behind him. A splash of color caught his eye, he looked down. On the emerald seat, in place of Santa, was a beautiful burgundy square. A small envelope rested on top. Dan's phone was next to it. He carefully slipped into the seat beside the present. His hand reached out, picking up the faded yellow envelope; it smelled of old parchment with a faint whiff of candy canes. Opening it, he found the note, written in a loopy but beautiful handwriting.

> *Dear Daniel,*
>
> *You're a bit older than my usual clientele, but I wished to show my gratitude. Remember, when holding onto the past, that you not lose sight of the present. This should assist you in seeing things more clearly.*
>
> *Your friend,*
> *K "SC" K*
> *P.S. She'll love the brick.*

Dan replaced the card in the envelope, setting it to one side. He stared down at the box and reached out to touch it. The box was wrapped in the softest velvet. He wondered what it could be. It was definitely a gift box, the seams almost invisible. He slipped the lid off, laying it to one side. He looked down at the box's contents for close to a minute before putting the lid back on.

Dan leaned his head against the wall, his mind racing. Finally, unable to stand it anymore, he stood up. He paced the room rubbing his face. The sound of a door opening made him pause, and he looked over to the nurse's station. A gorgeous woman decked out all in white scrubs, walked over to the desk and began rifling through the paperwork. She was wearing a silver Christmas tree pendant.

Dan was grateful for this bit of normalcy after Santa's vanishing act. He smiled at the flaming red hair, it glowed in the fluorescent light like burning embers. He cleared his throat. "Excuse me Miss," he called out. "I was wondering if you'd heard anything about my friend. Her name is Bernice Agnes Freeman?"

The nurse turned to the computer, typing away on the keyboard. She paused and then scrolled down a list of names. Dan leaned against the desk wondering why such a beautiful woman seemed so familiar. She was definitely the type he would remember. The woman stopped typing and looked up with a gleaming white smile.

"Abbey is doing just fine," the nurse said sweetly. "She's in Exam Room 8 if you want to go see her." Dan was struck by how brilliantly green her eyes were as they sparkled at him, laughing at some hidden joke.

"Thanks," he said, feeling an unsettling sense of déjà vu.

"No problem Danny-boy," she said.

Dan laughed and turned to grab his things. Maggie always called him that. He froze in midstep. "What did you call me?" he asked, turning back around. The desk was vacant. He stared for a moment, mouth open and then threw his hands into the air. "Screw it!" Dan shouted. "That's it. I'm tired of people disappearing on me." He walked over, grabbed the sweater and pocketed the phone before gently picking up the burgundy box. The card went in his pocket.

Turning on one heel, he stomped over to the ER entrance. He stopped, adopting a calmer air. He would sneak in if he had to and see if the vanishing woman was right. He thought about what he was going to say if he was stopped, and then decided it didn't matter.

The doors opened from the inside. Wheeling towards him, pushed by a scrubs bedecked young man, was Abbey, still wearing her elf costume. She smiled broadly at him and Dan breathed a sigh of relief.

Chapter 27

"Hey you," Abbey favored Dan with a million dollar smile.

The scrubs wearing man brought her to a halt. Dan wondered if he was a doctor. At the rate things were going, he was going to disappear in a minute so it didn't matter.

"She's fine," the scrubs clad man reassured him, his voice low and melodious. He handed Dan a clipboard filled with paperwork. "If you'll just sign these, our friend here should be ready to leave under your care." The man's whole posture was mellow, solid and very comforting. Dan shook his hand, partially out of gratitude and mostly to make sure he was real. The man had a solid grip, firm and warm.

"Thank you so much," Dan said. "No sign of concussion?"

"None whatsoever," the man confirmed. "We did an x-ray, CT, and an MRI to be sure. There was no sign of intracranial bleeding, no loss of function. The scratch on her head didn't even need stitches. Our friend here is in perfect health. But," he bent down so that he was at Abbey's eye level. "If you get a headache, feel dizzy, nauseous, have any kind of strange sensations…anything, come back immediately. We take head injuries very seriously."

"Thanks Patrick," Abbey was still smiling. She was lapping up the attention.

"I'll keep an eye on her," Dan assured him.

"Look Dan, it's Patrick!" Abbey gestured to the scrub clad man like a game show presenter.

"Nice to meet you, Patrick," Dan said.

"You too. Last time I saw you, you were flat on your back in bed."

"You'd be surprised how often I meet people that way."

Patrick laughed, "If anything is going to show up, it'll be within the next day or so. Symptoms normally appear within the first 24 hours. When she goes to sleep, make sure she's responsive to waking up. Tonight, try to wake her at least once."

"Right," Dan said, "tickle her awake."

"However you want brother, just make sure she has no trouble waking up."

"I'm pretty easy to wake up," Abbey said, with a wary glance at Dan, "It doesn't have to involve tickling."

"Well sure," Dan said to her, "it doesn't have to."

She sighed, and he never had heard a more wonderful sound. He signed the forms and handed them back. The man glanced at the empty desk and his shoulders drooped.

"Christmas party upstairs."

Dan nodded. "Merry Christmas." They shook hands once again.

"You too," Patrick replied, turned and walked back into the ER.

Dan watched him go, and then turned to Abbey. "Come on," he said, "before they come back for the wheelchair. This thing's a keeper."

"You're a goober," Abbey laughed. Dan began pushing her, and then stopped. "What?"

"This is from Santa," he bent to one knee, getting a nice look at those beautiful emerald eyes, handing her the felt box. "Merry Christmas." He kissed her cheek.

"Thank you," Abbey blushed, holding his eyes for a long moment. She studied the box, before carefully opening it.

It was something from a forgotten time. The handle was stained mahogany, the glass circle framed in polished silver; it gleamed as it caught the light. Gold lettering streamed down the handle of the beautiful antique magnifying glass. Abbey ran a finger down the words. "Partners in crime," she read.

"What do you think?" Dan asked, holding his breath.

She stared up at him, then back down at the gift. She picked up the magnifying glass, holding it up to her eye.

"I think," she said, examining him closely, "that you are the one with the head injury."

"What?" he asked caught off guard.

"Do you really think I would want to risk life and limb just because you asked?" Her voice was hard as steel.

"Well," he stammered, suddenly uncertain, "I hadn't thought…"

"I want a raise." She demanded, "And my own business cards."

Dan stared, blinked twice, and then threw back his head laughing, tears welling up.

"I so got you," she gloated.

"Yeah you did," Dan continued to push the chair toward the door. "Of course, you know what this means."

"What?" Abbey asked.

"I'm going to have to teach you everything I know."

"That shouldn't take long."

"For starters," he said, as the doors opened automatically, "I'm going to have to teach you what not to do when sniffing around dark rooms. And how to throw a punch."

"When I get out of this chair, I'll show you how I throw a punch." He laughed as they headed for the car. "Hey, what do you think of me having a super-detective alias? I'm thinking Bunny Hayes."

"I think they need to check again for brain damage."

Dan helped Abbey into the car. She didn't let him keep the wheelchair.

Chapter 28

A ringing sound woke Dan up with a start. It took a minute for his eyes to adjust. The gentle light of the TV was the room's sole source of illumination. Realizing the ringing was his phone, he groped for it, the leather couch squeaking and squelching. His fingers touched the phone and he flipped it open. He groggily pressed it against his ear.

"Uh, hello?"

"Hi Gertie," Julianne said, her voice distracted and exhausted.

"Hey ya Jules," he was out of sorts. "Uh…where are you? I'm at your house." He checked his watch. It was late.

"I'm at the office. Long night. Can you drop in for a bit? I have something I need to talk with you about."

"Right now?" He double-checked the time with the clock on his phone. It was very late. He glanced at the TV; it was still playing the DVD's menu music.

"Yeah," Julianne said more firmly, "quick as you can?" She hung up before he could argue.

Dan sighed, shutting the phone. He looked over at Abbey, fast asleep against his shoulder. Smiling, he shifted his weight to lay her down softly on the couch. She stirred but didn't wake up. That reminded him of his duties.

"Abbey."

She opened her eyes immediately, smiling sleepily at him. "Hey you."

"Hey you. It's after midnight."

"Yay!" She said softly. "Merry Christmas!"

"Merry Christmas Abs. You feeling okay?" She nodded. "I've got to run to town. Go back to sleep."

"Okay," she said, closing her eyes again. He reached over, adjusting the blanket over her. He bent down, picking up the bowl of popcorn. Jules fussed at him if he left food down here. Standing up, he stretched the kinks out of his body. The main menu was still playing Dan's Christmas present from Abbey.

The Moonlighting Season 1 DVD was playing the theme on a loop. Dan reached over, using the remote to turn off the DVD player and TV.

I am a very lucky man, Dan realized. The absence of light left him a bit disoriented. Fortunately he had this room memorized. He walked toward the stairs, shaking out his leg, trying to get it to wake up. At the foot of the stairs he turned back to watch Abbey sleep.

Her porcelain white face glowed in the darkness. She looked for all the world like an angel. One of those goofy porcelain angels old people collect, sure, but an angel nonetheless.

Dan headed up the stairs, trying to make as little noise as possible. Upstairs, the house was dark. Making his way to the kitchen, he decided to leave her a note. Dan turned on the light and began searching for something to write on. Jules always kept some scratch paper on the table in case inspiration struck. In addition to being a super genius, she was a mediocre poet. He jotted down a short note to Abbey, letting her know where he'd be. Pausing for a moment, he added that she should get ready for Christmas dinner at Mama Jones'. He was sure Gary wouldn't mind. Suddenly thirsty, Dan poured himself a glass of water from the tap. As he was taking a sip, he looked at the glass he was drinking from.

Dan almost snorted water. It was a Smurf mug, Smurfette to be exact. He didn't even know Jules still had these. She really is a packrat, he thought, as he finished his drink. A closet packrat. Apparently it runs in the family. Gazing out the window, he took in the beautiful landscape. It was starting to snow again, a beautiful blanket of white covering the lake front. He made a mental note to call the folks, wish them a 'Merry Christmas'. Though, not right now.

Ma and Pa Landis liked to sleep and would only panic if Dan called this early. Auntie Ruth might be up at this time of night, but she was a night owl. And collector of novelty mustaches. He finished off his glass, rinsed it, and put it on the edge of the sink. Double-checking the note, he set it prominently on the table, anchoring it with a paper weight. His phone buzzed with a text and he flipped it open.

Bernie had just landed in London. He sent her back a quick note wishing her a Merry Christmas and Happy Boxing Day. He walked out of the kitchen, catching one final glimpse of the Smurf mug on the counter. Smurfette batted her eyes back at him. The streets were quiet. Between the snow, the time of night and the low-key nature of the city, it wasn't a huge surprise that everyone was indoors. About now, Moms and Dads were probably assembling bicycles and doll houses. Or, maybe Santa was still making his rounds. Either way, Dan was grateful the streets were clear. He really didn't feel like keeping an eye on the other drivers. Even if they were in a reindeer driven sleigh.

Julianne's law firm was across town, a daily half-hour commute during rush hour traffic. Except she didn't keep normal hours. And of course, the way Julianne drove her little Ferrari, she always got to work in a matter of minutes. She'd only gotten a ticket once. She'd fought it and word had gotten out. No one wanted to face Boom-Boom in traffic court.

Dan pulled into the parking garage, waving to the poor guard on duty. He parked two spaces down from the black Ferrari, yet again admiring its sleek curves. That was some car. Heading past the beautiful machine, he continued toward the elevator. The garage was empty and he felt the familiar prickle of danger from the unknown.

Everyone knew parking garages were inherently dangerous and an empty one meant there'd be no one there to help. He wasn't too worried though. He was riding so high, he felt ready to take on the world.

The elevator took a minute to arrive. Thankfully it was empty. He pressed the button for the second to top floor. Julianne still hadn't made it to Senior Partner, but she was never one to complain about it. Leaning against the cool wooden wall of the lift, he couldn't blame her. You just couldn't stick it to the man if you were The Man. Or The Woman, in Jules' case.

Dan glanced at his watch, feeling the elevator was far too slow. For the money they raked in, you would think they could afford a faster lift. The doors opened to a brightly lit hallway. It was a power hallway, all strong colors and expensive decorations. Dan stepped out, instantly feeling appropriately weak and powerless. Precisely how they wanted you to feel. He headed for the receptionist's desk. It was solid oak, powerful and imposing.

No one was there but Dan stopped anyway. He stole a mint from the candy bowl, his mind flashing back to Karl. "This one's for you champ," he spoke to the ether, popping the mint into his mouth. It tasted bittersweet.

Dan tried to remember which way to Jules' office. It was always easier with people around; he usually kept a lookout for Marsha. Without that guiding light, he followed his nose. Marsha's desk always smelled faintly of cookies. Chocolate chip to be precise. He walked past her outer office to the big chief's office.

Julianne's door was open. She was working at her desk, surrounded by paperwork. She had her gold pen out, filling in some form or other. Julianne kept glancing from the paper to the computer screen and back. Dan rapped his knuckle against the open door, leaning against the frame.

Most offices had awards and achievements covering the walls. Jules didn't have any of those. You didn't get awards for keeping drug dealers out of jail. However, it did get you the second largest office in the firm.

"Hey," she said, looking up. Her eyes were bloodshot, the lamp barely illuminating the corner office. Dan thought about hitting the light switch, and then decided against it.

"You look rough," he said honestly.

She smiled at that, "Thanks. How's Abbey?"

"She's fine," Dan stepped inside. "Clean bill of health. She's asleep on your couch right now." Julianne nodded and then gestured to the seat across from her desk. It was a big, expensive looking desk, with comfortable plush chairs on both sides.

He slipped into the seat, looking into Jules' eyes. Both chairs were at eye level since she didn't go in for power games. Boom-Boom didn't need help with intimidation, she did just fine on her own.

"So," he made the first move, "What's up?"

Julianne put down her pen and sighed. She rubbed the bridge of her nose with two fingers. "I want to hire you," she stated matter-of-factly.

Dan took a breath and calmly replied, "No."

Julianne's surprise showed. Her pale eyes got wide.

"I know you and Gary are going through a tough time right now, but…" he began.

She held up a hand. "Hang on. You think Gary and I are going to get divorced?"

"Not going to happen," a voice rumbled behind Dan.

Swiveling his chair to the right corner, Dan saw Gary sitting in the shadows, one leg resting on top of another. He stared out with tired, bloodshot eyes before standing up. Gary walked across and stood behind Julianne, placing one massive hand on her shoulder. "I'm never going to leave this girl," he said.

Julianne rested her hand on his; it looked small and delicate compared to his massive mitt. "Never ever," she agreed.

Dan looked from Gary to Julianne, eyebrow arched. With her free hand, she picked up an envelope and tossed it to him. It was thick and heavy. When he opened it, he nearly fainted. Money, a whole lot of money, stared back at him.

"Like I said," she began, "I need to hire you.

Dan let out a long, slow breath.

"This should be interesting," he said grimly.

From the left side of the office, hidden behind the opulent door, came a voice. "You have no idea..." Doc gave a long, appraising look as he pushed on the stained wood. The door closed with a heavy snap.

***

The adventure continues in *The Cult of Koo Kway*, as we discover just what Dan has been hired to do, Tex rides into town, and we discover how Dan met Abbey.

And to think, it all started with a pair of fuzzy green handcuffs.

***